THE
DISCIPLE
OF
LAS VEGAS

THE DISCIPLE OF LAS VEGAS

AN AVA LEE NOVEL

IAN HAMILTON

SPIDERLINE

This edition published in 2011 by
House of Anansi Press Inc.
110 Spadina Avenue, Suite 801
Toronto, ON, M5V 2K4
Tel. 416-363-4343
Fax 416-363-1017
www.anansi.ca

Distributed in Canada by
HarperCollins Canada Ltd.
1995 Markham Road
Scarborough, ON, M1B 5M8
Toll free tel. 1-800-387-0117

House of Anansi Press is committed to protecting our natural environment.
As part of our efforts, this book is printed on paper that contains 100%
post-consumer recycled fibres, is acid-free, and is processed chlorine-free.

15 14 13 12 11   1 2 3 4 5

Library and Archives Canada Cataloguing in Publication

Hamilton, Ian, 1946–
Disciple of Las Vegas : an Ava Lee novel / Ian Hamilton.

(Ava Lee)
ISBN 978-0-88784-252-8

I. Title. II. Series: Hamilton, Ian, 1946– . Ava Lee.

PS8615.A4423D57 2011   C813'.6   C2010-907340-1

Cover design: Daniel Cullen
Text design: Alysia Shewchuk
Typesetting: Alysia Shewchuk

Canada Council Conseil des Arts
for the Arts   du Canada

ONTARIO ARTS COUNCIL
CONSEIL DES ARTS DE L'ONTARIO

*We acknowledge for their financial support of our publishing program
the Canada Council for the Arts, the Ontario Arts Council, and the
Government of Canada through the Canada Book Fund.*

Printed and bound in Canada

For my mother, Kathleen,
and in memory of my father, William.

WHEN AVA LEE WOKE UP, THE FIRST THING SHE FELT was a sharp pain shooting through her neck and shoulder. She stretched, causing the pain to become more intense, and then slowly relaxed her muscles. She knew from experience that the lashing she had endured wasn't going to cause any long-term damage.

She turned her head to look at the bedside clock. It was only 6 a.m. She had flown home to Toronto around midnight and had been in bed for less than five hours. She had thought that two melatonin capsules and a glass of Pinot Grigio would see her through the night, but the pain and a mind that was still a jumble of emotions were gnawing at her.

She lay quietly, hoping she could drift off again. After ten minutes she gave up and pulled herself out of bed. She kneeled to say a short prayer of thanks to St. Jude for her safe return, and then headed for the bathroom. Pulling off her black Giordano T-shirt, Ava turned so she could see her back in the mirror. The belt had hit her on the side of the neck and across her right shoulder, and then again on the same shoulder and partway down her back. The marks were a deep black and blue, yellowed at the edges. They looked worse than they felt, and in a few days they would start to fade.

Ava went into the kitchen, made herself a Starbucks VIA Ready Brew, and sat down at the small round table set against the window overlooking Cumberland Street and Avenue Road. She lived in the heart of Yorkville, the ritziest neighbourhood in downtown Toronto. Despite the early hour, the traffic below was barely moving as the January weather tried to decide if it was raining or snowing.

Normally she would have the *Globe and Mail* spread across the table, but she had been away for more than a week — travelling to Hong Kong, Thailand, Guyana, and the British Virgin Islands, tracking down and retrieving more than five million dollars that had been stolen from a client — and had cancelled the paper until further notice. So she opened up her laptop and turned it on to read the news online. That was a mistake.

After she signed on, Ava opened her email program, expecting to see messages from friends, a bit of spam, and not much else. She froze when she saw Uncle's name in her inbox. Uncle was her Hong Kong–based partner, a man in his seventies whose idea of high-tech communication was a Chinese knockoff iPhone he had bought for less than forty dollars at the Kowloon nighttime street market and used strictly for making calls. He had sent her two messages in the past eight hours; she couldn't remember receiving that many from him in the past year. She opened them. They were identical, simply stating that he needed her to call him. He didn't say it was urgent. He didn't have to — that he had sent two emails conveyed that fact well enough.

Ava groaned, went over to her hot-water Thermos, and made another coffee. She knew what he wanted to talk about. While she was in Guyana they had been offered a job by a Filipino-Chinese businessman named Tommy Ordonez. Ordonez was the wealthiest man in the islands. They had put him off so they could finish the job they were on. Ava had hoped he could be put off longer, because that job had turned nasty, with unforeseen complications. What was supposed to have been a straightforward tracking and retrieval of misappropriated funds had turned into extortion. She had prevailed, but not without difficulty, as the bruises and welts demonstrated, and not without stress, some of which still lingered.

Ava had turned off her cellphone the night before and thrown it into the bottom of her purse. She had intended to leave it there for a few days, or at least until she felt her head was in the right place. She went to retrieve it and saw that Uncle had called as well. She sighed. She had to call him back. She couldn't ignore two emails and a phone message without insulting him. Insulting Uncle was something she had never done — and never wished to do. It was just past six in the evening in Hong Kong, and Ava knew she'd probably catch him at a massage, an early dinner, or his Kowloon apartment.

"*Wei*," Uncle said. Ava could hear his little dog yapping and his Filipina housekeeper, Lourdes, telling it to be quiet. He was still at the apartment.

"It's Ava."

"You are in Toronto?"

"Yes, I got in late last night."

"And you are okay?"

"Yes, I'm fine."

"Good, I was worried about you . . . It is early there."

"I couldn't sleep, and then I turned on my computer and saw your emails."

"We need to talk."

Ava wondered if he thought she was being critical of his persistence, and she felt a bit uneasy about being perceived as even mildly rude. "No problem, Uncle. Is it about Tommy Ordonez?"

"Yes. He and his closest adviser, Chang Wang, each called me twice yesterday, after calling me twice the day before. I have been telling them they need to be patient."

"And how did they react?"

"Impatiently."

"Uncle, you did tell them we never do two jobs at the same time, and that I was still working on one?"

"Of course, but it only seemed to frustrate them more. Especially Ordonez. He is a man who does not think he should ever have to stand in a queue or have someone else's interests take precedence over his."

"Did he say that?"

"He didn't need to. Ava, the last time I spoke to him he could barely contain himself. I could feel him eating his anger, and I know that if he had been talking to anyone but me he would have exploded."

Ava finished her second coffee and, holding the phone to her ear, went to the counter and emptied another sachet into her cup. "What do we know about the job, Uncle?"

"Not that much. Just that it is a lot of money, that it involves a Canadian real estate transaction, and that one of

Ordonez's younger brothers, Philip Chew, is involved. They want to meet us face to face to provide the actual details."

"Is it a firm contract?"

"If we want to accept it."

"You haven't committed?"

"I thought it would be best for us to hear the full story before signing on."

"What I don't understand, Uncle, is why, with all the resources and power they have, they need us in the first place."

She had asked that question when the job offer was first made, and it had generated an awkward response from Uncle. Now he was just vague. "They will explain everything when we are in Manila."

"So you want us to go?"

"I told Chang Wang that we would discuss it with them, and they are insisting on doing that in person . . . I am told the sum of money involved is more than fifty million dollars. I think that is worth a trip to Manila, don't you?"

"Yes, of course it is," she said, and then realized that Uncle had twice referred to Ordonez's right-hand man by both his family and given names. It was a form of respect he rarely used for clients, and she guessed there was some kind of bond between the two men. "This Chang, Uncle, do you know him well?"

"He is from Wuhan, like me, and over the years we have done each other many favours. I would still have ten men rotting in Filipino prisons if it were not for him, and he would still be waiting for permits to build cigarette factories in Hubei province if it were not for me."

Ava was accustomed to Uncle's Wuhan connections.

He had been born and raised in a village on its outskirts, and he and the other men from there who had escaped the Communist regime had remained intensely loyal to each other. "And Chang hasn't confided in you about the nature of Ordonez's problem?"

"His first loyalty is to Ordonez. We need to understand and respect that."

"Earlier you mentioned that Ordonez was restraining himself when he was talking to you. I didn't think you knew him."

"Chang introduced us once, years ago, when I was at the top of my heap and he was scaling his. It was a passing encounter that seems more important to him than it is to me. I did not even remember the meeting until he mentioned it."

Ava was now standing by the kitchen window. The falling rain was beginning to freeze onto it. She watched a car skid into the intersection below and slide into an SUV. She hated this kind of weather. At least Manila would be warm. "Can you buy us an extra day or two?" she asked.

Uncle hesitated. She knew he didn't want to push her too hard. "I would like to get there as soon as possible. But if you need to spend more time in Toronto, then I will deal with Chang Wang and Ordonez as best as I can."

"Will they walk away from the deal if we delay?"

"I really don't know."

"Well, I guess that's something we shouldn't risk," Ava said.

"No, we should not. Their impatience could get the better of them."

She did a quick calculation. "If I catch the Cathay Pacific

flight late tonight, I can be in Hong Kong the day after tomorrow, early morning, your time. That at least will give me all of today to get caught up here, and I'll have a sixteen-hour flight I can sleep through."

"Good. We can leave for Manila the morning you arrive. I will have those flights booked. We can meet in the Wing lounge," Uncle said. "I will let Chang Wang know right away that we are coming. Ordonez's office is near the Ayala Centre in Makati City. The Peninsula Hotel is nearby. I will have them book us rooms."

"Okay, I'll call you when things are confirmed on this end."

"Fine. And Ava, I think this is the right thing for us to do."

She shrugged. "Ordonez is a big man and it's a lot of money."

"That does not mean we cannot still say no," Uncle said. "We will go and talk to them, and then you and I can discuss what we want to do. I have to tell you, I have a feeling that it will be worth it in the end."

"Yes, Uncle."

"Now I have to call Chang," he said.

As she hung up the phone, Ava tried to remember if she'd heard Uncle mention Chang's name before, and came up blank. That wasn't unusual. He had a network of friends and associates that spanned Asia, though his closest contacts were those who shared those long, deep Wuhan roots.

Is Ordonez from Wuhan as well? she wondered. She knew he was Chinese born, but nothing more specific than that. She'd find out soon enough, but her curiosity was far more aroused by the kind of problem a man as rich and powerful as Tommy Ordonez couldn't handle himself.

THE MORNING SUN GLISTENED ON THE SOUTH CHINA Sea as the plane descended onto the man-made island that was Hong Kong's airport.

She found Uncle at the rear of the Wing lounge, reclining in a Balzac armchair. He wasn't any taller than Ava and was nearly as lean. From a distance he looked almost like a child swallowed up in the chair. He was more than seventy, she knew, but his skin was still smooth, with only the faintest traces of lines around his eyes and on his forehead. His close-cropped black hair was streaked with just a touch of grey. Uncle was dressed as usual in a simple black suit and a crisp white shirt buttoned to the collar. His monochromatic style was part convenience, part camouflage. It made him easy to overlook — just an elegantly dressed old man, except to those who knew.

Uncle had been Ava's partner and mentor for more than ten years. They recovered bad debts for a living. Ava was a forensic accountant with degrees from York University, in Toronto, and Babson College, just outside of Boston. Before joining forces with Uncle, Ava had worked for a prestigious

Toronto firm, but she had found the bureaucracy that came with working in a large corporation stifling. She had left and set up her own small business, catering mainly to her mother's friends. When one of her clients was stiffed by a Chinese importer, Ava decided to collect the debt herself. In the process she met Uncle, who was chasing the same importer for a different customer. When their combined efforts proved successful, Uncle had suggested that Ava partner with him.

Uncle's reputation brought a wide range of clients to the table. What he lacked was Ava's accounting skills and the softer touch she could bring to the recovery process. Their customers were typically Asian, normally desperate, and often irrational by the time they signed up with Ava and Uncle. Their businesses were at stake, their families were being threatened by economic ruin, and they had already exhausted all the conventional methods of retrieving stolen funds. Uncle's mantra was "People always do the right thing for the wrong reason." Ava had become particularly adept at finding the wrong reason that would convince her targets to do the right thing, which in their case was return the money to its rightful owner. Ava and Uncle took thirty percent of everything they recovered.

When she spotted Uncle in the lounge, she glanced around to see if Sonny was with him. There was no sign of Uncle's driver-cum-bodyguard. He was as big as Ava and Uncle put together, and more vicious than anyone she had ever known. He had travelled with them in the past, most often to China, where a show of strength was never misplaced. Ava assumed that Uncle wasn't expecting to need protection in the Philippines.

She quietly approached his chair. His eyes were closed, and she thought he was sleeping until he said, "Ava, is that you?"

"Yes, Uncle."

"I thought so. I could smell that Annick Goutal perfume you like so much," he said, his eyes opening and a tiny smile tugging at the corners of his mouth. "You look beautiful, as always."

"Thank you."

"But the clothes —" he said, motioning to her black Giordano T-shirt and Adidas track pants. "You need to change. They are going to meet us at the airport and take us directly to Ordonez's office."

"I figured as much. I have everything I need here," she said, picking up her Shanghai Tang "Double Happiness" bag. "I'll take a shower and put on something suitable."

Ava walked into the lounge's private change rooms. She showered quickly, put on a fresh bra and panties and a pink Brooks Brothers shirt with a modified Italian collar, then debated whether to wear a skirt or slacks. She didn't know anything about Ordonez or Chang other than what she had read online in Guyana. To be on the safe side she opted for the trousers. A conservative look would never be seriously misinterpreted by powerful men.

She brushed her hair back and fixed it with her favourite ivory chignon pin. Then she applied some mascara and a touch of red lipstick. The last thing she did was slip her Cartier Tank Française watch onto her wrist. It had cost a small fortune, but she'd never regretted purchasing it. She loved its look and thought it established the perfect balance between serious and successful.

As she walked from the ladies' room back across the lounge, she could feel all eyes turn in her direction. Her pace was measured, never hurried, and she held herself erect, confident of her time and place.

Uncle was standing near his chair, in conversation with a man who looked about his age but was six inches taller and at least a hundred pounds heavier. His head was completely bald and he had a large, round face with jowls that trembled when he spoke. He wore a Burberry plaid shirt and slacks that rode too high over his belly. She could see a diamond-encrusted Rolex on his wrist, an enormous jade and diamond ring on his wedding-band finger, and a ruby ring on his pinkie. The contrast between the two men couldn't have been more striking. Yet as she watched them, she could see that the larger man was trying to make an impression on Uncle. She could read his desire to please in his body language, his rapid speech. Uncle was just listening, nodding every so often.

When he saw her, Uncle dismissed the man with a little wave of his hand and walked directly over to Ava. The man seemed startled to see her. Then he stared, his face impassive.

"I feel like some noodles," Uncle said, touching her elbow to guide her towards the restaurant.

They both ordered noodles with har gow, traditional shrimp dumplings. There was a delicious aroma in the air that Ava couldn't identify. "Snow pea tips fried in garlic," Uncle said when she asked. "It is too early to eat them. They attack my bowels."

As usual, he ate far more quickly than she did. She always wondered if his table manners were an indication of his true internal state, a contrast to the calm, placid exterior he showed to the world. "Who was that man you were talking to?" she asked when he had finished eating.

The question seemed to catch him off guard, and he closed his eyes briefly before answering. "He worked for me in Fanling years ago. Now he runs Mong Kok," he said. Before she could ask more, the boarding call came for the flight and Uncle slid out of his chair.

They walked to the gate and found long, disorganized lines of diminutive Filipino women carrying as much baggage as airline rules would allow. "It is that time of year," Uncle said. "Flights to Asia and to Manila are cheap, so all the domestics and nannies travel home now."

Ava knew the ritual. She and Marian had had a Filipina *yaya*, or nanny, until they went to Havergal College for high school. Every two or three years Yaya would buy a couple of *balikbayans* — boxes the size of small coffins — and load them with T-shirts, running shoes, and canned goods to carry back with her to the Philippines.

"How many are there in Hong Kong these days?" she asked.

"More than a hundred thousand, I think. On Sundays they go to Central or Victoria Park or to the Hong Kong Cultural Centre to socialize. I do not think Lourdes has missed a Sunday in ten years."

"Amazing women."

Uncle stared at the knot of people crowding around the boarding gate. "The Philippines would collapse economically without them. I read that there are about eight million overseas workers, and they remit money every month. If that is not the country's largest source of income, I do not know what is."

Uncle and Ava strolled past the lineup of people waiting impatiently to board the plane and showed their passports and first-class tickets to the Cathay Pacific attendant. When they boarded the plane, they were greeted by two attractive young flight attendants in cherry-red uniforms, who directed them to their seats. As Uncle settled into his, Ava noted that his feet just skimmed the floor.

As soon as the plane reached its flying altitude, Uncle eased his seat back. But before he could close his eyes, Ava asked, "Uncle, is Tommy Ordonez from Wuhan?"

"Not everyone we do business with is from Wuhan," he said with a small smile. "He is from Qingdao."

"And Ordonez is not his family name."

"No, his real name is Chew Guang. He took the Filipino name after he started doing serious business in the islands. He is what they call a Chinoy, a Chinese using a Filipino name."

Ava wasn't surprised by the name change. All across Asia, in countries such as Indonesia, Malaysia, Thailand, and the Philippines, economies were often controlled by resident Chinese. It created resentment among the indigenous populations, and in times of turbulence the Chinese were often targets of physical violence and looting. Changing their names was one way of trying to blend in, to disguise themselves from the xenophobes.

"Was he born in Qingdao?" Ava asked. She knew that Chinese people say they are from a particular city or province even if three generations removed.

"Yes, the eldest child in a family that includes two brothers and a sister. His father was an assistant brewmaster at the Tsing Tao brewery, and Chew apprenticed there when he was a young teenager. He was obviously smart and a very hard worker, because by the time he turned twenty-two he had been dispatched to the Philippines as an assistant brewmaster in his own right."

"How long before he went out on his own?"

"About three years. He started at a small brewery with a brand he called Philippine Gold. The beer was not of the best quality but it was cheap, and cheap worked. Within five years Chew Guang had the number-one beer in the islands. It was around this time that he changed his name to Tommy Ordonez and began — with help from the local Chinese, most of whom also had Filipino names — to expand and diversify. Chang Wang joined him then."

"And why did Chang keep his name?"

"He has no public visibility. He is the man behind the scenes, an operator, the key advisor, the one who helps Ordonez plot his business strategies and follow through on execution. He is a good man to have as a friend, and a monster when he is an enemy."

"Apparently Ordonez's brothers kept their family name as well."

"There was no reason for them not to. They live in places where it does not matter. Philip, the one in Canada — the one who has the problems — is the youngest. The other one, David, lives in Hong Kong and is the point man for the Chinese market. He finds homes for their cheap booze and cigarettes."

"From what I've read, the business isn't just beer and cigarettes."

"Not anymore. They own banks, trucking and cold storage operations, and the largest ocean freight business in the

Philippines. But it is the beer and cigarettes that underpin it all. In China they have moved from exports to manufacturing, and that is where I helped — getting them the approvals to build cigarette factories and distilleries."

"There is no home for those products in Canada."

"Of course not. Canada, from what Chang told me, is a source of goods and raw materials that they can sell into Asian markets. They own two jade mines, a host of ginseng farms, and a quasi-legal abalone fishing operation, and they have bought thousands of acres of timber rights. They also own a trading operation that ships scrap metal, chicken feet, cheap cellphones, and a variety of chemicals to China. The Chews are not fussy about what they buy and sell."

"But the problem they have involves real estate."

"It does. They have been building up a real estate portfolio, mostly in and around Vancouver, where Philip lives. Mainly apartment buildings, shopping centres, that kind of thing."

"It sounds like a very big business," Ava said.

Uncle shrugged. "Ordonez is worth at least five billion U.S. dollars, but he and Chang still run the company as if it were a two-man show. They do not trust anyone other than themselves. Even Ordonez's two brothers have limited authority, and now with their problems in Canada, that is not likely to change anytime soon. I asked Chang how they manage to keep on top of everything, and he laughed and said, 'Fear.' Ordonez is known inside the business as the Knife. Chang is the Sledgehammer."

"Nice."

"There is nothing nice about either of them," Uncle said, closing his eyes. "But most businesses are not built by nice people. You need a combination of greed, drive, brains, and paranoia. Between them, Chang and Ordonez have those bases covered."

3

A TALL FILIPINO MAN IN A GREY SUIT WAS STANDING just past the gangway at Manila's Ninoy Aquino International Airport, holding a sign that read MR. CHOW. Standing next to him was a senior Customs official.

Uncle identified himself. The man in the grey suit nodded and introduced himself as Joseph Moreno.

"We'll take you through Customs," Moreno said. "Do you have checked bags?"

"Yes," Uncle said.

"We'll have them cleared and brought to the hotel. Mr. Ordonez wants you to come directly to the office."

They skirted the long, ragged Customs lines. Ava noticed the airport's shiny tile floors, paint peeling off the walls, and a row of flowers in pots, a few of which had cracked and were spilling dirt from their bases. The Filipinos stood quietly, waiting patiently in line, while the Western tourists and businesspeople were sweating, red-faced, and visibly agitated by the almost casual disorganization.

The senior official who had met them at the gate led them to an empty Customs booth. He climbed in, turned on the computer, and held out his hand for their passports. Ava heard murmurs of angry disapproval from the Westerners waiting in line. It had probably taken them an hour to get where they were, and she knew it was making them crazy to see her and Uncle short-circuit the system so casually. *Welcome to the Philippines*, she thought. There were few countries in the world where connections mattered so much.

When they walked out of the airport, they were led to a parking garage on the other side of the roadway, where a black Bentley was purring right beside the exit door. The air was hot and heavy and smelled of diesel fumes. Ava was glad they wouldn't have to linger outside for any length of time.

Moreno opened the back door for Ava and Uncle. "We're only about fifteen minutes from the office, if traffic cooperates," he said. Ava's experiences with Manila traffic told her that fifteen minutes would more likely be thirty — and that was if they were lucky.

As they pulled out of the parking garage they merged with a chaotic crush of cars, buses, motorbikes, bicycles, jeepneys, and pedestrians, all jockeying for space with little regard for rules of the road. Manila's sixteen million people needed to get from point A to point B, and the jeepneys — bright, garishly painted old American military Jeeps converted into small buses that could carry more than thirty people at once — just made it worse. They wove haphazardly from one side of the road to the other, often stopping in the middle of traffic as passengers struggled to get in and out.

The Bentley's driver was being understandably cautious.

He was handling $300,000 worth of car — more money than he could expect to make in a lifetime.

"It's not too bad right now," Moreno said. "The rush hour — well, we call it crash hour — has been over for a while."

As they travelled towards Makati, the financial capital of the Philippines, the city landscape changed. Ava watched low-rise apartment buildings, small storefronts, and sidewalks jammed with vendor stalls and pedestrians give way to the city centre's bank towers, office buildings, Western-style shopping centres, and upscale hotels. The only street vendors there had spread their goods on the pavement and were selling their wares with one eye out for the police.

They passed the Ayala Centre, a massive commercial complex in the very heart of Metro Manila. Ava was remembering wandering its fifty or so hectares on previous visits when they pulled up in front of the Ayala Tower, an impressive V-shaped skyscraper sheathed almost entirely in glass. Moreno leapt out of the front seat and opened the back door for Uncle and Ava.

Outside the soundproofed Bentley they were confronted by the jarring sounds of traffic and a miasma of smoke that smelled of gasoline and ozone pollution. "Let's hurry inside," Moreno said.

There were two guards at the tower entrance, and each held an Uzi across his chest. Ava wasn't surprised. Manila was an armed camp. Every bank branch, every major commercial retailer, every office tower had security stationed at the door. Moreno led them past the guards and into the lobby. Ava veered towards the bank of elevators, only to be redirected. "Mr. Ordonez has a private entrance," he said.

They were led to a small alcove with a single elevator

manned by another guard with another Uzi. They rode the elevator to the top floor, where the door opened onto a semicircular reception area with oak floors covered by a scattering of old and expensive Persian rugs. To Ava's left were two maroon leather couches flanked by easy chairs and anchored by a long rosewood coffee table covered with magazines. To the right was a matching rosewood dining table that held a set of crystal glasses and a crystal decanter filled with water. Groups of eclectic original paintings hung on every wall.

Straight ahead was a young Filipino woman sitting behind a desk. She had a long, lean face and jet-black hair pulled back in a ponytail; she was wearing a sleeveless white blouse with a plunging neckline. There were two doors on her right and one on her left, guarded by a giant of a man in a black suit. He stood quietly, his eyes never leaving them. His weapon wasn't visible but Ava had no doubt he was carrying one.

"Welcome," the young woman said. "I hope the trip from the airport wasn't too difficult."

"It was fine," Moreno responded.

"Please, have a seat. I'll let Mr. Ordonez know you've arrived." She stood and walked to the door to the left. The guard opened it for her and she disappeared inside. Ava and Uncle had barely settled onto one of the couches when she re-emerged alone. "You'll be meeting in the boardroom," she said, motioning to the double doors on the right, and then opened them for Ava and Uncle.

The boardroom had the same oak floors as the reception area, but the soft, rich carpets and rosewood tables were replaced by ultra-modern leather and stainless steel chairs and a sleek glass-topped table. On the walls, a series of Chinese paintings depicting fountains, forests, and dragons made for a strange contrast to the slick, minimalist feel of the furnishings.

A distinguished-looking Chinese man, not much taller than Uncle, walked through a narrow side door almost as soon as they had sat down. He was wearing a red Polo golf shirt and a pair of black Hugo Boss jeans. He was small but sturdy, and his bald head shone in the light. "My friend," the man said, holding out his arms in Uncle's direction.

Uncle and Ava both stood to greet him. The two men hugged, whispering words in each other's ears. As they separated, the man nodded at Ava.

"Ava, this is Mr. Chang Wang," Uncle said.

Chang stared at her, his eyes moving up and down as if doing an appraisal. "Mr. Chang," she said.

"I have heard very good things about you from Chow Tung," Chang said, motioning for them to sit. Ava was surprised by his use of Uncle's given name. She hadn't met many people who were familiar enough with him to address him that way. "But it wasn't nice of you to keep us waiting so long," he said, in a playful tone that still conveyed some displeasure.

Before she could reply, the double doors swung open and Tommy Ordonez strode into the boardroom. He was close to six feet tall but slouched as he walked, his head down as if there were loose change to be found on the floor. She took in the rest of him, and her disappointment grew. He was wearing a casual yellow shirt and blue jeans and a Patek Philippe watch, and his fingernails were cracked and chewed down to nubs. He wore his black hair unfashionably long, flopping over his ears and hanging down well past his shirt collar. It was a huge contrast to the image he projected to the public. In the photos she had seen online, he was always wearing a three-piece suit and had a refined, distant look about him.

Everyone stood and Chang made the introductions. Ordonez gazed fondly at Uncle and then swung his attention to Ava, examining her from head to toe. "I wasn't told you were such a pretty young woman. I expected someone more like a bookkeeper." Ava was startled by Ordonez's voice. The words seemed forced from his mouth, as if an iron vise were gripping his larynx.

She glanced quickly at Uncle. His expression betrayed no reaction. Then she looked back at Ordonez, studying his face. It was certainly Chinese, the eyes smaller than the photos portrayed, the irises pitch-black and intense, but the whites were shot through with crimson patches of broken blood vessels. His face was round, his nose bulbous, his lips thick. High on his left cheek and partially covered by his unruly mop was a large black mole from which sprouted a single long, curly hair. It was a Chinese superstition to let such hairs grow — they were thought to bring good luck.

"I'm not sure what a bookkeeper should look like," Ava said.

Ordonez seemed surprised and shot a look at Chang.

"Let's sit," Chang said.

They took opposite sides of the boardroom table, Ordonez and Chang sitting with their backs to the window so the light shone directly on Uncle and Ava.

"This is a terrible mess," Ordonez said to Uncle. "I'm grateful that you're going to help us get to the bottom of things."

"Until we know exactly what happened, we cannot be sure how much help we can be," Uncle said.

"I have faith in you. When we met all those years ago, I never thought I would actually need to engage your services — or be able to."

Uncle dipped his head to acknowledge the compliment. "And I am honoured to meet you again. This is a remarkable enterprise you have built."

Ordonez took a deep breath. "Thank you. We have worked hard, my brothers and I and Wang, to bring it this far. There haven't been many setbacks, although, as you can imagine, there are always challenges in the Philippines, always some politician who wants to nationalize us, always another who wants us investigated for bribing his colleagues — though that kind usually disappears as soon as we add him to the payroll. All in all, it has been good."

Ordonez's attention was focused entirely on Uncle. Ava was used to that. Chinese men of Ordonez and Chang's background and position treated most women as window dressing. It irritated her, but she would never embarrass Uncle by overreacting. She waited until they had finished their little dance of compliments before inserting herself into the conversation.

"Excuse me, but is Philip Chew going to be with us?"

Ordonez gave her another sharp glance and then turned to stare at Chang.

"I'm sorry for asking, but since your problem seems to stem from the Canadian operation that Mr. Chew runs, I just assumed he would be here."

"Philip is ill. He can't travel," Chang said.

"He's in Vancouver?"

Ordonez glared at Chang.

"This isn't the time to talk about Philip," Chang said. "The records and the files are here, not in Vancouver. That should be a good enough place to start. Louis Marx, who is the comptroller for our Canadian business, is one floor below, in the boardroom there. He's been briefed and will give you all the assistance you need."

"How much money are we discussing?" Ava asked.

"Just over fifty million dollars," Chang said.

"Can you explain to me how you found out about the missing funds?"

"Marx can tell you," Ordonez snapped.

Ava glanced quickly at Uncle, whose steady gaze was on Ordonez. "I don't mean to be rude," Ava said quietly, "but I would like to get an overview from you before I meet with Mr. Marx. He may have a vested interest."

"Ava makes a good point," Uncle said.

Chang looked pained. "It's a swindle, plain and simple. Our Vancouver office thought it was investing in a golf course and residential complex in Kelowna — you do know where Kelowna is?"

"I do," Ava said.

"They worked through a supposed local developer named Jim Cousins. The plan was for him to purchase various tracts of land and to start clearing it and putting infrastructure into place. He fronted the first two million. Our Vancouver office sent him the balance on a purchase-by-purchase basis," Chang said.

"He bought the land first?"

"Yes."

"Then sold it to you?"

"Yes. Marx has all the paperwork downstairs."

"So what happened?"

"There is no land."

"And no fucking Jim Cousins," Ordonez hissed. He was sitting stiffly upright and his eyes were still on Uncle. She could feel him bristling under her gaze.

"How did you find out?" she asked.

"Deloitte is our outside accounting firm," Chang said. "They do an annual audit. This time they were particularly thorough."

"In what way?"

"They sent someone from their Kelowna office to the local land registry to confirm that we had title to the property."

"And you didn't?"

"No. Deloitte informed us that the land that we were supposed to be developing was actually owned by a whole bunch of people who had never heard of us or Jim Cousins."

"But didn't you have copies of the bills of sale, title transfers? Weren't the purchases papered from your end?"

"Forgeries."

"Wonderful," she said.

"That's a poor choice of word," Ordonez said, his eyes finally meeting hers.

"I'm sorry," she said.

"This man Marx," Uncle cut in, "he is completely knowledgeable?"

"As much as can be expected," Chang said. "Philip was the primary contact for Cousins. Everything flowed through Philip."

"And I can't speak with him?" Ava said.

"Ms. Lee," Chang said, "please, no more discussion about Philip. He is ill."

"We can talk by phone, email."

Ordonez interrupted. "My brother has had what my sister-in-law insists is something like a nervous breakdown. She says he isn't up to talking to anyone about anything."

She heard scorn, verging on disgust, in his tone. Ava guessed that Ordonez was someone for whom mental illness either betrayed a character flaw or was merely an excuse for failure. "That is regrettable," she said. "Have you spoken to him at all?"

"No," Ordonez snapped.

"Mr. Chang, have you?"

Chang shifted in his seat. "Louis Marx was the last person in the business to talk to him. You can ask him about what Philip had to say."

Uncle's eyes were still on Ordonez as he said to Chang, "Where is this man Cousins?"

"We have no idea. His office in Kelowna turned out to be a vacant apartment; he moved out about two weeks ago. None of his phone numbers work. His bank says he cleaned out his accounts. We hired a private detective agency to track him through family and friends, credit cards — anything and everything. They came up empty. Cousins has vanished."

"Did Marx meet him?" Ava asked.

"Twice, both times at our Vancouver office when he was dropping off papers."

"So he can describe him for me?"

"I imagine," Chang said.

She heard Uncle shift in his chair. She knew she was

trying the men's patience and that he was sensitive to it.

"I think that maybe Ms. Lee's time would be best spent with Marx," Ordonez said, his breathing rapid and heavy. "There is nothing more we can tell her."

"I agree," Uncle said, reaching over to touch her hand.

"I'll have my girl take her down," Ordonez said to Uncle, turning slightly away from Ava.

"We'll spend some time getting caught up, and we still need to finalize your fee," Chang said. "Then I'll have you taken to the Peninsula. Ms. Lee can join you there later."

4

LOUIS MARX LOOKED UP FROM HIS CHAIR. HE WAS in the boardroom one floor below Ordonez's office, surrounded by boxes and files strewn across the table.

"Hello," Ava said from the doorway.

Marx looked confused. "And what do you want?"

Ava took a few steps forward and stood across the table from Marx. "I've been brought in to help find the money. I thought they'd told you about me. My name is Ava Lee."

"They said they were bringing in an accountant. They didn't give me a name. They also didn't tell me you were a woman — a young woman."

"What did you expect?"

"Someone more like Dog the Bounty Hunter."

She smiled and extended her hand. "Well, I'm Ava Lee."

"Pleased to meet you," Marx said. He stood and reached across the table to shake her hand. His palms were sweaty. He was a large, flabby man, the kind who spent his life indoors behind a desk and had no appetite for exercise. His wrinkled grey slacks were half covered by the tail of his white dress shirt, and his stained blue tie hung loosely around his neck.

"Are you all right?" she asked.

"Not really," Marx said, his eyes darting manically around the room.

"Anything I can do?"

"Yeah, let's get this over with so I can get on a plane and get back to Vancouver."

"What's been going on?"

He waved a hand over the boardroom table. "They've been using me as a punching bag," he said. "I think they're trying to pin this entire fiasco on me. That's what's been going on."

"How so?"

"For the past three days I've been stashed away in this room getting grilled by Mr. Chang and one or another of the other senior financial people here. They come in together, ask questions, and then talk to each other in Chinese or Filipino or whatever language they're speaking, as if I'm not even in the room. Then they start up again. I've answered the same questions ten times."

"That must be unpleasant," Ava said.

"Really? Let me tell you how it started when I got here. They stuck the most incredibly detailed and one-sided non-disclosure agreement in my face and told me to sign it. I said I was an employee and that I'd already signed one in Vancouver. They told me I needed to sign that one too, and if I didn't they'd fire me and then sue me for the missing money. So I signed, of course, but things didn't get any easier."

"Well, it isn't my style to make threats, so why don't we sit and chat. Unless I'm completely misinformed, this is now my project, so you only have to concern yourself about dealing with me."

He seemed to relax as he looked down at the files. "There's a lot of information here, but truthfully, I'm not sure how relevant it is."

She sat at the table, removed a new Moleskine notebook from her Chanel purse, and wrote *Ordonez* across the top of the first page. Ava always used a new notebook for each case, and when the job was completed — successful or not — it was stored away in a safety deposit box at the Toronto-Dominion Bank a few blocks from her condo. "Let's forget about the files for now," she said. "Upstairs they told me a little about this land transaction. Why don't you tell me about this deal from your side. How did it start?"

His right hand ran through his thin sandy hair. "I'm the comptroller for the Canadian operation and the only non-Chinese member of the management board. We meet every Monday morning to review ongoing investments and discuss any proposals that come our way. It's a very static enterprise. We're not in sales or manufacturing, so the business is stable and more or less predictable.

"Well, about six months ago Philip — Mr. Chew, Tommy Ordonez's brother — brought a proposal to the table that was a bit unusual. In the ten years I've been with the company, he's never brought any business to the table. Most of the new initiatives originate from below or come as a directive from Manila. So it was a surprise when Philip informed us he had entered into an agreement to develop a residential community with a golf course in the Kelowna area. You know Kelowna?"

"I do. It's a prime vacation destination," Ava said.

"Lots of money, summer cottages, retirement homes, celebrities. It's tough to think how you could go wrong putting money into a development there. Anyway, Philip described it as a sweetheart deal. We were going to partner with a company called Kelowna Valley Developments, run by a man named Jim Cousins."

"Why 'sweetheart'?"

"KVD was fronting the first two million to secure the deal. We didn't have to put in a dollar until KVD had spent that money, and any money we put in would be to buy the land. The way Philip described it, Cousins would acquire various tracts and handle all that financing until the property was registered. We didn't have to put our money in until we had title. In terms of security, it doesn't get much better."

"How much land was involved?"

"About 1,600 acres that we acquired in dribs and drabs. There were fifteen separate land transactions. Normally we would have expected to get that large a tract in two or three buys, but Philip was happy with the way it was structured. He said it lessened our exposure to any fallout."

"Did the management committee approve the project?"

"It was strictly a formality. Philip was just being polite in keeping us informed. He made all the decisions for the company in Canada — at least, all the decisions up to an individual expenditure of five million dollars. Anything above that amount had to be approved at the head office in Manila."

"So Manila approved it?"

"No. They had never heard of KVD until Deloitte got involved."

"How is that possible? There was close to fifty million dollars invested. I thought you said Philip Chew had signing authority only up to five million."

"Philip told me to treat each land purchase as a stand-alone deal until we had purchased all 1,600 acres. At that point he was going to go to Manila to get approval to roll them up into one package."

"What if they had said no?"

"Not a problem, really. No one's ever gone wrong buying land in and around Kelowna. We could have sold it in a heartbeat."

"Assuming you actually owned the land."

"Yeah, assuming."

"And you never suspected that something strange was going on?"

Marx shook his head, and Ava could see how tired he was. She could imagine what Chang and the others had put him through.

"There wasn't really the opportunity. Philip told us about the deal on a Monday and a week later I was getting the paperwork to support the first purchases. It just kept rolling in. It wasn't until Deloitte started asking questions that I realized it was a bit off-centre."

"Who signed the cheques?"

"Philip and me."

"All under five million?"

"Yeah. Like I said, that was the threshold."

"Mr. Chang told me you met Cousins."

"Twice, both times in Vancouver. I offered to go to Kelowna but he put me off."

"He came to your office?"

"I met him in Philip's office, and they acted like the best of friends. Looking back, that was also kind of strange, because Philip isn't the most sociable character."

"Describe Cousins."

"Big, bluff guy in jeans and an L.L. Bean chamois shirt. I know about the shirt because I asked. He looked as if he had spent his life in construction or lumber. He had that outdoors look."

"Tall?"

"Over six feet."

"Any physical characteristics that would make him stand out in a crowd?"

Marx shuffled the files in front of him, then opened one and leafed through it. "Here, these are photos from the security cameras at the office. They'll give you some idea."

The photographs were grainy and the angles disjointed, but they were good enough for her to see that Cousins was rangy, rugged, and dressed like a cowboy. His face was blurred but she got a general sense that he was a handsome man with a thick black moustache and a full head of hair, combed straight back. "You never ran a credit check on him?"

"Philip gave him the green light."

"How did you discover you had a problem?"

Marx sighed and rolled his eyes skywards. "Deloitte was doing their audit and they came across the land trans-actions. They started off questioning whether or not we had violated the threshold limits. Philip argued with them, say-ing that we had been technically within our rights to do what we did. I know the lead auditor wasn't convinced, but he wasn't about to take on Philip head-on. So they did what auditors do: they burrowed deeper to make sure their asses would be covered in case this became an issue. Sending someone to the registry office in Kelowna was a bit extreme, even for them, but I think they had legitimate concerns about the way the deal was structured."

"Then what happened?"

"Deloitte called me first, then I called Philip. He freaked out and told me to hold off advising Manila until we were completely sure of the facts. I couldn't do that. I knew that Deloitte would report directly to Manila, and I didn't want it to look as if I was withholding information. So I called my counterpart here."

"Mr. Chang?"

"No way — he's the right hand of God. I called the CFO."

"So what happened?"

"I was told to go to Kelowna and meet the people from Deloitte there. We went to the registry office together and confirmed that the land we thought we had bought was owned by people we had never heard of. We went to Cousins' office, which turned out to be a vacant apartment. Then we went to the bank that had supposedly handled the transactions. They wouldn't tell us anything other than that KVD had an account there."

"Who set up the bank account?"

"Cousins."

"Who had signing authority?"

"Cousins."

"You didn't think to have at least two signatures on it?"

"Ava, we had the titles already. We were transferring money for property we had already purchased."

"Okay, so now Manila is involved."

"The CFO flies over to Vancouver, hires a private detective agency to chase down Cousins and the money, and spends two days going through the files with me."

"Where is Philip?"

"At home — devastated, depressed, and not much good for anything."

"You saw him?"

"I did."

"Was he really that distraught?"

"I thought so, and truthfully I didn't fault him. You know that bad cop/good cop cliché? Well, Chang and Ordonez are more like very bad cop and worse cop. Chang has almost reduced me to tears several times on his own. I'm not sure what I would do if I had both of them hammering at me. I'm sure Philip knew what was in store for him."

"And the detectives — they came up empty?"

"Can't find Cousins, can't find the money. All they can tell us is that the KVD bank account is empty and Cousins cleaned out his personal account too."

"How much was in his account?"

"We're told about two million."

"That's a lot of money."

"He fronted the two million to start the project, so he had to have some money," Marx said, and then caught himself. "Of course, he really didn't front anything, did he?"

"No," Ava said softly.

The room went quiet. She had been making notes as Marx spoke. She circled the words *two million* and *personal bank account*.

"Now what?" Marx asked.

"I'd like to spend some time alone with the files. I'm sure

I'm not going to find anything other than what you've told me, but you never know — I could get lucky."

"Be my guest. I'll be glad to get out of this room."

"Do we need to call anyone?"

"To get permission for me to leave, you mean?"

"Yes."

"They told me to do whatever you asked."

"Good. Then why don't you go back to your hotel, have a drink, get a massage, get whatever. Just relax. Louis, we're colleagues now. I'm not the inquisitor. I'm here to figure out what happened and to try to fix it." She shook her head. "I think you should get back to Vancouver as soon as you can. You're like a red flag to these guys. Every time they look at you they're reminded of what went wrong, and they need to lash out. Go home. I'll tell them I need you in Vancouver."

She watched him leave the boardroom, his suit jacket slung over his shoulder, his shirttail hanging out the back of his trousers. She didn't give him another month with the company. If he didn't quit they'd fire him. Someone was going to have to take the blame for this fiasco. And Louis Marx wasn't Chinese and his brother didn't own the company.

HER PHONE RANG AT SEVEN IN THE EVENING. IT WAS the wake-up call she had booked after leaving Ordonez's offices and before crawling into bed with a glass of Pinot Grigio. Ava showered herself into relative consciousness before calling Uncle, who had left a note for her at the front desk, asking her to call him when she checked in.

"*Wei*," he said.

"Uncle, it's Ava."

"I'm in suite 1040. Come and see me."

His door was open when she arrived. The room was beautiful, with gleaming teak floors, elegant bamboo furniture of a quality she knew you couldn't buy anymore, and a king-size four-poster bed with a snow-white down comforter. Uncle was sitting on a bamboo chair, his feet barely touching the ground, a bottle of Tsing Tao beer in his hand. "I have some white wine on ice for you," he said, pointing to a credenza.

"You're spoiling me," she said.

"It is by way of an apology."

"I'm sorry, Uncle, I don't understand." Ava couldn't think

of anything he'd done that required an apology. Even if there had been a slight, their relationship was such that he would have made amends in a more subtle and less direct way.

He waited until she had poured herself a glass and seated herself next to him before leaning towards her. He caught her eye, and she flinched when she saw the anger in his face. "I was very unhappy with the manner in which Chang Wang and Tommy Ordonez treated you today," Uncle said. "I had words with Chang after you left the room. I told him I was not certain we wanted to take the job and that I would leave it up to you."

Ava was surprised by his reaction. She hadn't found Ordonez and Chang more offensive than some of their other rich Chinese clients. *There's something else at play here*, she thought. "Is there a problem with our fee?"

He smiled. "You are so practical."

"Is there?"

"No, just the opposite. After the way they behaved, I insisted on our usual rate. They agreed."

"So what's the issue?"

"Their behaviour," he said. "Chang Wang is waiting downstairs to have dinner with us. I told him that if we are not there by eight o'clock it means we are going back to Hong Kong tomorrow."

"You and Chang Wang — how far back do you go?" she asked, realizing that this had nothing to do with her.

"We are both from Wuhan, and we grew up together as boys in the same village."

"And you've kept in touch all these years?"

Uncle stalled by taking a sip of beer. "We have done

favours for each other," he said slowly. "Chang helped me get to Hong Kong. After I was established, I helped him get to the Philippines, where he had a brother. From time to time our businesses — my old one — needed help, and we were there for each other. In China today, Tommy Ordonez would be nothing but an ink blot if it were not for my connections. And Chang helped me make a lot of money in these islands."

"Such old friends, and close friends. There can't be too many men from that village who made it out, let alone became so successful."

"Only a few of us, and that makes it worse."

Now she understood. By being rude to her, Uncle thought they had been disrespectful to him. He was at times overly sensitive to slights, and as he got older she noticed he was more easily irked. She also knew he didn't care about Ordonez's behaviour; it was Chang's attitude that bothered him. "Uncle, Chang Wang was in a difficult position today. Tommy Ordonez is obviously in a rage over this Canadian business. His own brother, whom he obviously trusted, has failed him. You wouldn't expect Chang to openly chastise or oppose Ordonez. Maybe by being a little rude to me himself, he managed to moderate Ordonez. I'm sure that his actions towards me meant no disrespect to you."

Uncle leaned back in the chair and closed his eyes. "Ava, if you want to go back to Hong Kong we will leave Ordonez to sort out his own mess," he said quietly.

"Uncle, that would be the wrong reason to go back to Hong Kong."

"What do you mean?"

"From what I've read and heard, Philip Chew is up to his

neck in this thing. That's obvious to me, to you, and I'm sure to them. So why do they want to use us at all?"

He took another sip of beer. "You are probably right, of course. They do suspect Philip, Chang more than Ordonez. Ordonez is still willing to give his younger brother the benefit of the doubt. They want us to eradicate that doubt."

"And then what, push us aside?"

"No, I was firm about that and they agree. Even if we discover that Philip was responsible for the loss, there is the matter of determining what he did and why he did it. And then there is still fifty million dollars — or part of fifty million dollars — that we need to find and recover."

"Why hasn't Ordonez confronted his brother?"

"He wants to be one hundred percent sure of the facts."

"I'm not sure I believe that," she said.

"Neither do I, but Chang did say that when they sent their CFO in Manila to Vancouver, Philip Chew would not meet with him or talk to him on the phone. The CFO even went to his house but was not allowed through the front door. Chew seems to have barricaded himself inside. So maybe Ordonez has not talked to him because he cannot," Uncle said. He paused and looked down at his beer. "Ava, Ordonez is a very proud man, and I know that is another reason why we are involved. He wants to keep this whole affair as private as possible. Inside the company they are blaming this Jim Cousins for concocting the scheme and they are saying that Louis Marx did not do his job properly. That is the official line, and I am not sure anything we find will change that, internally at least. You need to understand that, in Manila, Ordonez is a superstar in the business community. He has hardly put a wrong foot forward. If it comes out that he was swindled by his own brother, he will become a cheap headline in the *Manila Star* and every other newspaper in the country. And in the Philippines image is important. The idea of people laughing behind his back makes Ordonez crazy."

"Chang told you all this?"

"Most of it."

She sat quietly for a moment, calculating costs. "Uncle, what if we prove Chew's culpability? What if I find out where the money went and there is no money to be retrieved?"

"We have a standby fee of one million dollars."

"How much time do they expect us to devote to this?"

"I told them that if we could not find answers within a week, then we would part ways."

"There isn't much downside to that," she said.

"I think not."

"Then let's take the job."

He smiled. "As I said, a practical girl."

"And a greedy one. I want that fee."

She started to rise, assuming their conversation was over, but Uncle remained in his chair. "There's something else I don't know?" she asked.

Uncle sipped his beer. "The fat man you saw me with at the airport in Hong Kong."

"Yes?"

"His name is Lop Liu."

"You implied he ran the Triad in Mong Kok."

"He does."

"What does that have to do with me?"

"Do you remember Jackie Leung?"

"The toy manufacturer just outside Guangzhou? The one

who tried to move the business to Vietnam without telling his partner? I caught up with him in Ho Chi Minh City."

"You beat him, yes?"

"He came at me with a crowbar."

"All he remembers is that you beat him and took his money. Lop told me that Jackie has become very successful, and he has *guanxi* — connections and influence — with some of my old adversaries. The fat man told me that Jackie wants repayment for the misery we put him through."

Ava was accustomed to threats and wondered why Uncle was taking this one to heart. "You're not nervous, are you?"

He waved his hand. "Me, they would never think about harming. It is you that pig Leung has targeted."

"Uncle, why are you telling me this?" she asked.

"I want you to be careful."

"I always am."

"Ava, these are serious and competent people who have been well paid, with promises of more if they can kill you. You need to be alert until I can resolve this."

"And how will you do that?"

"I am going to have Leung taken care of."

"Then what do I have to worry about?"

"I have to find him first."

BALD-HEADED CHANG WANG SAT LIKE A SMALL BUDDHA in the hotel lobby, where he was being fussed over by female staff. When he saw Uncle and Ava, he pushed himself to his feet. "I made a reservation for us in the Old Manila restaurant here in the hotel," he said without a flicker of emotion. "They have excellent filet mignon. You do eat red meat, I hope, Ava."

"I'm Chinese, Uncle Chang. I eat everything," she said.

He noted her show of respect with a slight smile. "It has been a difficult day for all of us," he said. "I appreciate your patience."

They all ordered Caesar salad and the filet mignon. The two men drank beer with dinner; Ava had white burgundy from the bottle Chang insisted on ordering for her. He waited until they had finished eating and were contemplating cognac before turning to business. "How was your time with Louis Marx?" he asked.

"I found him entirely believable," she said.

"What do you mean?"

"Being a comptroller has to be one of the most thankless

jobs in the world. It's a constant juggling act. On the one hand you have a set of professional guidelines and a code of ethics that you try to adhere to, and on the other you have a boss who is constantly pressuring you to cut corners. Then if that weren't enough, there's outside scrutiny from companies like Deloitte, ready to point fingers at the slightest misstep. And when they do, of course, your boss forgets that he pushed you to compromise the law and lets you take all the blame. I think Louis Marx did what Philip Chew wanted him to do. Nothing more, nothing less."

"So you think the fault for this loss lies with Philip Chew?"

"Of course, and so do you," she said to Chang.

Uncle interrupted. "I spoke frankly to Ava."

Chang didn't seem surprised. "But what about this Cousins — what do you think about him?"

"He's an important part of this," Ava said. "If we're lucky he'll turn out to be the villain. In any event, I need to track him down. As a starting point I want to see the reports from the detectives you hired. They weren't in the files I saw today."

"I'll have them for you in the morning."

"I also couldn't find any record of incorporation for Kelowna Valley Developments. Didn't anyone check to see who actually owned it?"

"We did," Chang said. "It's owned by a numbered company, also incorporated in British Columbia. But when we traced it, we found that the shares are being held in trust by a Vancouver lawyer."

"In trust for whom?"

"We don't know and he wouldn't tell us. We assumed it was Cousins."

"I'll need the name of the lawyer."

"Of course."

"And there were no banking records for KVD?"

"We don't have any. The account was opened by Cousins and he had sole signing authority. We've requested information, but the bank is not forthcoming."

"Which bank?"

"Toronto Commonwealth."

Well, that's a break, she thought.

The two men ordered cognac. Ava was only halfway through the bottle of wine and wasn't about to finish it. She waited until the snifters arrived before saying, "Uncle Chang, Louis Marx told me you made him sign a non-disclosure agreement. Do you need me to do the same?"

"Of course not. You work with Uncle and you have his absolute confidence. And now you have mine. No one doubts your discretion."

"And discretion seems to be very important to you and Mr. Ordonez."

Chang held the snifter to his nose. "Tommy Ordonez is a Chinoy. Do you know what that is?"

"Yes," Ava said.

"The fact that he is the richest man in the Philippines doesn't change that. He has never been and never will be accepted by the six or seven old Spanish families who have run this country for centuries, families whose members take turns being president. They respect him to his face, of course, and they're afraid of the power he can exert. But they will never accept him and they would like nothing more than to see him shamed. You noticed, I assume, that Tommy has a very unusual voice?"

"Of course."

"He had a throat ailment when he was a boy, and it was badly treated. No more damage can be done and it doesn't affect his health in any way, but he knows that in private they mimic and mock him. The condition is something he can't change and their ignorance doesn't affect him, but the way they perceive him as a businessman and as the head of his family does matter to him. He's viewed as a man who never puts a wrong foot forward. That's not true, of course, but that's his image, and there is a lot to be gained from maintaining that image. And it's a great source of pride to him as well as being a matter of practicality. Public knowledge of discord in the family, let alone that a younger brother might have cheated him, would cause Tommy almost unbearable humiliation."

"Assuming there was cheating."

"I'm not a man who puts his head in the sand," Chang said. "Fifty million dollars or more is missing from our company's coffers, and Philip's signature is on every agreement." He knocked back his cognac in one shot and looked at Ava. "Find out what happened, find out why it happened, and find as much of the money as you can."

(7)

IT WAS JUST PAST NINE THIRTY IN MANILA, WHICH meant that offices in Toronto were open for business. Ava turned on her laptop and went into her phonebook. She hadn't spoken to Johnny Yan in three months but she hadn't heard of any change in his employment status at Toronto Commonwealth Bank through their mutual friends from York University.

When Ava attended York, almost a third of her class were of Chinese origin. Some of them had naturally gravitated towards one another, and bonds were formed. By the time she graduated her group was down to ten close friends, all of them committed to succeeding and all of them committed to helping each other. It was the Chinese way — not much different from the ties that Uncle had forged over the years, although the scale was obviously much smaller.

She called Johnny on the hotel line and he answered on the second ring. "This is Ava," she said.

"Where are you? I don't recognize that country code."

"Manila."

"Lucky you. It's snowing like hell here."

"Johnny, I need a favour. Can you talk?"

Johnny knew what Ava did for a living, so nothing she asked for surprised him. "Shoot," he said.

"The company is called Kelowna Valley Developments and it had an account at one of your branches. The sole signee was a guy named Jim Cousins. The account would have been opened about six months ago, and over those six months around fifty million dollars was deposited and withdrawn. I need to know where the money went."

"Do you have an account number?"

"No."

"God, you always make me do extra work."

She laughed. "Johnny, one more thing. I think Cousins had a personal account there as well, and I'd like to know how active it was. You may have to go back further. In fact, it would be helpful if you could go back as far as you can."

"Two years is about the maximum the system will allow."

"That's fine."

"How quickly do you need this?"

"Now."

"Of course," he said, laughing. "I have a meeting starting in ten minutes and I'll be tied up most of the morning. I won't be able to get to it until lunch time."

"I'll wait up."

Ava hung up and signed into her email. There was a note from Derek saying he had moved into her condo for a few days and that he intended to contact Mimi. And by the way, he wrote, is she the short, chunky brunette or the tall blonde with large breasts?

Before leaving Toronto, Ava had barely had enough time to get things sorted. She had been reduced to firing off last-minute emails to her sister, Marian; her mother, Jennie; and her best friend, Mimi. However, she did have time to talk to one of her closest male friends, Derek Liang. Derek was the only other person she knew who practised bak mei, one of the oldest and deadliest martial arts, and she employed him from time to time in her work. He lived in Richmond Hill, a northern suburb of Toronto that was predominantly Chinese, and had expressed interest in moving downtown. What he really wanted was to meet some women who weren't the usual Chinese princesses he dated. She had left a key to her condo for him with the building manager and told him she would let her friend Mimi know he was moving in. The moment she had said it, she felt a flutter of regret.

Ava deleted Derek's message and opened an email from Mimi. The subject line read MARIA.

Ava,
I gave your name and email address to a woman last night. Her name is Maria Gonzalez and she's an assistant trade commissioner at the Colombian consulate. I met her at a business function and we chatted. She flirted with me in a nice, shy kind of way. I asked her if she was gay. She is. So I talked about you and told her she should contact you. I know how private you are and I'm sorry if you think I was being indiscreet, but Ava, this is a wonderful young woman. She's beautiful, tall, graceful, and smart. Don't be surprised if she contacts you. And don't worry, I'll take care of Derek.
Love,
Mimi

Ava sighed. The last thing she needed was for her personal life to get in the way of business. She lay on the bed and tried to nap, but her mind was racing. Uncle's information about Jackie Leung had caught her off guard, and now as she digested it she felt surprise and a touch of alarm. She had been threatened before by people she had rousted, but it had always amounted to nothing. She wondered if this could be different.

Leung's case had been a nothing job, a simple matter of the active partner in a business trying to move the company's assets before the passive partner, the investor, caught on. She had cornered Leung in Ho Chi Minh and forced him to give everything back. That had meant keeping him locked in a hotel room for most of a day and dunking his head in the toilet every hour or so. She was new at the game then, less sure of herself and less sure about what tactics would work. When he finally capitulated, they drove in his car to the bank to make the money transfer. Just outside the bank he said he needed to get some papers from the trunk, and then he charged at her with a crowbar.

Ava had broken his arm and his nose. She took him to a hospital to get patched up and then drove back to the bank to conclude the business. When they returned to his car, she locked him in the trunk. She had no idea how long it took for someone to find him.

She thought she had handled Leung with only as much force as was needed. If he hadn't attacked her he wouldn't have been hurt at all, except for his ego and his wallet. Just as she was wondering what part of the ordeal had made him angry enough to pay people to come after her, her phone rang.

"This is an interesting account," Johnny said.

She noticed he was using his cellphone. "What did you find?"

"It looks like it was used as a transit account — money in and then, just as quickly, money out."

"Can you give me the amounts and dates?"

"Do you have a notepad? There's quite a bit of detail here."

"In front of me."

"I'll give you the deposits first."

"Go ahead."

There were fifteen deposits, all of them less than $5 million, just as Louis Marx had described. The dates were random. In one week three deposits had been made and there was a gap of close to three weeks between two others. The very first deposit was for $4 million, Ava saw. Marx had said that Cousins fronted $2 million. That meant that the $2 million Cousins was supposed to have put in the account was never deposited. As Johnny gave her the deposit amounts, Ava kept a running tally. They totalled $58 million, a bit more than Chang had said.

"What a strange pattern," Ava said.

"The withdrawals are even weirder," Johnny said.

"How so?"

"The day after each of these cheques was cleared, a wire was sent to Costa Rica for almost that exact same amount."

"Costa Rica? That's hardly an offshore haven."

"I know, and what's stranger still is that the money was sent to six different banks and to fifteen different individuals. Crazy, huh?"

"Give me the details," she said.

As she copied the names and the amounts withdrawn, a

pattern began to emerge. "Johnny, those wires weren't the only withdrawals, right?"

"No. Every time a wire was sent, money was transferred on the same day to another Toronto Commonwealth account."

"Jim Cousins' personal account?"

"Yep."

"And if I'm doing my numbers correctly, it looks like it was for three percent of every deposit."

"More like three and a half."

"A commission?"

"Why not?"

"For laundering money?"

"That's a logical conclusion."

"So, Johnny, why didn't alarms go off at the bank?"

"Read the list I just gave you. Six banks. Fifteen people. Costa Rica. How does that fit any money-laundering profile you've ever encountered?"

She read the names Johnny had given her. Wilma Castro Hernandez. Maria Rodriguez. Jose Villanueva. And so on. "It doesn't."

"Exactly. So the bank wouldn't have picked up on anything."

"So we're either dealing with a very sophisticated money-laundering operation or something entirely different. How about Cousins' account?"

"Closed about two weeks ago."

"How long was it open?"

"About six months."

"Was there ever two million in it?"

"Not until these transfers started, and it didn't get to two million until they came to an end. And then, of course, the account was closed and the money was moved out."

"Where did Cousins send it?"

"Jersey."

"New Jersey?"

"You should be so lucky. Jersey in the Channel Islands. Although . . ."

"Did you find something?" she urged.

"There are some attachments to the Jersey wire transfer file. Give me a minute."

Please be good to me, she thought.

"If this guy Cousins is trying to hide money he must be an amateur," Johnny said when he came back on the line. "Two days after his money went to Jersey he must have tried to do something with the account there, because we got a request from the bank to reconfirm the account holder's status with us."

"And?"

"They provided us with a copy of his passport and, believe it or not, his Kelowna address and a forwarding address in the U.S."

"I love you, Johnny Yan," she said.

"And so you should. This is going to cost you a dinner," he said, and then gave her Cousins' San Francisco address.

Ava hung up, hardly believing her luck.

She went online and found the building, an apartment/ hotel with units available for rent by the week and month. She checked the time. It was mid-morning on the U.S. west coast. She dialled the number on the website. A pleasant, young-sounding woman confirmed that there were vacant apartments. Ava gave the woman her name and asked if she could stop by to see them the following day. That wouldn't be a problem, she was told.

"And by the way," Ava said, "I have a work colleague named Jim Cousins who said he was moving into the building. Is he in residence yet?"

"He is, indeed," the woman said.

Ava emailed her travel agent and asked her to book a seat on the first flight out of Manila to San Francisco. She would call Uncle in the morning. She just wasn't sure how much she was going to tell him.

8

IT WAS ALMOST 9 A.M. BY THE TIME AVA GOT TO THE airport and began the slow, torturous process of getting to the boarding gate. She had planned to go to the first-class lounge before her flight, but by the time she got through security there was only fifteen minutes before departure, so she went directly to her gate. She turned on her cellphone to call Uncle and saw that he had left two messages. She chastised herself for not calling him earlier.

"Uncle, I'm sorry," she said when he answered his phone. "I left the hotel early this morning and I didn't want to wake you."

"You worried me," he said softly. "Where are you?"

"At the airport. I've located Jim Cousins. I'm on my way to talk to him."

Even over the phone she could hear his breathing change, his spirits rise. "Good God, so soon. Even for you, Ava, this is fast."

"I was lucky, and if my luck holds he'll be exactly where I think he is."

"Where?"

"In an apartment in San Francisco."

"How did you do it?"

"That doesn't matter. You can tell Chang if you want, but it might be wise to wait until I actually get there and confront him."

"I think he should know."

"No promises, though."

"What do you mean?"

"Just because I've located Cousins doesn't mean he'll be there. And even if he is, it doesn't mean we're any closer to recovering the money. So be careful about what you say. Don't let them draw the wrong conclusion."

"Where is the money?"

"I have no idea," she half-lied.

She could sense his doubt — he knew she wasn't telling him everything. "When you find out, call me in Hong Kong. I am going to fly back today after meeting with Chang and Ordonez," he said.

"I will," she promised. The call for first-class passengers to board the plane came over the PA. Ava was guided to her seat by a series of flight attendants. When she had settled in with a cup of coffee in hand, she reviewed her notes, trying to make sense of the information Johnny Yan had given her. Aside from the fact that all the money had gone to Costa Rica, the amounts and the recipients and the banks seemed to be almost completely random. The same wasn't true for the three and a half percent that had found its way into Jim Cousins' bank account. It was obviously for services rendered, but what services?

She sat up straight and gingerly stretched her arms. Her shoulder still ached, and a combination of wine, Tylenol, and the comfort of the Peninsula's bed hadn't blunted the pain. She tried to distract herself by focusing on the documents Chang had sent early that morning. The detectives' report was long on verbiage and short on substance. *Maybe they're getting paid by the word*, she thought. Most of it focused on Cousins. They had come up dry at the bank and had run into a brick wall with the lawyer, who wouldn't breach his trust.

She shorthanded the information on Cousins into her notebook. Calgary born, educated at the Southern Alberta Institute of Technology. Worked in the Alberta oil fields, Saskatchewan oil fields, Texas oil fields, and Indonesian oil fields, then back to the northern Alberta tar sands. No wife. No kids. No mention of Kelowna until just over six months ago. He had arrived there out of nowhere, and then he was gone.

The people in Kelowna who met him had thought he was a cowboy and a gentleman. Cousins didn't seem to have a job but he paid his rent on time, and most nights he dropped a couple of hundred dollars at the local casino without getting bent out of shape. He didn't drink, do drugs, or do women. He paid his taxes and had no criminal record. He also had no credit cards, which must have complicated the detectives' work no end, since credit card usage was their favourite trail. They had included a copy of his passport and several photos with the report. She took them out and slipped them into the back of her notebook. The rest of their work went into the garbage.

Ava turned to the file on Kelowna Valley Developments. The company had been incorporated in British Columbia just before Jim Cousins arrived in Kelowna. He was listed as president. The work had been done by the law firm of McDougal, Fraser, and Ling. The registered owner was a B.C. numbered company and the shares in the numbered company were held in trust by Edward Ling. The law firm's offices were in the Pacific Tower in downtown Vancouver. Edward Ling was listed as a senior and founding partner.

Ava put her notebook away and reclined her seat. She needed to take a break. She searched for a movie to watch and found Wong Kar Wai's classic *In the Mood for Love*. It was a slow and introspective story about unrequited love, starring two of Hong Kong's most famous actors, Maggie Cheung and Tony Leung. Ava wasn't accustomed to seeing Leung in anything but action movies, but he held her interest, although not as much as Cheung, who, long and languid and dressed in the most exquisite cheongsams, stole every scene she was in.

Ava fell asleep as Leung and Cheung misconnected for the last time. When she woke, the plane was less than an hour outside San Francisco, where, she hoped, she would find her next target.

9

SHE HAD BEEN TO SAN FRANCISCO TWICE BEFORE, once on a job and the second time with a lover who wanted her to see the gay scene's Mecca. Unfortunately Mecca was too out there for Ava, and the trip went badly. She flew home early, and alone.

It was a grey, dismal day, promising rain. Driving a silver Audi A6 she had rented at the airport, Ava exited the highway and started to work her way through Japantown and the Fillmore area to Lower Pacific Heights. She was impressed by how attractive the city looked, even in such gloomy weather. The twisting, climbing streets were lined with trees; colourful, quirky storefronts; and rows of red-brick Victorian-style houses.

She turned onto Post Street, which was mostly apartment buildings, and parked the car at the end of the road. She looked at herself in the rear-view mirror and realized she was a bit dishevelled from the flight. She brushed her hair back and fixed it with the ivory chignon pin, retouched her makeup, and smoothed out the front of her shirt, tucking it into her slacks. *Presentable, professional*, she thought.

The doorman smiled at her when she was still twenty paces away. He was positively beaming by the time she reached the entrance. "Hello, my name is Ava Lee. I called yesterday about viewing one of the apartments. Could you ask the rental office if they have time to show me a unit?"

He called inside on his walkie-talkie. Ava heard a woman's voice answer that she was in a meeting and hoped Ms. Lee wouldn't mind waiting. The doorman looked at Ava, his eyebrows raised.

"I have a colleague staying here — Jim Cousins. I could visit with him for a while. Could you ask if that's okay?" she said.

"Certainly," the woman said. "Mr. Cousins is in apartment 306. Tell Ms. Lee to come by my office on the ground floor when she's ready."

This is too easy, Ava thought as she walked through the door and into the building.

She felt a touch of nerves as she approached apartment 306. This was the time when expectations gave way to reality. If he was home she hoped he would be reasonable, if not accommodating. But she was prepared for just about anything. Over the years she had experienced everything — shouting, cursing, crying, threats, even physical attacks.

She knocked on the door and waited. Nothing. She knocked again and counted to twenty. She was about to turn and leave when the door opened. Jim Cousins stood in front of her, his hair tousled and pillow creases stamped on his cheek. He was taller than she had expected, definitely over six feet, and more handsome. He wore jeans and a white T-shirt that failed to hide his strong, lean physique.

"Can I help you?" he said, not unkindly.

"Mr. Cousins, my name is Ava Lee."

"I'm sorry, am I supposed to know you?"

"No, but I know you. I've been sent by the Ordonez organization to have a chat with you about the Kelowna Valley Developments project."

She braced herself, preparing for her body to be slammed against the wall, for a fist to be thrust at her face, for a kick to be aimed at her groin, all accompanied by a shower of obscenities. This was when it always happened.

He shrugged. "Sure. C'mon in."

Ava blinked in surprise and walked past Cousins into the living room. There were boxes everywhere. "I haven't finished unpacking," he said, closing the front door. "You want coffee or anything?"

"Instant is fine," she said, still unsettled by his casual manner.

"We'll sit in the kitchen," he said.

Ava followed Cousins into the kitchen and sat at a small round table with two chairs. She pulled out her Moleskine notebook while he fussed with two mugs. "I just take it black," she said.

He put a mug in front of her and then sat down. "Could you tell me your name again, and do you have any ID?"

"My name is Ava Lee and I'm an accountant. Here's my business card."

"An accountant, eh? You aren't what I was expecting."

"You were expecting someone?"

"Yeah, but not someone like you, and not this soon."

"They hired detectives when they couldn't find you on their own."

"I borrowed a buddy's car, drove to Saskatchewan, then crossed the border into North Dakota. They just wave you through there if you look like a local. I also don't use credit cards or debit cards. That's just my lifestyle — nothing sinister. I figured I'd be hard to track."

"But why would you want to be so evasive in the first place?"

He smiled. His eyes caught hers and she saw no fear, no hesitation in them. "Philip asked me to stall for him, give him some time to get things sorted."

"Philip Chew?"

"Who else?"

There were times when Ava wished her instincts were wrong. "I expected as much," she said.

"Really? I'm surprised."

"You don't exactly have the background of a scam artist, and on first impression I don't think you're a good enough liar to get Philip Chew to buy in to some bogus land deal."

"Why, thank you."

They sat silently, drinking their coffee. "Could I have another?" she asked.

"How did you find me?" he asked, his back turned as he poured water into her mug.

"Through the Jersey bank," she said.

"Shit. I told Philip I didn't want to jump through hoops and loops, but he told me if I moved my money directly from Canada to the U.S. it would be caught in no time. So he sent me to this Jersey bank as a kind of halfway house. Some of my money actually just got here yesterday."

"Your two million or so?"

"I was paid $2,030,000," he said.

She opened her notebook. "Do you mind if I write this down?"

"Be my guest."

"You're an oil-field worker, I understand."

"I was an oil-field worker. A technician, but still working outside," he said. "I've worked all over the place. The last job was in bloody Fort McMurray — northern Alberta — those horrendous tar sands. I put in six months without a break, built myself a very nice bankroll, and decided to treat myself to an extended holiday in Las Vegas. That's where I met Philip."

Ava's heart sank. There was no worse combination in the world than Las Vegas and a Chinese gambler.

"I play poker for relatively high stakes — ten- to twenty-dollar no-limit hold'em. I started off at the Bellagio but there's a real pecking order there. If you're not a high roller or a professional player you get treated like shit. So I moved my action to the Venetian and got in with an okay crowd. We played in a private room just to the side of the main area. Philip was one of the regulars. He and I played together for six or seven consecutive days.

"Everybody thinks poker is cutthroat but, you know, you can only play so many hands, and when you're not playing a hand or you're between hands, there's a lot of chit-chat. It actually gets kind of social. That's when Philip and I got to know each other."

"What kind of poker player is he?"

"Not bad, not bad at all. He tended to play a little too tight and that worked against him, especially in Vegas, where they pick up on your tendencies really quickly. But it didn't kill him. When he drank, well, that was another story. The more he downed, the looser he got and the more money he lost. He didn't drink that often, though. I figure he was down maybe thirty or forty thousand for the week we played together. Not that he gave a shit. He never lost his cool."

"How did you do?"

"I was up two thousand. It should have been more, but I lost a couple of monster pots the last two days I was there."

"So you and Phillip played poker together."

"And we talked. He told me about his business, about his big-time brother. I told him about my rather crappy existence. Despite the difference in our lifestyles, we hit it off. On my fourth day at the table, Philip asked me to join him for dinner. We ate at the Chinese restaurant in the Venetian, comped, of course, and he opened up a bit more. We did the same the next night and the night after that. On the sixth night he asked me if I wanted to do some business with him. I told him I wasn't a businessman. He said not to worry, that he would look after all the details. All I had to do was follow his lead and act like I owned a company.

"I told him I needed to know exactly what I was getting myself into. He told me that he hadn't finalized his plans yet and said he would like to contact me in a week or two if that was okay by me. I had no reason to say no. I wasn't back in Fort McMurray more than a week before he called. He asked me to fly to Kelowna to meet him. And I did."

"He had set up Kelowna Valley Developments by then?"

"Yep."

"Why Kelowna?"

"He said it was far enough from Vancouver to discourage casual visits."

"From whom?"

"His wife."

"His wife?"

"Yep, that's why he was doing all this shit. He had money he needed to move out of the country into some investments, and she was all over him. He said she wouldn't care if he was putting money into land in Kelowna."

"And he wanted you to be the middle man. That's all, right?"

"That's all."

"And you leapt at the chance?"

He looked at her as if she were crazy. "Have you ever been to Fort McMurray?"

"No."

"Have you ever spent an entire winter working outdoors in minus-twenty-degree weather?"

"No."

"Well, you're goddamn right I leapt at the chance."

"So you became president of Kelowna Valley Developments."

"I did. He brought the articles of incorporation with him and gave me a cheque for ten thousand dollars to open a bank account."

"And then how did it work?"

"Philip would send me all the paperwork I needed. I just turned around and sent it back to his office. They'd cut me a cheque, I'd deposit it, then Philip would tell me where to wire it. It was real simple."

"And you kept three and a half percent."

"That was the deal."

"Didn't you think that was a lot of money for simply shuffling paper around?"

"The wife sounds pretty fierce," he said, with a slightly sheepish grin.

"That's bull," she said.

He averted his eyes.

"You knew what you were doing was probably highly illegal."

"But I didn't know for sure."

"You're no idiot. You could have guessed."

Cousins tapped his fingers on the table, his attention wandering. "Wait here," he said.

She watched him as he walked towards what she guessed was his bedroom. She wondered if the cooperative phase was over.

When he came back into the kitchen he was carrying a large brown envelope. "Let me finish the story, and then I'll show you this," he said.

"Go ahead."

"Everything went smoothly for about five months, and then two weeks ago Philip called me in a fucking panic. He said his wife's auditors were all over the deal and that it might be best for me to get out of Kelowna. I told him I wasn't scared of his wife or her auditors, because as far as I was concerned I hadn't done anything wrong. That's when he told me that it was company money I'd been sending to Costa Rica.

"He told me he needed to go to Manila to sort things out, and that if I just laid low for a few weeks everything would be fine. He told me to take my money with me. I told him I still had an account with one of the big U.S. banks from my days working in Texas. He said that would be too easy to track, and gave me the name of the bank in Jersey."

"Did he tell you to come to San Francisco as well?"

"Hell, no, that was my decision. I'm gay." Her surprise must have registered on her face, because he asked, "Do you have a problem with that?"

"Hardly," Ava said. "Let's get back to Philip. How was his mood during this period?"

"Progressively wackier."

"When was the last time you spoke to him?"

"I called him after I crossed the border."

"And?"

"He told me not to worry."

"Strange advice, given the circumstances."

"I don't see why," he said.

She was impressed again by his calmness and then moved to roil it. "You know you're going to have to give that money back, don't you?"

His face was impassive. "I'm not giving anything back," he said. "I earned it. I'm keeping it."

"Philip Chew stole it."

"Not that I knew."

"You knew, but you just didn't want to admit it. Why do you think the money was sent to all those individuals if he was investing in a business? What sense does that make?"

"He said that was the way they wanted it done."

"And you actually believed that?"

Cousins looked away and shifted uncomfortably in his chair. *He had wanted to believe it*, she thought, *but he knew.* He opened the envelope and took out a document. "Here, this is a contract I had a lawyer draw up with Philip," he said, slipping it across the table to her. "I'm not a total fool. It outlines exactly what I was to do and why I was to do it. There's an affidavit at the back signed by Philip that swears the money is his to do with as he wishes. He's specific about investing money in Costa Rica. My lawyer put in a paragraph that absolves me of any responsibility for the project. I was simply an employee, performing a task based on Philip's sworn and notarized statement that everything was completely legal and above board."

She read the document, aghast at how dumb — or desperate — Philip Chew must have been to sign the contract. Jim Cousins' lawyer had done a very good job.

"Can I keep this copy?" she asked.

"Sure, I have others."

"What a mess this is," she said to herself.

"Go and talk to Philip."

"I'm not sure they'll leave you alone, you know, the guys in Manila. They're capable of deciding that, contract or no contract, you have their money. It could get ugly."

"Is that a threat?"

"No, a friendly warning."

"I'm not giving it back," he said again.

She could tell he was uneasy, but the truth was she didn't want to push too hard. The two million wasn't going to make much difference to Ordonez, and Cousins had been cooperative. She could always explain to Manila about the contract and tell them she didn't want to risk having Cousins go public.

"Fair enough," Ava said. "Tell you what, we'll leave it like that for now, under the condition that you don't show that contract to anyone else. This is strictly between you and me."

"Why would you do that?"

"You've been honest with me when you could have lied."

He looked dubious.

"I'm not lying to you," Ava said.

"And all I have to do is bury the contract?"

"Basically."

He extended his hand across the table. "It's a deal."

10

AVA SAT IN THE RENTED AUDI OUTSIDE COUSINS' apartment building, going through her options. About one thing she was certain: if she went to Chang Wang and Tommy Ordonez with the information she had, her involvement would be over. They would circle the wagons around the family and deal with Philip in their own way. She did not want that to happen. For one thing, she was curious, really curious, about the Costa Rica connection. Even if there wasn't any money for her to reclaim in Central America, she wanted to understand the how and the why of what Philip had done. And then there was the money — maybe a lot of money — and she wanted her chance to go after it. The job still had the potential of being one of the biggest paydays she and Uncle had ever had.

It was just past one thirty in the afternoon, which meant that it was four thirty in the morning in Hong Kong. Still too early to call Uncle, but the perfect time to call Vancouver. She needed to confirm for whom the shares were being held in trust. She didn't have much doubt that it was for Philip Chew, but it would be a way for her to start a conversation with Edward Ling, and he might help get her access to Chew.

The receptionist at McDougal, Fraser, and Ling informed her that Mr. Ling was not in the office and asked if she wanted to leave a message. "This is a matter of some urgency involving a member of his family," Ava said. "I need to speak to his assistant."

"To whom am I speaking?" Ling's assistant asked.

"My name is Ava Lee. I need to speak directly to Mr. Ling."

"What is this concerning?"

Ava knew she wasn't going to get anywhere by being evasive. "I'm an accountant, a forensic accountant, and I've been engaged by a multinational corporation to investigate the improper transfer of a considerable amount of their money. I believe that your law firm has an involvement in this transaction. Specifically, I believe Mr. Ling has an involvement through a client of his."

When the assistant didn't respond, Ava made things clearer. "I need to talk to him to straighten this matter out, one way or another, before I submit my report and various authorities, *legal* and otherwise, get dragged into it," she said.

"He's in conference and won't be back for another hour or two."

"Please have Mr. Ling call me as soon as possible. I'll be waiting."

Ava sat in the car looking up and down Post Street for a restaurant, but she didn't see one that interested her. Then she realized she was only a short ride from Chinatown.

At one time San Francisco's Chinatown was pre-eminent

in North America. But with a growing Chinese diaspora across the continent, the Bay area could no longer boast having the best Chinese restaurants. Maybe she was just being biased, but Ava didn't think any city could surpass Chinatown North in Toronto. In fact, she and Uncle sometimes argued about whether Toronto was on par with Hong Kong. A thousand of the best Hong Kong chefs were now practising their trade in Toronto, and they hadn't lost their skills in moving to the West.

Ava parked her car in a lot on Bush Street and walked two blocks east to Grant. The southern entranceway to Chinatown was framed by two sets of double pillars connected by an archway crowned with a traditional green tile roof. She headed north and was immediately immersed in the sights and smells of every Chinatown she'd even been in: restaurant windows displaying barbecued ducks and pigs; porcelain, fabric, and furniture stores selling "genuine" Chinese antiques; herbalists and tea merchants; fruit and vegetable stands spilling out onto the sidewalks; and clinics offering acupuncture and whole-body massage. She admired the quality of the architecture. The Bank of America's columns and doors were tattooed with gold dragons and there were fifty or sixty dragon medallions on its façade. She stood in front of the Bank of Canton and studied its triple-tiered green slate roof with upward-sweeping eaves, the edges painted poppy red.

She walked the entire eight blocks to Broadway Street, turned, and then headed back. She stopped at the Sing Chong Building, a jewel of old Chinese-style architecture and the first structure to be erected in Chinatown after the 1906 earthquake, before entering a neighbouring restaurant that advertised dim sum for four dollars a plate.

She ordered hot and sour soup, chicken feet, steamed cow stomach, and salty fried scallops. The dishes came in quick succession. *The food is good*, she thought. *Maybe not quite Toronto good, but good.*

She was halfway through her meal when her cellphone rang. The screen displayed a Vancouver area code, and she guessed it was Ling.

"Ava Lee."

"Ms. Lee, this is Edward Ling."

"Thank you for calling me back —"

"I'm not sure what game you're playing," Ling said swiftly, "but you caused some distress to my assistant."

"I assure you, Mr. Ling, this is not a game."

"Then what is it? I'm a senior partner in this law firm, and my client list is exceedingly short and select. I'm not aware that any of them have engaged in the kind of activity you described to my assistant."

"I'm in San Francisco. I flew here this morning from Manila. My plan is to catch a plane to Vancouver either late this afternoon or early this evening. I would like to meet with you when I get there."

"Manila?"

"Yes, Manila. I've been hired by a company with its headquarters in Manila."

"Do I have to guess who it is?"

"I think it's best if you don't. I just want to assure you that right now I am party to information that I haven't yet shared with my client. There are questions that still need answers, and I think you can help me and perhaps help your client as well."

"And which client of mine are you trying to assist?"

"Mr. Ling, let's not say any more than we have to over the phone. We can discuss the situation when we meet."

"I really don't like doing this," he said.

"Me neither, but the alternative is almost guaranteed to be less palatable."

He sighed. "I have a working dinner at six o'clock at the Pan Pacific Hotel. Meet me in the lobby at eight o'clock."

"Do you know anything about the flight schedules between here and there?"

"There will be a flight every hour or so, and the flying time is only an hour."

"Then I'll see you at the Pan Pacific," she said. "I'll be wearing a blue button-down dress shirt."

"This is my cellphone number," he said, reciting it. "Call me if there are any changes in your plans."

She called her travel agent in Toronto, and within five minutes she had a flight to Vancouver and a room at the Pan Pacific. She decided it was time to call Uncle.

"*Wei*," he said.

"It's Ava."

"Did you find him?" he asked.

She was surprised by his abruptness. "I did."

"And the money?"

"No."

There was a heavy silence. *Uncle told Chang Wang more than he should have*, she thought.

"Do you know what happened to it, where it is?"

"Jim Cousins doesn't have it. He was a just a conduit," she said.

"You are certain?"

"I'm one hundred percent certain. Cousins was hired to be the front man for this piece of work."

"By Chew?

"Of course."

"I was hoping for something else — anything else."

"Not to be."

"This is very bad," he said.

She wondered what he meant by *bad*. "The thing is, I don't want you to say anything to Chang Wang or Tommy Ordonez just yet."

"I told Chang that you had located Jim Cousins."

"Now tell him that Cousins wasn't in San Francisco when I got there. Tell him that I'm on his trail and I'm confident I'll catch up to him in a day or two. Buy me a couple of days."

"Why, Ava?"

"Because I don't know what happened. I mean, I do know what Chew did and I have the documents to prove it, but I don't know why he did it and I don't know where the money is. It will take some time to figure it all out. If you mention that we have proof Chew did it, Ordonez won't be able to contain himself. He'll be on the first plane to Vancouver and the situation will degenerate into a family brawl, and any chance we have of collecting our fee will be dead."

"I trust Chang," Uncle said.

Ava took a deep breath. "Uncle, you told me that Chang is Ordonez's creature. He may be an old and dear friend, but you know his primary loyalty is to Ordonez."

It wasn't often that Ava argued with Uncle, partly out of respect for his position and his age, but also because she accepted that he had tremendous judgement when it came to understanding situations and people. Uncle had gone quiet after her outburst, and she feared she had offended him.

"Do you have a plan?" he finally asked.

"I do."

"A few days, you said."

"Hopefully."

"I would like to collect our fee as much as you would."

"Then let me run with this," she said softly.

"I will tell Chang that Cousins has not been run to ground yet."

"Thank you, Uncle."

He paused, and Ava was wondering if he was angry at her when he blurted, "How could Philip Chew do this to his family?"

In Uncle's world, *family* extended far beyond blood relations, and disloyalty, even to the remotest fringes of the group, was cause for dismay. Causing harm to your immediate family was unthinkable to him. "That is what I hope to find out," Ava said.

She was expecting him to criticize Philip Chew some more, but instead he said, "Ava, I have not found Jackie Leung yet, but I know who he contracted with. I have confirmed that there are two men looking for you."

"I see."

"The gang is from Guangzhou. I have been negotiating through an intermediary to have the contract cancelled. So far they have resisted, but I am not done yet. Either way, Jackie Leung will be located and dealt with. In the meantime, stay alert."

AVA WAS SITTING IN THE LOBBY OF THE PAN PACIFIC Hotel in black slacks and a powder-blue Brooks Brothers shirt with her jade cufflinks. Her hair was still damp from the shower she had taken after checking in. She glanced at her Tank Française watch. It was just past eight o'clock.

She saw Edward Ling before he saw her. A bulky man with a shock of white hair, wearing a tailored navy-blue pinstriped suit and a blue Hermès tie loosened at the neck, he was walking down a staircase from the mezzanine, scanning the lobby.

Ava stood so he could see her. He acknowledged her with a nod and walked towards her.

"Are you Ava Lee?" he asked.

"Yes, I am," she said, offering her hand.

"You aren't what I expected. Not at all what I expected." He slurred ever so slightly, and she knew there had been alcohol with dinner.

"I don't know what you mean."

"You're so young."

"I'm not as young as I look."

"Do you have a business card?" he asked.

She opened her purse and handed one to him. She also pulled out her Moleskine notebook and the envelope that contained Jim Cousins' contract. Sitting down, she placed the papers next to her on the couch. Ling sat down across from her. She could tell he was agitated, and wondered how much he knew.

"Are you a daughter of Marcus Lee?" he asked.

"Yes," Ava said, startled. "I am."

Ava was the second daughter of Marcus Lee and his second wife, Jennie. Jennie had become Marcus's wife in the old style, which is to say he had never left or divorced the first. Ava and Marian had become his second family, acknowledged and cared for but with no hope of inheriting anything more than their names and whatever their mother could put aside for them from Marcus's generous allowance. Their father had four children by his first wife, who lived in Hong Kong, and another two with wife number three, who lived in Australia. It was — at least to Westerners — a strange approach to family life. But in Chinese eyes it was traditional and therefore acceptable. It was also not a lifestyle for a man without wealth.

"I met you when you were two years old."

"I beg your pardon?"

"I met you in Hong Kong when your father was still living with your mother. You have an older sister, right?"

"Marian."

"When I heard your name earlier today, I had a vague recollection. And then I called a friend in Hong Kong and he made the connection for me. I wasn't sure until I saw how young you were."

"How do you know my father?"

"We were schoolmates in Hong Kong, and then later we knew each other in Australia."

"What a coincidence."

Ling stared at her and she began to feel uncomfortable. "You look a lot like him," he said. "Although looking like your mother wouldn't be so bad. She was a real beauty."

"She still is," Ava said.

"Do you stay in touch with your father?"

It was a rude question, designed to humiliate her. "Yes, and I'll be sure to tell him we met and that you inquired about our relationship."

Ling flinched. He realized he had gone too far. Marcus Lee wasn't a close friend anymore, but he was a man who had too much wealth, power, and influence for Ling to dare offend him. "Well, anyway, it's such a small world, isn't it?"

"I'm here about Philip Chew," Ava said.

"I thought as much when you mentioned Manila."

"You incorporated a company called Kelowna Valley Developments for him. A man named Jim Cousins was designated president but the shares were held by Chew."

"Are you always so direct?" he asked with amusement.

"It saves time."

He shrugged. "As I remember, the shares in that business were held in trust by our law firm."

"You incorporated the company for Philip Chew. It's logical to assume that the shares are being held in trust for him."

"I haven't actually admitted incorporating the company for Philip. That is your assertion."

He's a bit tipsy but he's not slow, she thought. "Do you deny it?"

"Ms. Lee, where is all this leading?"

"Mr. Ling, I had several choices when I found out what had been going on. Coming to you was the one I thought would cause the least amount of damage to everyone involved."

Ling pinched an eyebrow between his thumb and index finger. "The thing is, I have no idea what you're talking about. I may have incorporated Kelowna Valley Developments, and I may have done it for Philip, but that's where my involvement ends. I had nothing to do with the company after its inception and I don't have the slightest idea why you're talking about damage."

"Do you care about Philip Chew?" she asked.

"What kind of question is that?"

"Is he a valued client? Is he a friend?"

"Both, and what of it?"

She picked up the notebook and the envelope and placed them on her lap. Ling stared at the envelope. "I would like to have a very frank exchange of information with you, but I need to know that it will remain between the two of us unless we both agree otherwise."

"Do you trust me?"

"If you really are a friend of Philip Chew, then I think I do."

"I am."

She patted the envelope. "Over the past six months, Philip Chew orchestrated the removal of more than fifty million dollars from company accounts. He did it through Kelowna Valley Developments and he used Jim Cousins as the front man. I've already met with Cousins and he's admitted to his role in the affair. This is a copy of the contract that existed between Chew and Cousins. It outlines quite precisely what was to transpire."

Edward Ling didn't flinch. His eyes bored into hers, searching for any shred of a lie, any hint of exaggeration. Ava didn't turn away. "That's ridiculous," he said loudly.

"It's the truth."

His head swivelled in the direction of the stairway he had just descended. "Why would he do that? It's his own company, for God's sake."

"It's his brother's company," she countered.

"I've known Philip for close to twenty years."

"So?"

"You're cynical for someone so young."

"I chase bad debts for a living. You can't be cynical enough."

"Why would he do something like this?"

"That's what I'm trying to find out."

"And you want me to help you?"

She picked up the envelope. "I'm prepared to give you a copy of the contract. It will satisfy you that what I'm saying is true. What I want in return is confirmation that Philip did indeed incorporate the business and ask you to hold the shares in trust."

"And then what?"

"I want to speak to him. I want you to call him and persuade him that it's in everyone's best interest if he meets with me."

"You won't go directly to Tommy Ordonez with this information?"

"Do you know Tommy?"

"Not really," he said, with a shrug. "I don't do any of their corporate work. They use a Manila law firm for most of their legal work and another law firm here that's affiliated with it. Philip was a personal client."

"If I go to Tommy, all hell will descend on Philip. He'll hardly be able to breathe, let alone explain himself — assuming there is an explanation for fifty million dollars wandering off from corporate coffers."

"Why should you care?"

It was a fair question, and she knew her answer couldn't be glib. "I have several reasons, all of them more or less self-serving. First of all, I was hired to find out what happened to the money. I think I've taken that between seventy and eighty percent of the way, and I'm professional enough to want to finish the job. Second, I get paid a fee for every dollar I recover. I can't recover anything unless I know what's left and where it is. Third, I have taken a certain dislike to Tommy Ordonez. I think he's the kind of operator who uses people. If I went to him with what I have, he would cut me out without a thought. I don't want to give him that opportunity. And finally, I really am intrigued by the way Philip handled this deal and the story he spun to Jim Cousins. He's been very creative, and I want to know the truth."

Ling looked at the envelope, and she knew he was anxious to view its contents. "You see, it is interesting," she said.

He shook his head. "Yes, Philip did incorporate the company and asked me to hold the shares."

"I want it in writing."

"No problem."

"Good. I'll give you a copy of this contract when I get your letter confirming the shares."

"How about arranging a meeting with Philip?"

"That's not a condition," she said. "I just want you to do

the best you can. I am serious when I say that I'm his best chance to avoid his brother's anger."

"Jesus, you remind me of your father," Ling said. "Every deal he ever negotiated left something on the table for the other party."

"There's no point in being unreasonable," she said.

"Maybe you should say that to Tommy Ordonez."

"I will, when I know exactly what happened."

"You don't think Philip just made off with fifty million dollars?"

"You know him better than I do. What do you think?"

Ling shook his head again. "Not a chance."

12

AVA WOKE AT 7 A.M. WITH A START. THE TIME CHANGES and jet lag were beginning to get to her. Her mind was alert but her body felt like a sack of potatoes that had been tossed about in the back of a truck. She rolled off the bed, knelt, and said a small prayer to St. Jude. Then she got up and grabbed a couple of pouches of Starbucks VIA instant coffee from her "Double Happiness" bag. The coffee didn't energize her nearly enough. She needed a good, brisk run to give her body a real jolt. As she stripped in the bathroom she looked at the still-dark bruises on her body. She sighed, put on her Adidas running gear, and walked over to the window.

The ground was wet but the rain had stopped and the mist had cleared. The Pan Pacific Hotel was in the Canada Place complex on Vancouver's inner harbour, overlooking Burrard Inlet. Ava could see the Coast Mountains to the northeast and Stanley Park to the northwest. She put on her running jacket and grabbed her cellphone before leaving the room.

Stanley Park was more than four hundred hectares

— larger than New York's Central Park. Within the park, more than two hundred kilometres of trails and roads wound around half a million centuries-old trees, some of them seventy metres high. Ava jogged the perimeter, which was encircled by a seawall close to nine kilometres long that offered breathtaking views of the inlet. It began to rain again, ever so slightly, but the scenery around her was so beautiful that she hardly noticed.

Just as she was passing under Lion's Gate Bridge, a massive construction that spanned the inlet, connecting the downtown area to wealthy West Vancouver, she heard her cellphone ring. She stopped to retrieve the phone, leaning against the seawall.

"This is Ava Lee."

"Edward Ling. Good morning."

"Good morning."

"You sound winded."

"I'm running in Stanley Park, halfway around the seawall."

"In this weather?"

"It isn't so bad."

"Well, while you've been running, I've been working. I have that letter you wanted. I'm going to send it to your hotel by courier and, if you don't mind, I'll ask the courier to pick up the envelope you promised me in return."

"That's fine, but I'll be at least another forty-five minutes."

"There's no rush on my end."

"How about Philip Chew? Did you manage to arrange a meeting?" Ava asked.

"I'm afraid I had no luck with that. When I called the house, Philip wouldn't even come to the phone. I spoke to his wife. She said he was quite ill and not up to handling any business, legal or otherwise. I must say she sounded distressed herself."

Ava remembered what Chang had said about Philip in Manila. It sounded like it hadn't been an exaggeration. "That's unfortunate. I guess we'll just have to proceed as best as we can without him for now."

"My letter?"

"If I'm satisfied with it I'll send the envelope back with your courier."

"You will be."

Ava slipped the phone back into her pocket and resumed her run around the seawall, but now her mind was less on the scenery and more on Philip Chew. She considered her options. Call the Chew residence? Go directly to their home and try to worm her way in? Contact Louis Marx to see if he could broker a meeting? She knew that unless she was willing to get on a plane to Costa Rica and traipse from bank to bank, trying to locate those fifteen different recipients, her only real chance of finding out what had happened to the money was to talk to Philip Chew.

It was ten thirty when she walked, wet but energized, into the hotel lobby. When she got to her room, she saw a white envelope on the floor. There was a note and a phone number on the front: *I'm waiting in the lobby. Call me when you want me to pick up the paperwork for Mr. Ling.*

Ava ripped open the envelope. Ling's letter was short and to the point, confirming that KVD had been incorporated by Philip Chew and that McDougal, Fraser, and Ling held the shares in trust for him, and only him. It was what she wanted. She called the courier's cellphone number and told the woman who answered that the envelope for Edward Ling would be waiting outside her door.

Ava stripped and stepped into the shower. As she was standing under the hot spray, trying to relax her aching muscles, her mother came to mind.

Jennie, Ava, and Marian had relocated to Canada from Hong Kong when their father had taken on his third wife. For two years before moving to Toronto they had lived in Vancouver, where Ava knew her mother had had an active social life and a wide circle of friends. Mah-jong players, other second wives, Vegas junketeers — women with money, looking to fill their days with fun. Ava also knew that, true to her mother's social nature, Jennie had kept in touch with many of them.

It was close to eleven when she left the bathroom, two o'clock in Toronto.

"Yes," Jennie Lee said. Ava could hear mah-jong tiles clicking in the background.

"Mummy, it's Ava."

"Where are you?"

"Vancouver," Ava said. "I think I need your help."

"Give me a minute." Ava heard her mother talking to her friends, and then the phone went silent. When Jennie came back on the line, there was no background noise. "I went outside so we could talk properly. What is going on?"

"You still have a lot of friends here, don't you?"

"Of course. Auntie Grace, Auntie Lily, Auntie Kimmy — lots of them."

"Could you make some calls for me?"

"Why?"

"There's a very wealthy man here named Philip Chew.

Could you find out if any of the aunties know him or his wife?"

"Why?"

"Because I need to talk to him, and I think if I try to do it directly I won't have any luck. It might actually be best if I could talk to his wife first, and I was hoping maybe one of the aunties knows her and could help make that happen."

"Her name is Kitty."

"Who?"

"Philip Chew's wife."

"You know her?"

"I met her once. She is a good friend of Auntie Lily. They play mah-jong together. She's a bit of a snob, though. Lives in West Vancouver, in the British Properties, with all the rich *gweilos*. She thinks she's too good to live with the other Chinese in Richmond."

"Could you call Auntie Lily?"

"What's the time there?"

"It's just past eleven."

"I doubt she's up yet. She's a night owl."

"Could you at least try?"

"What is it you want me to say to her?"

"Auntie Lily needs to convince Kitty Chew that I'm a friend and that she should convince her husband to talk to me. She should start by telling her who I am. The fact that I'm female, Chinese, and connected to her group should help the cause. Now, Mummy, listen. Philip Chew is in deep trouble. The only chance he has to work his way out of it is to talk to me. Auntie Lily needs to understand how important this is for the Chews."

"He's in that much trouble?"

"He is."

"All right," her mother said slowly. "It isn't that often that you ask for my help."

I've never asked you to help, Ava thought, but she stopped herself from saying it out loud. "Thanks. Call me on my cell. I'll be waiting, so please don't let this drag on."

"And don't you nag. I'll try to reach her right now."

With a towel wrapped around her damp hair, dressed only in a black Giordano T-shirt and panties, Ava went to her computer. Mimi had emailed with two pieces of news that evidently warranted three exclamation marks each.

The first message said she was having dinner with Derek that evening. Ava felt an unease that she knew was irrational.

Derek wants to meet some women who aren't Chinese and who aren't named Mimi, Ava wrote back. Please introduce him to some women who have at least a modicum of intelligence. You are my best girl friend and he is my best guy friend and there are times I need to involve him in my business. There is no way I want to jeopardize either of those relationships, and the quickest way to do that is to have the two of you screwing each other.

Ava sent the reply and then opened the second message Mimi had sent. She reported that she had spoken to Maria Gonzalez that morning and urged her to contact Ava. *And say what?* Ava wondered. She deleted the email.

Ava pushed Derek, Mimi, and Maria out of her thoughts and opened a message from Marian. On Ava's last trip to Hong Kong she had met up with their father. He had told Ava he wanted the family to go on vacation together. Although he and his wife had been living apart for thirty years, Marcus still spent two weeks a year with them in Toronto.

I'm really happy about the idea of a holiday together, Marian wrote, especially with my girls, but I'm afraid of what Mummy will choose. She always wants to go to Las Vegas or the Bahamas or anywhere with a casino that she can spend all of her time in.

Why don't you communicate with Daddy directly? Ava wrote. Work it out with him yourself. She wasn't sure if Marian would. Her elder sister was more easily intimidated by their mother than Ava, and had a more distant relationship with their father.

She wandered into the bathroom to dry her hair. She had inherited her five-foot-three, 115-pound frame from her mother. But Edward Ling was right; when she examined her features, she found signs of her father in her eyes, her nose, the shape of her face.

She turned off the hair dryer, walked back into the room, and put on the second pair of training pants she'd brought with her. She was pulling on a pair of white socks when her cellphone rang. She leapt at it. Her mother's number lit up the screen.

"Well?" Ava said.

"Write down this phone number," Jennie Lee said.

"Kitty's?"

"No, her daughter, Maggie. Kitty doesn't want to talk to you and says her husband is in no condition to either, but Lily convinced her that someone from the family should. Maggie is their only child and is very close to them. So, Ava, don't be aggressive with her; it sounds like the family is going through a difficult time. Lily said Kitty was upset and kept asking Lily what she had heard. Lily told her that she had heard nothing, that she was just calling for you. She said you were her niece."

It wasn't true, but Ava appreciated the small white lie. "Thanks, Mummy, and please thank Auntie Lily for me."

"I will. Now, remember what I told you about Maggie. She is their only child, and she's still in school."

"I'll be as nice as can be."

13

ACCESS TO MAGGIE CHEW WASN'T WHAT AVA WANTED, but it was all she had. Most traditional Chinese parents shielded their children from the realities of their lives, and Maggie was a student and an only child. *Well, I'll try her anyway,* she was thinking, when her phone rang. She looked at the screen and saw a number she didn't know, although the country code was familiar.

"Hello," Ava said. She heard someone breathing, and then a rough wheeze. She felt her shoulders seizing up. "Who is this?"

"Where are you?"

She looked at the time. It was close to twelve in Vancouver, which meant that it was three o'clock in the morning in Manila. "Mr. Ordonez," she said.

"Where are you?" he repeated.

"Vancouver."

He paused. Ava could hear his breathing become louder. "Have you spoken to my brother yet?"

"No, I haven't, and it isn't likely that I will. He doesn't seem prepared to speak to anyone, except maybe Louis

Marx. And, Mr. Ordonez, from what I hear, your brother is genuinely ill. Even Marx may not have access to him anymore."

"Chang fired Marx last night."

"Oh," Ava said, noticing that Ordonez had bypassed her remark about his brother's health.

"Did you find the man Cousins?"

"No."

"Chang said you knew where he was."

"Except he wasn't there when I arrived."

"Chang said he was in San Francisco."

"Yes."

"So why are you in Vancouver?"

It was more of an accusation than a question. Ava hesitated. Her first instinct was to strike back. Instead she calmly said, "I wanted to confirm who incorporated Kelowna Valley Developments and who the shareholders were."

"And did you?"

"Not yet."

"When will you know?"

"Maybe later today."

"Call me when you do."

Ava sat upright. "Mr. Ordonez, I'm not going to do that."

"What?"

"I don't work that way. When I'm on a job, I don't contact clients with progress reports. I keep Uncle generally up to date and he passes along to the clients all or part of what I tell him, when and how he sees fit."

"I am not your regular type of client," he said, his voice rising.

"I'm sorry."

"What do you mean?"

"I'm not going to call you."

The phone line went dead.

Ava stared at her cellphone, trying to decide if she should call Uncle. *No*, she thought, *it's too late*. Then she waited another minute, almost certain Ordonez would call back to remonstrate with her. When he didn't, she stood and walked to the desk, where she had written Maggie Chew's phone number into her notebook. She shook off her conversation with Ordonez and dialled the number.

"Hello."

"Hello, this is Ava Lee."

"You didn't waste any time," the voice cracked.

"Auntie Lily said I could call."

"I know, but it was only yesterday that I heard your name for the first time. Louis Marx called the house to speak to my father and ended up talking to me. Louis said he met you in Manila. And now Aunt Lily says you're here in Vancouver already."

Ava felt a tiny surge of optimism. If she had been speaking to Marx, then Maggie Chew knew something was going on. "What did Louis tell you about me?"

"He said you'd been hired by my uncle but, despite that, you seemed to be fair."

"I try to be."

"After talking to Louis I was going to try to contact you anyway. You didn't have to drag Aunt Lily into this. Her call upset my mother. She doesn't want her friends to know that my father is going through a rough patch."

"I'm sorry. How was I to know?"

"You couldn't, I guess."

"I'm sorry anyway."

"Are you really in Vancouver, like Aunt Lily said?"

"Yes."

"You move fast."

"It's what I do," Ava said.

"She said you wanted to meet with my father."

"If it's possible."

"It isn't."

"I see."

"He isn't making any sense right now. I think he's had some kind of nervous breakdown. My mother and I have been trying to get him to see our family doctor or go to the hospital, but we can't get him to listen to us. He seems totally lost, like he's burrowed into himself."

"Louis said he was distressed."

"Catatonic is more like it."

"I'm sorry."

"You keep saying that."

"What would you prefer me to say?" Ava asked.

Maggie hesitated and then said, "I'll meet with you if you want. I have some understanding of what's been going on, and I know my Uncle Tommy will be howling for blood. Maybe there's a way we can manage all of this better."

"It certainly can't hurt," Ava said, her optimism notching up another gear.

"Where are you calling from?"

"The Pan Pacific Hotel."

"There's a very good Chinese restaurant near there, the Emperor's Crown, in the Marine Building in the inner harbour. Could you meet me there in about an hour? I'll be wearing a powder-blue sweatsuit."

"Black Adidas nylon jacket and training pants," Ava said. "And Maggie, I wish I didn't have to ask you to do this."

"Well, I know sooner or later we'll have to talk to someone, and better you than some other people I can think of . . ."

"I'll see you in an hour," Ava said softly.

14

AVA GOT TO THE RESTAURANT AT EXACTLY ONE O'CLOCK.
From the entrance she scanned the room for a powder-blue
sweatsuit. When she didn't see one, she asked for a table for
two by the window. She put the envelope that contained the
information from Cousins and Edward Ling on the table
and then sat for ten minutes watching float planes land and
take off from the marina in the harbour.

A server was placing a pot of jasmine tea on the table
when Ava saw a silver BMW pull into the lot. It was a high-
end Series 5 or 6, and the driver was wearing a powder-blue
sweatsuit. It was the kind of car she would expect the only
daughter of wealthy Chinese parents to drive. She was no
stranger to the breed. Not all of them were spoilt, arrogant,
and manic about acquiring the latest fashion in clothes,
cars, shoes, and purses. But more than enough were.

When Ava saw the BMW, she assumed Maggie Chew
would fit the bill. But as she watched the short, pudgy girl
walk into the restaurant, the image disappeared.

Ava stood up, and when Maggie saw her, she walked
towards the table with her head down, her eyes fixed upon

her unlaced white running shoes.

"Thank you for coming," Ava said.

Maggie raised her head. Ava saw that her skin was marred by bright red pimples high on her cheeks and small pits beneath them. Her eyes were large, with dark circles around them. "I didn't think I had much choice," she said.

"Shall we order?" Ava asked, a believer in the calming quality of the dim sum ritual.

"I don't know how much I can eat."

"What would you recommend?" Ava persisted.

Maggie picked up the dim sum menu. "The sticky rice is good . . . the chicken feet in black bean sauce . . . turnip cake."

"How is the har gow?"

"I prefer the shrimp-and-chive dumplings."

When their order had been taken, Ava poured tea for Maggie. Maggie tapped her middle finger gently on the table as a sign of thanks. *She has manners*, Ava thought.

"I'm sorry I had to reach you through Auntie Lily. I tried Edward Ling first."

"Aunt Lily is just about my mother's closest friend, and my mother can't stand Edward Ling. Besides, when he called last night, he insisted on talking to my father and didn't even mention your name."

"Did he speak to your father?" Ava asked.

"No. I told you, my father is not in a state to talk to anyone."

"Maggie, do either you or your mother know what's happened to your father?"

"My mother knows that something has gone wrong with the business, but she isn't interested in all the gory details.

She couldn't handle them anyway. I'm a bit stronger."

"So you know something? I mean, you know what happened? You know the details?"

Maggie closed her eyes, squeezed them tightly, then shook her head. "I've spent the last week at my parents' home trying to keep my father sane and trying to get my mother to stop crying," she said, waving a hand to indicate her sweatshirt. Ava noticed the cuffs were badly frayed. "I usually don't dress like this, but I haven't been getting much sleep and I've let myself go. When you called, I was at my condo getting some clean clothes to take back to West Van. That's where my parents live."

"The British Properties?"

"Yes. That was my mother's choice."

"And I hear you're a student."

"Law school. My father's wish."

"I'm an accountant."

"I know; Louis told me. He said you were hired by Uncle Tommy's company to look into some missing money, and he was shocked when he met you. Young, good-looking, female, capable — not my Uncle Tommy's normal type of employee. Louis said some of the people in Manila were actually afraid of you, that you have some amazing connections."

Ava didn't want to talk about her connections. Instead she patted the envelope that held her paperwork. *There isn't much point*, she thought, *in being coy*. "The money that's missing — your father took it. I have all the records here."

Maggie's eyes flicked over the envelope. "I know he did," she said.

Ava blinked. "Well, since you know," she pressed, "I'd

like you to tell me why he did it. And I'd like to know where the money is."

The turnip cake arrived. Maggie Chew slathered chili sauce on a slice and bit into it. "Why haven't you gone to my uncle with your information?"

"How do you know I haven't?"

"Because if you had, there's no force on earth that would keep him from descending on my father, with every ounce of malice and viciousness he could muster. There are only two things he cares about: his position in the family and his money. When it comes to family, my Uncle Tommy talks a good story, but the reality is that he thinks of it as *his* family. He thinks that everyone should be grateful to him — the oldest son, the trailblazer — for whatever they have in life, and should express their thanks by being obedient, subservient, and loyal as a dog. Then there's his money — he's married to it. My father and my uncle in Hong Kong were supposedly partners in the business, but the truth is, all the purse strings are held tightly by Uncle Tommy. He decides how much money they need and then doles it out as he sees fit."

"You've obviously done a lot of thinking about this," Ava said.

Maggie laid down her chopsticks. "It's all I've thought about for the past week. My father has committed two cardinal sins. He's stolen from my uncle's precious money hoard and in the process he's betrayed the family. I'd be surprised if Uncle Tommy didn't want him dead."

"Do you know how much money your father appears to have taken?"

"He said it was more than fifty million dollars."

"You say that so calmly."

"It's so big a number it hardly seems real."

"Where is it?"

"It's gone."

"How can more than fifty million dollars just disappear?"

Maggie picked up her chopsticks and plucked a chicken foot from the bamboo steamer. Then just as quickly she put it back. "I really don't think I can eat."

"Me neither," Ava said. A lump the size of a grapefruit was lodged in her chest. Any hope of a giant fee had been quickly dashed. "Tell me what happened."

Maggie closed her eyes again. "My mother told me last week that my father had been acting strangely for months. I was so busy at school that I hardly saw them. She told me she would nag at him about what was wrong but he wouldn't talk to her. He'd just retreat into his office at the house and spend hours on the computer playing online poker."

"It's popular these days."

"That's hardly the word for it," Maggie said. "It's become a life-sucking addiction. That's how he lost the money."

"Oh no, please don't tell me that," Ava said, struggling to believe it.

Maggie opened her eyes. The tears welling in their corners were threatening to spill over. "I know it sounds absurd. I know it sounds absolutely insane and improbable," she said.

"You're saying he lost fifty million dollars playing online poker? How is that even possible?"

"He was playing no-limit Texas hold'em at a table where the minimum blinds were $1,000 and $2,000. You can't sit at a table like that without a starting stack of at least $100,000, and according to my father he normally started with $200,000."

"Still —"

"And then multiply that by five, because that's how many tables he would play at one time."

"A million dollars in one sitting?"

"Sometimes more. If he lost he would just reload," Maggie said, wiping her eyes. "It started, I think, slowly. He began with his own cash but he quickly ran through that. When it was gone, he dipped into company money — always, he swears, with the intention of winning the money back. Of course, he never did, and it just got worse and worse. Some weeks he lost close to ten million dollars."

"He didn't always lose, did he?"

"No, just most of the time. Enough of the time."

"Then why didn't he stop?" Ava asked, realizing the second she did that it was a stupid question.

"He was addicted."

"Of course," Ava said softly.

Maggie Chew sensed doubt in the reply. "No, really, he was. He became completely irrational."

"Then what was all this nonsense with Costa Rica?" Ava asked.

"The Costa Rica thing is, I think, part of a bigger puzzle. Ava, would you believe me if I told you that my father was cheated?"

In her own life Ava had heard more than enough of the lies and rationalizations that helped the Chinese gambler sleep at night. "I would like to," she said.

"I think he was."

Ava sat quietly. The lump in her chest stopped throbbing. *Money that was gotten illegally is money that needs to find its way home*, she thought. "I'll need more than your opinion."

Maggie stroked her right cheek. "We'll have to go to my condo in Yaletown. There's a guy named Jack Maynard you need to talk to. He can explain what went down, or at least what he thinks went down. If you believe him, you can come back to West Van with me and I'll let you sit with my father."

"Why would you do this?" Ava said slowly.

"If the money was stolen, then you can get it back, right?"

"And what makes you think I can do that?"

"Louis Marx — he heard them talking about you. He said that's what you do. He said you're the best."

Ava nodded and thought, *One phone call*.

"Okay," she said. "Let's go to Yaletown."

15

YALETOWN WAS ON THE OPPOSITE SIDE OF DOWNTOWN Vancouver from Ava's hotel. Once an industrial area, its proximity to False Creek had been a lure for developers in the late 1980s. The rows of brick warehouses had been converted into trendy offices and loft apartments that sat on top of restaurants, art galleries, bars, and boutiques.

"The parking spot costs me five hundred dollars a month," Maggie said as she pulled her car into the underground garage off Mainland Street. "I have classmates who spend less than that on accommodation."

They took the elevator to the top floor of the four-storey building. As Ava entered Maggie's open-concept loft she was struck by the living area's sixteen-foot ceilings and ten-foot wall-to-wall windows that flooded the space with light. The kitchen counters were empty, the walls were bare, and the only furniture in the living room was a beige leather couch and matching chair and a glass coffee table.

"We'll call Jack from my study," Maggie said, motioning Ava to follow her.

Ava walked into the room and was visually assaulted

by piles of books and paper strewn everywhere. Pictures of Maggie's family covered every wall and framed the flat-screen television. Empty mugs and glasses lined the windowsill next to the desk, which held a large Mac. Ava stood by as Maggie leafed through some papers spread over a loveseat. "Sorry for the mess. I kind of live in here," she said. She held up a sheet of pink paper. "Here we are."

"Just a second," Ava said. "Before you call, why don't you tell me a little about Jack Maynard."

"Sure. Do you want to sit down?"

Ava sat on the loveseat. Maggie took the office chair and rolled it closer. "He's a young guy, late twenties maybe, and he's a professional poker player. Believe it or not, he graduated from MIT with a master's in math. He started playing, strictly online, while he was in university, and he discovered he was very good at it. He's well known in the professional gambling world. A couple of the poker magazines rate him among the top twenty online players in the world."

"How much did he tell you he lost?"

"Just under six million, and there were two other regulars who lost in the three- to four-million-dollar range."

"Not as severely damaged as your father."

"They're professionals, not addicts. They knew when to stop."

Ava nodded sympathetically. "I remember when my mother made my sister and I sit in the car in a casino parking lot for five hours while she lost her monthly household allowance playing baccarat. My sister asked her why she did it, and she said that she just couldn't help herself."

"My father took my mother and me to Vegas once,

dropped us off in a room, and then disappeared for four days. She said he almost lost the house."

"If this Jack Maynard is so good, how did he lose all that money?"

"That's exactly what he's going to explain to you."

"One other thing before you call him," Ava said. "I know next to nothing about Texas hold'em poker."

"You understand something about poker, though?"

"Just the basics. I mean, I know how the hands are ranked."

"We'll look online," Maggie said.

She turned on the computer and clicked an icon that looked like a waterfall. "This is The River, the gambling site that my father and the others played on." She signed in and opened up a page that listed table after table of hold'em poker options. She hit one that read *$10/$20*. "We don't have to gamble at a table to be able to watch it. Jack told me that when my father and the others were playing, there would be several hundred onlookers. Morbid fascin-ation, I guess."

There were six people at the table, each with an avatar. "People don't use their real names?" Ava asked.

"No. Jack played under the name Brrrrr, and my father was Chinaclipper."

"Then how did they get to know each other's real identity?"

"Maynard was so famous that everyone knew who was behind Brrrrr. My father was just an anonymous player until he and Maynard and some of the others began to share personal information on the chat line. Over six months they got to know each other quite well."

As Maggie was speaking, Ava watched the play of cards and quickly began to understand the basics. Each player got two cards, face down. Five cards were then turned face up in the centre — first three, and then one and one. Players bet after they had received their first two cards, then after the first three cards were turned over, and then again after each of the single cards was exposed — four betting rounds in all. Players could use any of the seven cards to make a five-card hand.

The table she was watching was no-limit hold'em. That meant that players could bet every dollar they had in front of them at any given time. She was amazed by how quickly some of the pots grew. At the $10–$20 table they were watching, two pots were raised to more than a thousand dollars each. She began to grasp the multiples that must be involved at tables with antes of $1,000 and $2,000.

"Let's call Maynard," Ava said.

Maggie punched in the number and turned on the speaker. "Maynard lives in Virginia," she said.

"Hello? Is that you, Maggie?"

"I'm here, Jack. I have you on speaker phone. I'm with that woman I mentioned to you this morning. Her name is Ava Lee."

"Ms. Lee," he said.

"Call me Ava."

"Maggie tells me you're some kind of special accountant."

"I guess you could call me that."

"She says you recover money for people."

"Sometimes I can, but not always."

"Just how do you that? Get it back, I mean."

"Persuasion," she said.

He laughed, more disbelieving than amused.

Maggie interrupted. "Jack, I don't think we need to

quiz Ava. Why don't you start by explaining to her what happened."

She could hear him breathe, and in the sound she felt his tension. A bottle cap popped. "Have one for me," Maggie said.

"I've been drinking every day for the past couple of months. I need to stop," he said.

"Talk to me," Ava said, pulling out her notebook. "But before you do, please understand that I have only the most rudimentary knowledge of poker."

"I'm a pro," Maynard began. "I've been playing poker for a living for the past five years, mainly online. I was putting in a minimum of eight hours a day, five days a week."

"You use the past tense," Ava said.

"I'm giving it a break — the losses crippled me. I need to rebuild my self-confidence, and my bankroll."

"Where did you play?"

"On several sites, but in the past year I played primarily at The River. There was always good high-stakes action there."

"Maggie mentioned the amount of money her father gambled. Is that what you mean by high stakes?"

"Yeah. There were about fifty of us who played for those kinds of stakes on a regular basis. And then of course people were always coming and going, testing their talent at a higher level. Those were the ones we usually took to the cleaners."

"'Talent'?"

"It isn't just a game of luck when you're playing poker for that kind of money. Maybe in the short term luck will hold, but over the long haul your ability to read people — to understand who you're playing against and what their tendencies and habits are — sometimes matters more than the cards you're dealt. And then there's the mathematical element, which is one of my strong points. I can get into it if you want, but it gets complicated."

"No, I believe you. The thing is, if talent prevails, how did you and your friends lose all that money? Did you run into someone more talented?"

"No fucking way," he said, his voice rising.

"Is that ego talking?"

"No fucking way."

"So who was winning when you were losing?"

"There were two of them. Their poker names were Buckshot and Kaybar. They never played together at the same table, but we never thought that was strange until we started looking back. We also never found out their real identities, which is also strange, because ninety-five percent of the guys knew each other."

"Just those two were winning?"

"No, but they were by far the main beneficiaries of our supposed bad run."

"Maggie tells me you believe you were cheated."

"I'm certain of it."

"How can you be so sure?" She heard paper rustling in the background. "Is there someone there with you?" she asked.

"No, I'm alone. I'm just going through my notes."

"So, again, how can you be so sure?"

"I'm a math grad and so is Felix Hunter, who played under the name Felix the Cat. Like I said before, mathematics plays into this, and understanding the basic math of no-limit poker is fundamental to playing well. I mean, there are odds attached to every hand, risks attached to every bet, but let me say that the way we lost ran completely counter to the laws of probability.

"At first I wrote off my losses as just a run of very bad luck. It doesn't matter how good you are — everyone hits bad streaks, and I thought I was just going through a particularly long one. But when it continued and I kept losing to those same two guys, I started to think that maybe it had nothing to do with luck. I talked to Felix about it first, and he felt the same way. So we backtracked. We traced the hands we had played over the past few months. When you look at just one hand, it doesn't mean a thing; two aces can lose to a two and four at any given time, and even a number of losses like that can be rationalized. But when we looked at literally thousands of hands, we saw a very clear pattern."

"You have all those hands on record?"

"Of course. All the hands are displayed after they're finished, and I have software that stores and files them by date and time. I mean, this is my job, the way I earn my living — I apply myself to it. Going back and studying how you played a hand or how you played against a certain individual, that's the only way you can improve. So, yeah, I had the hands, and so did Felix."

"So what did you find?"

"We were cheated."

"How?"

"We think — no, we're convinced — that they could see everyone's hole cards."

"The two cards turned face down?"

"Yeah. We think they could see all the cards on the table."

"And what makes you think that?"

"I'll try to keep it simple," he said. "Basically, they knew exactly when to bet heavy and, just as important, they always seemed to know when to fold. And bluffing either of them — well, it was impossible. It didn't matter how much money you bet, they always called and they always won. I'm looking at a hand I lost more than a hundred thousand dollars on. I had an ace of clubs and the king of hearts, a great starting hand. The flop was the three of spades and an eight and nine of hearts. I raised. Buckshot called me. On the turn, the fourth card was a ten of hearts. So now there was a possibility on the board of a straight and a flush. I raised again. He called. The river card was the two of clubs, which didn't change anything. There was fifty thousand dollars in the pot; I bet another fifty. It was a huge bet even for a bluff. He had to give me credit for having a straight or a flush, or at the very least a high pair or even two pair. He called, and when his cards were exposed, he was holding the three of diamonds and the six of spades.

"He won a hundred thousand dollars with a pair of threes. Do you have any idea how unlikely that is? He called a fifty-thousand-dollar bet with garbage, and into a board that nearly every poker player in the world would think had him beat. And let me tell you, it wasn't the only time."

"Yes, I can see the improbability of it," Ava said.

"Another thing Felix picked up on was the number of hands they played. It was an inordinately large percentage, and it stuck to a pattern. They seemed to want to see just about every flop, the way Buckshot did with the three and six that beat me. They played rags — cards such as a deuce and seven of different suits, the very worst starting hand in poker — all the time. They'd call the opening bet and even call raises so they could see the flop. In reality, your opening two cards don't mean much until the next three cards are flopped and your hand starts to take shape, but there are hands like the deuce and seven that are so bad statistically that hardly anyone ever plays them. These guys were playing them all the time, and naturally, when they got lucky, they cashed in in a big way because the other players never gave them credit for starting with cards that bad.

"When Felix pointed that out to me, I went over the data myself and found something else. Buckshot and Kaybar seemed to fold before the flop every time someone else had a monster opening hand — a hand such as two aces or two kings, which is really difficult to beat. And what I also noticed was that they folded against those hands even when the other player didn't raise before the flop. We call that slow playing. When you have a big hand and you want to maximize it, you bet small to avoid scaring off the other players. Both Felix and I did that often enough. The thing is, when we looked at the numbers, guess what?"

"I have no idea."

"I had pocket aces or kings more than eighty times during that losing stretch. Felix had them more than a hundred times. On nearly every single occasion, those guys folded before the flop. It didn't matter how little or how much we bet, they folded. Can you imagine, statistically, what an anomaly that is? It's fucking impossible that they'd fold that many hands. They had to be seeing our fucking hole cards. There isn't any other explanation."

Ava could feel Maggie's eyes on her. "Jack, if you're so certain about this, why haven't you done anything about it?"

"I tried."

"And?"

"I went to the local FBI office first. They told me that none of the online poker sites were American companies — they're all offshore. Strictly speaking, they're illegal in the U.S. They said they had no jurisdiction and kind of implied that I was an idiot for even going to them. So then I called a couple of guys I know who do promotions for The River. I told them what I thought had happened and asked them to put me in touch with some senior people at the site."

"Did they?"

"Yeah. I had several tense conversations with some English guy named Jeremy Ashton. He sort of nudged me along during our first talk, trying to find out what my beef was, and then he asked me to send him my analysis of the play. I did, and when I didn't hear back after about a week, I called him again. He wasn't so nice this time. He basically said I was just a sore loser and that they had decided to ban me from the site. I went off on him, screaming, swearing, threatening to go public with my information. He told me to calm down and that he would take another look at my material."

"To what end?"

"I never heard from him again."

"And did you go public?"

She heard a big sigh. "No, I didn't. The night after my rant at Ashton, my car was blown up in the driveway."

Did you know this? Ava mouthed to Maggie. Maggie nodded.

"And you think it was them?" Ava said.

"Who else would have done it? The car was blown up at

four in the morning, and the state police said it was a professional job."

"Why didn't you tell the police of your suspicions?"

"I'm a coward, plain and simple. If they could blow up my car once, they could do it again, and this time maybe with me in it," Maynard said. "And Felix had a worse experience. He went to Ashton about the same time I did. He lives in Vegas, and two days after he called Ashton, his apartment was trashed. They left a note on his front door that said *We can get to you anytime.* I thought I should tell you that before you go chasing after them."

"That was thoughtful. Thank you."

"You don't sound too concerned."

"These kinds of things happen from time to time. I don't pretend they don't; I just don't let them paralyze me."

"So you're going to help Philip? Is that what I'm hearing?"

"I'm not working for Philip, but if getting some money back for my client helps Philip, then I guess you could say I'm going to try to help him."

"How about trying to get my money back while you're at it?"

Ava hesitated. She was tempted by the idea of another fee, but then she thought of the complications that would entail. "I can't do that," she said. "I'm under contract and I handle only one client at a time. If I'm successful, though, there should be some side benefits. We can talk then."

"I guess that'll have to do," he said.

"In the meantime, are you willing to help me?"

"How?"

"I want a copy of your paperwork. I want whatever analysis you and Felix did. I want a signed statement from you,

Felix, and whoever else was involved on the losing end, attesting to the fact that you think you were cheated and how you think it happened."

"I can do that."

"Now I also need to understand how these sites operate. For example, how are the hands constructed? I imagine there's some kind of sophisticated computer program at work here."

"Yeah, there is. The River created its own software but the site is managed by a First Nations band on an island near Kingston, Ontario. The company is called the Cooper Island Gaming Commission."

"How do you know that?"

"It says so on the website," he said. "First Nations are exempt from all U.S. and Canadian gambling laws — that's why we have so many casinos on Native land in North America. It's just a natural extension to have them administer online gambling. The Cooper Island Gaming Commission supposedly has a hell of a server capacity."

"So they supply the servers and administer the site."

"Yeah. There are more than ten billion poker hands in the River system, all dealt on a random basis."

"And no issues, no problems until about six months ago?"

"That's right."

"So if you're right about Buckshot and Kaybar seeing your hole cards, someone has obviously messed around with the software."

"That's what had to have happened."

"Have you approached the band?"

"They were next on my list, until my car blew up."

"Do they handle the money as well?"

"No, that all goes offshore. For a few years it went to Cyprus, then for about nine months it was Madagascar, and for the past year it's been Costa Rica."

"Ah, I was wondering where Costa Rica fitted into this. That's where Philip was sending his money."

"Like the rest of us."

"What was the procedure for transferring money in and out?"

"They'd take money any way you wanted to send it and they'd pay you just about any way you wanted as well. I never had any problems putting money in or getting it back."

"Philip's money was sent to a variety of banks, and to a different person each time. Why was that?"

"For security. When you wanted to send a wire, you had to email them from an address they had on record to let them know what you were planning. They would email you back with the name of the bank and the individual the money was to go to. Once the wire had gone, you had to send them its number and the exact amount of the transfer. You were given detailed directions not to use the words *gambling*, *poker*, or *The River* in any of your communication with the banks. They were trying to avoid any possible problems with the U.S. government."

"Where does this Jeremy Ashton work? Costa Rica?"

"Shit, no, he's in Las Vegas. Amazing, isn't it? A company that's incorporated in Cyprus, has its operations centre on a Canadian reservation, and flows its money through Costa Rica, and the operations are directed from Vegas. God bless cyberspace."

"Is it a public company?"

"No."

"Shareholders?"

"I couldn't find out."

Ava drew a circle around the word *software*. "The First Nations band, could they be investors in the company?"

"No, they provide a service, that's all. Their main interest is in supplying the server support. A lot of their customers are gambling sites but they make it very clear that they have no financial involvement with any of them."

"You would think they would know if the software had been penetrated," Ava said, as much to herself as to Maynard.

"You would. That is, if they had a reason to investigate it."

"And they should know who Buckshot and Kaybar are."

"They'll know."

"What's the name of the band?" she asked.

"The Mohneida First Nation. Their reservation is on Cooper Island, which I'm told straddles the U.S.–Canada border about twenty minutes from Kingston."

"And you didn't approach them?" she repeated.

"No."

"Did anyone else?"

"Not that I know of. Felix and I were the only ones doing the forensic work until they dumped that shit on us."

"That's good," she said.

"So what are you going to do?" Maynard asked.

"I don't know. I need to think about it. And Jack — and I'm saying this as much for Maggie's benefit as yours — my interest in this revolves around my client. Any reporting I have to do I'll do to him, and believe me when I tell you, there won't be much of that anyway. So neither of you should expect to hear from me unless I need something. I'll make sure that when it's over, you'll know the result, good or bad."

"Are you going to talk to Philip?" he asked.

She looked at Maggie. "Not unless Maggie wants me to. I have enough information here to get me started. Do you think Philip will have anything else to add?"

"Not really."

"Then I'll get on with things."

"The information you want me to send?"

"Send it to my email address," Ava said.

"I'll get it off to you in the next hour or so, and I'll send Felix's as well," he said. "You will talk to the Mohneida?"

"It seems to be the logical starting point."

"Try to keep our names out of this, will you? We're both still a bit nervous."

"I'll do what I can," Ava said, and signalled to Maggie that the conversation was over.

"Jack, we have to go now," Maggie said, turning off the speaker.

Ava went over to the computer, where the River website was still open. She clicked over to the administration section and found the gaming commission's phone number and email address. She would need to find out more about them before making contact. She would also need to decide whom to contact.

Her thoughts were disrupted when she felt Maggie leaning over her shoulder.

"What do you think?" Maggie asked.

"Maynard is credible. Let's see if his numbers hold up," Ava said.

"And you really don't want to speak to my father?"

"Let's leave him alone for now. Why cause him more distress?"

"So what happens now?"

"Maggie, go home and look after your parents. Hopefully in a few days, a few weeks, I'll get Tommy Ordonez his money back and your father can work out his issues with him on a different footing. Now I need to get back to my hotel."

"I'll drive you."

"That's not necessary."

A cellphone rang in another part of the loft. "That's mine," Maggie said, going to answer it.

Ava remained in the study to copy Jack Maynard's phone number into her notebook. When she walked into the living room, Maggie had her back turned. Ava thought she heard a sniffle and was about to ask if everything was okay, but before she could speak, Maggie spun around. Tears were running down her cheeks.

"That was my mother. She's hysterical. Uncle Tommy phoned our house and she made the mistake of answering. He bullied her into putting my father on the phone. My mother said my father didn't talk to him — he just listened, and then he started to shake. Our doctor's on his way. I need to get home."

16

AVA TOOK A TAXI BACK TO THE PAN PACIFIC HOTEL.
She tried to focus on the Mohneida, but Tommy Ordonez
kept wedging his way into her thoughts. It was three
o'clock in the afternoon in Vancouver. That meant he had
phoned his brother at six in the morning in Manila. Did
he ever sleep?

When she got to her room, she sat slumped at the desk.
It had already been a long day. She thought about calling
Uncle with the information about Philip Chew, but it was
too early for that. Then she tried to construct a conversation she might have with Ashton, assuming he'd take her
call. When she couldn't find one that didn't result in his
hanging up on her, she gave up and began to research the
Mohneida online.

Ava knew her Canadian history, and the story of the
Mohneida was the story of most North American First
Nations bands. They were a small tribe, an adjunct of the
great Mohawk nation. Their home territory was in the
middle of the Thousand Islands, on the St. Lawrence River
about two hundred kilometres west of Montreal. Like the

lands of the Mohawks near Montreal and Cornwall, their territory straddled the American and Canadian borders — a geographic quirk that gave them dual citizenship. It was an isolated region, which had kept them out of most wars, and until the European settlers began to spread across North America, their isolation had protected them from disease and the addictions that afflicted many of the larger tribes. Eventually European influences began to erode their traditional lifestyle, which was rooted in fishing and hunting. As the twentieth century advanced, the Mohneida — like so many other First Nations peoples across North America — were decimated by alcoholism, drug addiction, and all the violence and poverty that went with them. Then Ronald Francis landed in their midst.

According to *Maclean's* magazine, Francis had been born on the reserve. His father, an alcoholic, died when he was two and his mother moved to the city of Kingston. Francis was incredibly bright; he attended Queen's University, one of Canada's finest post-secondary institutions, and graduated with a degree in social work. He was hired by the Department of Indian Affairs, who assigned him to the Mohneida reserve. It took Francis six months to realize that social work wasn't what his people needed. They needed jobs — sources of income other than government handouts — and some sense of purpose. He resigned his post and set out to help his people achieve economic independence, using their dual citizenship and treaty rights that exempted the band from paying duties or taxes on either side of the border.

Francis didn't invent this new economy. Some of the bands upriver were already exploiting their duty-free, tax-free status by buying cartons of cigarettes, worth forty dollars on the open market, for five dollars each, then selling them in the general marketplace for twenty dollars. The same kind of profit margins were being made on another tax- and duty-laden product: liquor. However, while it was legal for the bands to buy these products, it was not legal for them to export them. Police on both sides of the border were trying to enforce the law, but the St. Lawrence River offered too many crossing points, and the Thousand Islands area, with its maze of channels, was particularly difficult to patrol.

Within three years of beginning their new enterprises, the various bands along the river were supplying an estimated thirty percent of all the cigarettes sold in the province, and only a slightly smaller percentage of liquor. When the Ontario Provincial Police went public with a list of the worst offenders, the Mohneida were at the top, and Ronald Francis was named as the man behind it all.

The federal and provincial governments were losing tens of millions of dollars in tax revenues and duties, so they came down hard on the cigarette companies. The supply line began to dry up. By then Francis — now chief of the Mohneida — had prudently stashed away much of the profits and was looking for ways to diversify. The band opened a water-bottling plant and then built a cigarette factory, manufacturing and selling their own brand at well below normal prices. And they were considering building a casino.

Just as they were exempt from taxes and duties, First Nations weren't bound by provincial and federal laws when it came to what they did on tribal land. Using this protected status, many bands across the country had partnered with investors and built casinos. Ronald Francis wanted one for the Mohneida and had worked hard to achieve it. Ava read story after story about investors from Asia and the Middle East making the trek to Cooper Island, but ultimately none of them would invest. The problem was that the island was too isolated. Bridges would have to be built from both the American and Canadian shores, and the cost was prohibitive. No matter how Francis spun it, the population base wasn't large enough to justify that kind of expenditure.

It was around the same time that online gambling was introduced to the world market. Within months there were countless websites dedicated to blackjack, roulette, and Texas hold'em poker. It was an unregulated market, one that had appeared virtually out of nowhere and then spread like a virus. The American government banned the sites outright, forcing any U.S.-based operations to move offshore.

Ronald Francis watched all this happening from Cooper Island and saw an opportunity. If it was legal for the Mohneida to build a casino on their land, then it had to be legal for them to host online gambling sites. He brought in some consultants, former senior executives of the Nevada Gaming Commission, with the initial idea of running his own site, but they pointed out a potentially more secure and profitable route for him to take. They recommended that he provide a home for the websites that had been forced offshore and were struggling to establish credibility. So Francis set up the Cooper Island Gaming Commission, which registered, licensed, and regulated online sites.

Initially the Gaming Commission had issued more than twenty permits, and now it was estimated that sixty percent of the world's online gaming was run on the Cooper Island servers. Ava was impressed with Francis's business acumen. Turning a tiny island in the middle of the St. Lawrence River into what was in reality a global business leader had been a definite feat.

She found the Cooper Island Gaming Commission's website and read the list of gambling sites they administered. As expected, The River was one of them. Then she read their self-proclaimed mandate. The commission was dedicated, it said, to ensuring that online gambling was secure and fair and that all participants would be fully paid.

Ava turned back to some of the newspaper articles she'd been reading; in one of them she found a recent photo of Ronald Francis. He was standing outside, his right hand pointing at the Cooper Island Gaming Commission's offices. His face was large and round, with thin lips and small, dark eyes. His most striking characteristic was his long black hair, which hung in a braid halfway down his back, secured with a clasp decorated with a feather. He was wearing jeans and a plaid cowboy shirt.

It was now late afternoon, and just after 7 a.m. in Hong Kong. Uncle would be up now, drinking tea and working his way through the two or three Chinese newspapers he read every morning. She knew she should call him and confirm the fact and the details of Philip Chew's theft. But the matter of The River was still hanging in the air. It was one thing to tell Uncle she had found out how and why Philip Chew had stolen more than fifty million dollars, but it was another to state with any certainty that Chew had been cheated and that it was still possible to recover all or part of the money. She decided to hold off calling until she had reviewed Jack Maynard's data and, if it held up, until she had a chance to formulate a plan for approaching the Mohneida or The River.

As if on cue, her computer signalled an incoming email from Jack Maynard. All it said was, Here's what you need. There were two attachments. She opened the first, which was from Maynard himself: six pages of data along with a covering letter summarizing his analysis. Felix Hunter's work was as thorough as Maynard's, bare-bones and to the point. Across the top Hunter had written in capital letters: THESE NUMBERS ARE STATISTICALLY ANOMALOUS. *Words that would strike fear in the heart of any mathematician*, Ava thought with a small smile.

She read through the summaries, making notes as she went. Anyone with even the most basic math skills could see the pattern. She transferred the data from both attachments to a memory stick, with the intention of printing them later. She believed the printed word still made a bigger impact than any electronic version.

It was mid-evening in Ontario, and the Cooper Island Gaming Commission's offices would be closed. She logged on to a website that cost her twenty-five dollars a year in exchange for access to personal information on about ninety percent of the North American population. Ava had no idea how they acquired the data, but all she had to do was type in a name and part of an address and the site would spit out a full address, phone numbers, family members, employer, and estimated annual income. She typed in RONALD FRANCIS, COOPER ISLAND, ONTARIO, and out it came.

Francis's wife's name was Monica and they had no children or siblings. He made approximately $300,000 a year.

She believed everything except the income. The website didn't provide a cellphone number but it did list his home number. Ava debated calling it. She tried thinking of an approach that would excuse her disturbing him at home, and she came up with one that might work. Francis's phone rang four times. Ava was ready to give up when a woman answered.

"Mrs. Francis?"

"Yes."

"I'm sorry for calling so late. My name is Ava Lee," she said. Conscious of what Monica Francis might think about a woman calling her home, she quickly added, "I work for a Hong Kong investment firm that has an interest in doing business with the Mohneida band. I've just arrived in Vancouver and I wanted to get in touch with Mr. Francis as soon as I could."

"Chief Francis isn't here."

Ava noted the title, and the fact that Mrs. Francis didn't seem annoyed by her call.

"Do you know when he'll be home?"

"In four days," she said. "Did you say you were in Vancouver?"

"Yes."

"The Chief is in Victoria attending a First Nations conference."

"Do you know where it's being held?"

"The Empress Hotel. He's staying there as well."

"That's wonderful — so near."

"Was he expecting your call?"

"No, not specifically. I wasn't sure when I was going to make it over."

"Well, call him at the hotel. I'm sure he'll be glad to hear from you."

I'm not so sure about that, Ava thought as she hung up.

17

VICTORIA WAS ONLY HALF AN HOUR AWAY BY AIR FROM
Vancouver. Ava emailed her travel agent and told her to
book an early-morning flight into British Columbia's capital city. Then she sat back in her chair and thought again
about calling Uncle. Now that Maynard's and Hunter's data
was in hand and looked solid, she knew he needed to be
briefed. She reached for her cellphone. As she did, it rang.
He must be reading my mind, she thought as she picked up
the phone.

"My father . . ." a voice sobbed.

"Maggie?"

"My father —"

"What is it?"

"He tried to kill himself." The sob turned into a wail.

Ava closed her eyes. "Is he okay?"

"He jumped from the roof of the house. My mother saw
him as he went past the living-room window."

"Maggie, is he okay?"

"They don't know yet. They just took him to the hospital."

Ava didn't want to know any more. "Maggie, go and look

after your family. I'll be in touch when I have something to tell you."

"My uncle did this!"

"Go and look after your mother," Ava said.

"I'll never have anything to do with that son of a bitch again, and neither will my mother. And if my father lives I'll make sure he doesn't —"

"Maggie, if I can get some of the money back, maybe that will help make things right. Your father had to be racked with guilt about this."

"I don't care about the money anymore. It's my uncle's money. It can stay lost, for all I care."

"Okay, I understand how you feel, but please, Maggie, go and tend to your family."

"I will . . . and if you talk to Tommy Ordonez, tell him never to contact any of us again."

Ava sat at the desk for several minutes, still in shock. What could Tommy Ordonez have said to his brother? Surely Maggie had told her father about Ava's involvement and the information Jack Maynard had passed on to her. Surely he must have realized there was some light at the end of the tunnel.

She picked up the phone and dialled Uncle's number.

"*Wei*," he said.

"Uncle, it's Ava. I'm sorry for calling so early."

"*Momentai*, my dear."

"Uncle, there have been a lot of developments on this side, and not all of them are in our favour."

"I am listening," he said.

Ava took Uncle through her day, from the phone conversation with Edward Ling to her meeting with Maggie Chew, her conference call with Jack Maynard, and her attempt to contact Ronald Francis. Uncle listened quietly. When she had finished the business side of the report, he said, "You have made tremendous progress. Did that Maynard send you his information?"

"Yes, and I've gone through it. It holds up. His conclusions are fully supported by the data."

"So now what?"

"I need to talk to the Mohneida. I need them to tell me who Kaybar and Buckshot are."

"I have confidence in your powers of persuasion."

"And if it takes more than that?"

"Meaning?"

"Financial incentives."

"Do whatever you have to do. I will make it work from this end."

"Uncle, there is one more thing that may affect how, and even if, we proceed," Ava said.

"What is that?" he asked, caution in his voice.

"Philip Chew tried to kill himself about an hour ago. He jumped from the roof of his house in full view of his wife."

Uncle paused, and then said deliberately, "Is he dead?"

"Injured. How badly, I don't know."

Uncle said slowly, "He has brought such disgrace upon himself and his family. It had to be a terrible burden to bear."

"Uncle, Tommy Ordonez called his brother yesterday, and from what I'm told he berated him so severely that Chew was reduced to a trembling mess. Maggie blames him for her father's reaction."

"Who is to know what causes men to do what they do?"

"If Chew dies?"

"The damage he has caused can still be mitigated if we get some of the money back. I will talk to Chang about making sure that the wife and daughter are not abandoned."

"So you think Ordonez will want us to keep pursuing this course?"

"Once he knows that the money was definitely swindled from his brother, and from the company, he will want it back. In his mind I am sure he can separate the money from his brother's tragedy. If anything, it might make our case for getting the money back even more compelling."

"And you don't think he'll feel any guilt about his brother's attempted suicide?"

"Ava, Ordonez is the kind of man who thinks people get whatever they deserve in this life, and that their characters are what they are. I am sure he will believe that his brother jumped because his character was too weak to withstand the guilt he carried, and that whatever he said to him had nothing to do with it."

"And you're comfortable with our continuing to work for him?"

"Ava, since when did our clients have to be nice people?"

"True enough."

"As long as they honour their agreement, we should honour ours."

"Yes, Uncle."

"I know you do not like Ordonez, but men like him do not care whether we like them or not, and any emotion spent in that regard is wasted."

"I understand, Uncle," Ava said. "I forgot to mention — Ordonez called me today as well."

"Chang did not mention anything about that."

"He may not know. The call was at three o'clock in the morning, Manila time. He wanted me to call him with updates."

"What did you say?"

"I said no."

"How did he take it?"

"Not well."

"I will talk to Chang."

"Uncle, if Chang can't get him to back off, I may need you to speak to him. I can't work like this. I'm going to Victoria in the morning to meet with Chief Francis, and I want to have a clear head. I don't want to be worried about answering my phone."

"I understand," he said.

Ava knew he did. What she didn't know was whether Tommy Ordonez would listen.

18

AVA CAUGHT THE FIRST FLIGHT OUT, AT 7 A.M., AND BY eight she was walking up the front steps of the Fairmont Empress Hotel. Behind her Victoria's inner harbour glittered in the morning sun.

The hotel was designed to look like a monstrous French chateau; its golden brickwork was shrouded in ivy and topped with a blue slate roof. It was more than a hundred years old, and to Ava's critical eye it wasn't showing many signs of its age. She walked into the lobby and admired the seamless marriage of marble and wood and the huge overhanging chandeliers. She could understand why the hotel was still on the Condé Nast Gold List.

She walked over to the reception desk and checked her luggage with the concierge. Ava then went to the house phone, called the hotel operator, and asked to be connected to Chief Francis's room. The phone rang five times and then went to voicemail.

"Good morning, Chief Francis. My name is Ava Lee, and I represent a Hong Kong investment firm. You were recommended to us by a colleague who met you several years ago when you were considering building a casino. We have other, more diverse interests, and I'd appreciate the opportunity to sit and talk with you. I was in Vancouver yesterday and called your home last night to make an appointment. Your wife graciously told me you were in Victoria, so I flew over this morning, hoping we could connect. I'm at the hotel, and I'll leave you with my cellphone number."

Ava retreated to the lobby and settled into a leather chair. There was nothing to do but wait. She gave herself until one o'clock. If she didn't hear from him by then, she would go looking for him and engage him as best as she could.

She picked up the *Vancouver Sun* and was scanning the front page when her cellphone rang. An eastern Ontario area code lit up the screen, and for a second she thought it was Marian calling, until she noticed that the number was unfamiliar. "Ava Lee."

"This is Chief Ronald Francis."

"Thank you for returning my call."

"Do I know you?"

"No, sir, you don't," she said and paused. She didn't want to lie to him, nor did she want to raise the Philip Chew problem over the phone. So she said nothing.

"And you want to meet?"

"If that's possible. I'd really appreciate even ten minutes of your time."

She could hear him mumbling to someone. "We have a small boardroom on the mezzanine level," he said. "I have an opening in half an hour."

"I'll be there," she said.

Ava stood up and walked to the business centre. She printed out the data Maynard and Hunter had sent her and went through it with a black marker, obliterating any mention of their real names and their player names.

At five to nine she was at the boardroom door. She pulled at the cuffs of her crisp white Brooks Brothers shirt and then absentmindedly fiddled with her gold crucifix pendant. A thin young man wearing a Western shirt and jeans opened the door. "Could you wait a minute?" he asked.

She stood outside for fifteen minutes, listening as an active discussion went on inside the room. She thought she heard the word *river*, and then the door opened. The same young man poked his head out. "You can come in now."

She walked in and saw two men sitting at a round table. The man she recognized as Chief Francis was leaning back in his chair, his feet up on the table, displaying his cowboy boots. The other man was big and broad and had arms as thick as Ava's thighs. The two men stood and looked at her with disinterest.

"Sorry to keep you waiting," Francis said, extending his right hand as his left reached back to adjust his braid. "This is a busy time for us. I'm Chief Ronald Francis. This is Martin," he said, pointing at the young man who had let her in. "And Harold," he went on, motioning to the large man.

"Thank you for seeing me," Ava said as Martin's warm brown eyes caught hers. She waited to be asked to sit. When no one spoke, she sat down, opened her Chanel purse, and took out her Moleskine notebook, along with the envelope that contained Maynard's and Hunter's data.

"I wasn't expecting a presentation," Francis said. He resumed his seat, put his feet back on the table, and motioned for Martin and Harold to sit down.

"My name is Ava Lee and I'm an accountant," she said. "I'm here on behalf of perhaps the largest multinational company in the Philippines, and one of the largest in Asia."

"I thought you said you were Hong Kong–based."

"I work for a Hong Kong firm that's been hired by the Filipino company. I was brought on to look into a rather substantial fraud case that may indirectly involve your band," she said.

"What the hell are you talking about?"

"The River."

Francis's look of disinterest evaporated, and she found herself the subject of a prolonged and menacing stare. "This is crap," he said. He looked at Harold as he said to Ava, "This meeting is over."

Ava didn't move. "Chief Francis, if you can give me about ten minutes of your time, I think we can work together at resolving what is basically a business issue that my people would like handled as discreetly as possible."

"This meeting is over," he repeated and nodded at Harold, who stood up and reached for Ava. He grabbed her by the left bicep, and when she didn't immediately respond to his touch, he increased the pressure and yanked her to her feet.

Francis was turning away when Ava's right hand shot out and connected with the elbow of Harold's extended arm. He spun around when the man screamed and staggered backwards, his arm dangling uselessly by his side.

"I'm sorry, I can't stand being mauled," Ava said. "All I want is a ten-minute discussion. If you want me to leave after we've had it, I will do so without any fuss."

Harold collapsed into a chair, his face contorted and blooming with pain. "What did you do to him?" Francis asked.

"He has a particularly sensitive nerve in his elbow. He'll be okay in about thirty minutes."

He stared at her again. She didn't flinch. "Who are you?" he said.

"Someone you need to talk to."

Francis took his feet off the table and motioned to Martin. "Martin, despite his age, is one of my senior financial people. He's also the most computer literate of us."

"So we can talk?"

"I'm listening, but I'm not sure for how long. We've been briefed already."

"You've already been told about the problem?"

"Obviously."

"By whom?"

"Some people from The River."

"I don't know what they told you, but our position is that someone seems to have breached the security of the software attached to The River's poker program and manipulated it to cheat other players."

"It isn't our software. We just administer it for them," Francis said quickly.

Martin interceded. "Ms. Lee, to follow up on what the Chief said, I got a call from one of the techies at The River a little while ago, and he told me they suspected there had been a breach. He said they had identified what they thought was the problem and that they would have it corrected. He made it sound like something quite minor."

"Then why were you discussing the situation so intently while I was outside? I couldn't help overhearing how concerned you all seemed."

"That was me being paranoid," Francis said.

"About what?"

"We license and regulate online gambling. We have a trust to maintain. People are sending their money into cyberspace with only our assurance that it's safe and secure and that any gaming they do is above board. Anything that undermines that trust is of the ultimate importance to me."

"As it should be."

"I called Jeremy Ashton at The River after Martin told me about his talk with the techie. He assured me it was just a glitch that they had caught and fixed. He said that some of the players were grumbling but they were handling the problem, and we shouldn't talk to them if they approached us. He said it was mainly a public relations issue and that they were on top of it."

"So why were you still talking about it this morning?"

Francis stared at her. Again Ava met his gaze. His eyes were dark brown, so dark that the lack of contrast made his irises look abnormally large.

"I can understand your reasons for wanting to keep this quiet. What you need to understand is that we have our own reasons for wanting exactly the same thing."

She sensed Martin squirming in his chair and turned to him. "Did you do some investigating on your own?" He looked at Francis.

"Tell us what you know," Francis said to Ava.

"No," she said. "We need to have an agreement first."

"You want to drag lawyers into this?" he asked.

"Of course not."

"Then what?"

Ava opened the envelope and placed the copies of Maynard's and Hunter's work in front of her. "We hired two experts, mathematicians from MIT and Stanford. We had them analyze high-stakes play on The River's website for the past six months. The raw data was provided by some of the players involved. These are their reports. In their minds, the numbers are statistically anomalous."

Francis looked to Martin. "Chief, that means the numbers are bullshit — they don't make any sense," Martin said.

"Would you give us those reports?" Francis said.

"Yes, that could be arranged."

"Martin, how long would it take our people to do their own examination of the data and to cross-reference everything?" he asked.

"To do it properly, it could take months."

"I don't have months," Ava interrupted.

"Then why give us the reports?" Francis said.

"I want to trade."

Francis leaned back, balancing his chair on its rear legs. His pulled at his braid again. "What do we have that you need?"

"The real names of a handful of players who were involved in the high-stakes action."

"How many players?"

"Five."

Martin leaned over to Francis and whispered in his ear. The Chief nodded and turned to Ava. "How much money do you think was scammed?"

"Does that matter if your main priority is preserving the integrity of your system?"

"Don't be a smartass."

She smiled. "I do understand that there are degrees of damage," she said. "In this case I think we're talking about somewhere between sixty and eighty million dollars."

Francis glared at Martin, who shook his head slowly from side to side.

"Jesus fucking Christ," Francis said. "Is that true?"

"It's outlined here," she said, tapping the documents.

"So Ashton was blowing smoke?"

"It would seem so, unless he really thinks that sixty million dollars is inconsequential."

Francis closed his eyes and leaned his head back. He didn't stir for a minute or more, his lips moving from time to time.

"Chief, as I said, we have no interest in going public with this," Ava said finally. "I can also say that we have no doubts about your integrity, and I'm prepared to give the band complete indemnification from any fallout, legal or otherwise."

"You can do that?"

"Yes."

"In writing?"

"If you need it."

"So I give you the names and you give me what? The reports, a commitment not to go public, and complete indemnification from any future legal action?"

"Yes."

"What are you going to do with the names?"

"Go after them for the money."

"How can you do that and keep us out of it? I mean, I don't care how good your lawyers are —"

"We don't use lawyers," she said. "We use more traditional, less expensive, and more time-sensitive methods."

"Who is 'we'?"

"Mainly me, but I have support if it's required."

"I'm not sure I believe what I'm hearing."

Ava shrugged. "Let me tell you what the alternative is. The people in the Philippines are incredibly wealthy. They are also vindictive, particularly when members of their family are affected. And one has been — he's already tried to commit suicide. So we're talking personal here as well as money. If we can work out an arrangement, I guarantee you will never hear from them."

"And if we don't make an agreement?"

"They'll get the lawyers involved. They'll bring in public relations companies. They'll cost you millions in expenses and they'll drag your name through the mud. They'll make sure that no one in Asia considers even a ten-dollar investment in the band. It will be your standard train wreck."

"I wondered how long you were going to be sweet and reasonable."

"I still am. I just don't think it's fair to lie to you, to leave you with the idea that there's no cause and effect."

Francis looked at Martin. "What do you think?"

"I think Ms. Lee has made us a sound business proposal," Martin said.

"Five names?" Francis said.

"Yes."

"Then we've heard the last of this?"

"You will never hear from us again."

He tugged at his hair. "Give the names to Martin."

She extracted a slip of paper from her notebook. "China-clipper, Brrrrr, Buckshot, Felix the Cat, and Kaybar. I need to know who these people are, and I want addresses, phone numbers, email addresses — everything you have on file for them."

"I don't want to go to my lawyer to draft anything," Francis said. "He's a stickler for the fine points of the law, and he might think we're compromising ourselves by giving you those names."

"I'll send you an email with my commitment in it. Print it and I'll sign it."

"Assuming you actually have the authority to sign anything."

"If you need to call Hong Kong, I'll gladly provide you with a number."

"No," Francis said, writing down his email address and handing her the paper. "For some reason I trust you."

Ava stood. "The trust is mutual," she said. "Although I do need to ask that no one from the band contact anyone at The River. I think it's best all around if they think this issue is behind them."

"All right," Francis said.

"You'll have my email in half an hour," she said.

"I'll make a phone call. You'll have the names by then as well," Martin said.

Francis and Martin stood, and each in turn extended a hand. Harold was still slumped in the chair, holding his arm. Ava realized she might have jabbed him a little more forcefully than she intended.

"I have to say, I didn't expect this to happen when you walked through the door," Francis said.

"Sometimes meetings take on a life of their own," Ava said, nodding at all three men.

19

AVA LEFT THE MEZZANINE, WENT TO THE CONCIERGE TO retrieve her bags, and checked into a room. Her cellphone had been off during the meeting, and when she turned it on, her mother's number was at the top of the missed calls list. *The bamboo telegraph has been working overtime*, Ava thought. Philip Chew's attempted suicide would be the talk of countless mah-jong tables. She just hoped her mother didn't think that they or Aunt Lily had pushed him over the edge.

When Ava got to her suite, she went to work on the memorandum of agreement for Francis. It took longer than she thought to get the wording right. She couldn't help slipping in phrases that created loopholes; in the end she took them all out. There was no point in risking his alienation by trying to act the amateur lawyer.

When the email had been sent, she waited twenty minutes and then went downstairs to the mezzanine level. Martin stood outside the boardroom, talking on his mobile phone. She saw a copy of her email in his hand. *This is good*, he mouthed, and passed her the piece of paper.

She held it against the wall and signed it, then kept her distance until he had closed the phone. "Here," she said, handing the paper to him.

He took the email from her and disappeared into the boardroom. He was back in less than five minutes. "These are the names you want, and here's my card. The Chief asked that you call me if you need anything else. Or if you think there's anything we need to be warned about."

As she handed him her card, Ava noted that Martin's family name was Littlefeather. "How old are you?" she asked.

"Twenty-eight."

"So young."

"We're the first generation to benefit from the Chief's work. He has faith in us."

"I'm impressed."

"But I can't take Harold out and I can't control the Chief the way you did," he said.

"I'm older than you are."

"Bull," he said.

She leaned forward and offered her hand. "I'd like to stay in touch with you."

"Me too," he said, taking her hand and holding it. She smiled, then turned and walked towards the elevator.

She opened the slip of paper when she was alone in the elevator. There were four names on it. *Philip Chew. Felix Hunter. Jack Maynard. David Douglas.* Where was the fifth? Then she saw that Douglas's name was written next to both *Buckshot* and *Kaybar*. She needed to talk to Jack Maynard.

"David Douglas," Ava said, when she got to her room. She sat down at the desk and opened her notebook.

"What about him?" Maynard asked.

"Who is he?"

"The Disciple."

"Who?"

"David 'the Disciple' Douglas, one of the greatest poker players in the world. A fucking master."

"I think he's also Buckshot and Kaybar."

"Impossible," Maynard said, dragging the word out.

"Why?"

There was a long pause. "I don't know. Maybe *unthinkable* is a better word."

"Did you play online with him?"

"A couple of times."

"Did he win?"

"Yeah, but he's the Disciple. Him winning isn't exactly a surprise."

"Check all your records and see if he ever played against you at the same time as either Buckshot or Kaybar, and then call me back."

"Wait," he said. "I can correlate that in a few seconds."

She waited, her head already halfway to Las Vegas.

"Son of a bitch," he said finally.

"Jack, you can't discuss this with anyone, not even Felix."

"I can't believe this shit. Douglas beat me, Philip, and Felix for maybe five or six million combined, but we never thought twice about it. It was Buckshot and Kaybar who made us freak out. Now I'm looking at my records and kicking myself for not seeing the obvious. None of them ever played together. Ever. And I'm telling you, when you factor Douglas's play into the numbers we ran on Buckshot and Kaybar, that ninety percent certainty we had that we were screwed jumps to one hundred. And do you know what hurts most?"

"I can guess."

"We were fucked over big time by the very guy Felix and I almost model ourselves after."

Ava was beginning to regret the phone call. "Jack, for the last time, please don't discuss this with anyone."

"What are you going to do?"

"I'm going after him."

"For Philip?"

"For my client."

"Well, fuck that," Maynard said. "Get our money back at the same time. Then we can all bury that son of a bitch so deep he won't be able to show his face anywhere in the poker world."

She knew she had lost him. Douglas's name had set off a firestorm in Maynard's head. "Listen to me, Jack. Maybe I can get some money back for you and Felix, but — and please hear me — I made a commitment to the Mohneida that I would keep this quiet. In exchange, they've made it possible for us to go after Douglas. Without them we would be nowhere. And I don't go back on my word."

"Okay, then don't. Just get our money."

"And you'll stay quiet about Douglas?"

"If I have to."

"You do."

"And you'll take my word for it?"

"Yes, I will. With one caveat."

"I'm listening."

"If you cause me to lose trust with the Mohneida, I'll take it very personally. And my people don't do car bombs. They do face to face."

"Shit. I won't do or say anything, I promise," he said.

Ava wasn't sure she believed him but she had no other choice but to go along. "Okay, then I'll do what I can to get your money back as well."

"Thank you."

"Send me an accounting of how much they took from you and Felix."

"Will do."

"And then send me your take on David Douglas. Pretend he didn't screw you. Pretend it's two weeks ago and you were asked for an objective assessment of him."

"Can do."

"I can see from the information the Mohneida gave me that he lives in Vegas. Where does he play?"

"When he's there, he plays the cash game at Wynn's. I played with him there myself. They told me he shows up just about every day."

"Do the people at Wynn's know who you are?"

"Yeah."

"Then do me a favour. Call Wynn's right now and ask if Douglas has been playing there, and then call me back."

"Okay."

It took less than ten minutes for Maynard to call Ava back. "He's been there every day for the past month or so. In fact he's sitting at one of the tables now."

"Well, I guess I'm going to Las Vegas," Ava said.

It was almost five o'clock. She doubted that there would be any direct flights from Victoria to Vegas, and she had no idea if she could get back to Vancouver and catch one from there. She went online and, to her surprise, saw there was a nine-o'clock flight from Vancouver to Seattle that connected with an eleven-o'clock flight that got into Vegas just past midnight. Ava phoned her travel agent in Toronto, but when she couldn't reach her, she went back online and booked the flights herself.

She was packing her bags when her cellphone rang. The 613 area code again — eastern Ontario. "Ava Lee," she said.

"It's Martin Littlefeather."

"How are you?"

"I'm fine. I just wanted you to know that I've finished going over the data you gave us. At first glance it seems to hold up very well. It'll take time to confirm, of course, but it's so well organized that it should take less time than I thought."

"That's good."

"I was also calling to see if you'd like to join me for a drink later."

"Actually, Martin, I'm flying to Las Vegas tonight."

"Vegas?"

"Yes, I think that David Douglas is my man, and that's where he is."

Ava heard noise erupting from his end. "Just a second. I'm with people and they've decided to start to party."

When he came back on, she heard a toilet flushing. "Sorry about that. Did you say David Douglas?"

"Yes."

He hesitated. "I can't say I'm surprised."

"Why?"

"He's a shareholder in The River, along with Jeremy Ashton. The company is registered in Cyprus."

"Why didn't you tell me earlier?"

"You left before I had a chance to say anything."

"I did, didn't I. Well, now that we're talking, tell me what you know about him."

"I've never met Douglas. We've only dealt with Ashton, which is not unusual. A lot of these poker sites have well-known professionals attached to them to attract players. They're normally not involved in any of the day-to-day administration."

"Then talk to me about Ashton."

"He's English, a bit of a snot, and demanding as hell. I've actually talked to the Chief a few times about cutting them loose. When we started this business, we were so anxious for customers that we were more flexible with our standards than we should have been, and we didn't always do the kind of due diligence we do now."

"Are you saying there's something odd going on with The River?" she asked.

"I'm saying I don't know if there is or not, but that there shouldn't be any doubt."

"Fair enough. Although it's a bit late in the day now."

"I know," he said softly.

"Hey, I'm sorry. I'm not trying to second-guess you." Ava checked her watch. "Martin, I know I didn't clear this with the Chief, but can you send me everything you have on Ashton and Douglas and their businesses — The River and the holding company and whatever else you have on file?"

"I can."

"Tonight, if possible."

"Okay."

"Do you need to discuss it with the Chief?"

"I don't think so. He did ask me to handle communications with you. I don't see how your request is out of the ordinary."

"Thanks, and I'll talk to you later."

"Good luck."

Funny, she thought, *luck* wasn't a word she normally associated with her job, but this time it seemed to fit.

20

EVEN AT MIDNIGHT, MCCARRAN AIRPORT WAS A ZOO.
Serving a city with a population of only a million people, it
was the sixth-busiest airport in the world, handling more
than 600,000 planes and 45 million passengers a year.
Hordes of people slumped towards the departure gates,
tired, depressed, defeated, and broke. Moving past them in
the opposite direction were thousands of confident, eager,
energetic new arrivals.

Ava's plane landed at the main terminal and she walked
out to the taxi stand. The lineup looped back and forth like
one for a Disney World ride in peak season. She shivered,
the cool desert air penetrating her nylon Adidas jacket. She
spotted a limo driver with a sign that read DOWNTOWN
and headed towards him. A tall, lean black man got there
just ahead of her. "The Venetian," he said.

"Can you take two people?" Ava asked, poking her head
around him.

"Up to him," the driver said.

"Where are you going?" the man asked.

"Wynn's."

"Okay," he said, nodding at the driver.

McCarran Airport was in the southeast part of Vegas, only eight kilometres from the downtown area and about four kilometres from the heart of the Strip. Its outer boundary was mainly desert. On previous trips it had taken Ava not much more than ten minutes to get from the airport to the main Strip, but tonight traffic was unbelievably heavy. After crawling along Tropicana Avenue for fifteen minutes they still hadn't reached Las Vegas Boulevard.

"Is there something going on tonight?" Ava asked.

"There's always something going on," the driver said.

The man she was sharing the limo with spent the first ten minutes of the drive working his BlackBerry. Whatever he was reading had brought a smile to his face. Ava thought he looked slightly familiar. She gazed at his long, lean frame. He wore a black silk jacket over a white T-shirt, black designer jeans, and a pair of expensive white sneakers. When he had put the BlackBerry away, he turned to her and said, "Hi, I'm Gilbert Jackson."

The driver twisted his head to look back at them. "I thought I recognized you. Great to drive you."

"I'm Ava Lee," she said to Jackson.

"You in the movies?" he asked.

"No."

"You didn't do that *Crouching Tiger* thing?"

"No."

"You sure?"

"I think so."

"Okay," he said, smiling at her.

"What do you do?" she asked.

"I played basketball, and now I'm an agent."

"He's *the* agent," the driver said. "He represents the best."

"I was lucky," Jackson said. "I wasn't much of a player but I learned how the system works. And I made a lot of friends."

"I'm an accountant," Ava said.

"I have one."

"I wasn't looking for a job."

He shrugged. "I'm here for an agents' meeting. You?"

"I came here to get some money."

"Then you've come to the wrong place," Jackson said. "They didn't build Las Vegas to give money away."

Traffic lightened as they moved closer towards the Strip. As they turned north on Las Vegas Boulevard, four massive hotels — the MGM Grand, the Tropicana, New York–New York, and the Excalibur — lit up the night sky. Those hotels alone, Ava knew, held twenty thousand guests at any given time. Most of them, it seemed, had spilled out onto the jammed sidewalks.

It had been a few years since Ava had been to Vegas. On previous trips, always with her mother, she had done her run along the Strip in the early morning. She would start at Sands Avenue and work her way south, past Flamingo Road, Harmon Road, and Tropicana Avenue, out to Russell Road, where she was greeted by the famous WELCOME TO LAS VEGAS sign at the tip of the boulevard. Just beyond had been patches of vacant desert, small strip malls, and stand-alone restaurants. Now Ava saw that the gaps had been plugged. On the west side of the Strip, New York–New York ran into the Monte Carlo, and beside it was the massive new City Center complex and the Bellagio, on the southwest corner of Flamingo Road.

"Hardcore Disneyland for adults," Jackson said.

"If you like to gamble," Ava replied.

"Hell, not many of my guys are into that. They come here to party — which, if anything, is worse. Vegas has the best club scene in the country, and there's more trouble to be found there than on any casino floor."

"Women?"

Jackson laughed. "These guys are in the NBA. They use women the way you use dental floss."

"Nice," Ava said.

"No offence."

"A bit late for that."

"What I mean," he said, as they neared the northwest corner of Flamingo Boulevard, "is that things get more complicated here. Yeah, there are women, but there's also drugs and booze and cash. Some of my guys really believe that shit about what happens in Vegas stays in Vegas. When the NBA All-Star game was held here, it got so bad they had to shut down some of the clubs early on a Saturday night."

"How bad could it have been?"

"Three shootings and a couple of near riots inside the clubs."

"Geez."

He smiled at Ava. "Yeah, geez. That's why I never let any of my guys come to Vegas alone, or with friends. I send a babysitter along with them. A big, tough babysitter."

As the limo got close to Sands Avenue, the Venetian loomed into view. St. Mark's Square had been transplanted to Las Vegas with everything but the pigeons. They drove around the canal to the entrance. As Jackson left the limo, Ava said to him, "Just leave a tip. I'll pay for the ride."

He looked at her as if she was joking. "That's a change."

"I told you — I don't need a job," she said.

The limo left the Venetian, glided past the Palazzo, and entered Steve Wynn's world. Wynn Las Vegas was, by Vegas standards, the epitome of class. The only theme was luxury. The forty-five-storey hotel had close to three thousand rooms and had cost almost three billion dollars to build. Its curved exterior was sheathed in bronze glass, with *Wynn* written in gold across the top. Inside, its marble and glass walkways were lined with high-end boutiques, including Cartier and Chanel. Overhead hung hundreds of light fixtures and chandeliers made of colourful blown glass. The casino occupied more than 100,000 square feet and was serviced by cocktail waitresses whose breasts almost touched their chins.

Ava had booked a deluxe resort room. It was more than six hundred square feet and decorated in soft creams and modern furnishings. She imagined that the floor-to-ceiling, wall-to-wall windows would flood the room with natural light during the day. The bellboy spent a few minutes showing her the high-tech controls for the drapes, the massive flat-screen TV, and the en suite bathroom. She was less enthralled when he told her that if she put anything in the room's mini-fridge it would result in a charge. She also didn't like the idea that if she picked up a can of cashews for more than sixty seconds, she owned them. *As classy as they try to be in Vegas*, she thought, *there's always a hint of a tart.*

She booted up her computer to find emails from Martin Littlefeather and Jack Maynard. She pulled out her notebook and copied the corporate and personal information that Martin had provided on The River, David Douglas, and Jeremy Ashton.

Maynard's email was long and rambling, and he had attached a photo of David Douglas.

Ava now saw why Douglas was called "the Disciple." He was older than she had imagined — she guessed around sixty — and had a strange build: tall, narrow in the shoulders, and with a hollow chest that swelled into a large, pronounced pot belly. His face was bony and angular; he had a sharp chin, a pointed nose, and eyebrows that were thickets of curls. The look was topped off by a head of long, wiry silver hair that had been coiffed into a puffy Afro resembling a halo. Maynard had written, The hair is his trademark. He thinks it makes him look saintly.

Maynard explained that Douglas was considered an elder statesman of the poker community, someone who took his wins and losses calmly, never gloating, never whining. He had acquired his nickname from his unique coif, as Ava had thought, but also from his habit of casting his eyes skyward whenever he had a difficult decision to make at the poker table.

Maynard closed his email with a comment that Ava found telling. It is every poker player's fantasy to be able to see his opponents' cards, to be completely in control. That prick Douglas took that fantasy and made it a reality. He must have felt like he was some kind of god, fucking around with us miserable mortals.

Martin Littlefeather's email was more concise and all business. The River was controlled by a holding company that was registered in Cyprus. It had three shareholders: Douglas, Ashton, and a company called Duncon LLP. There was no mention of who owned Duncon. Littlefeather had included the names and addresses of the banks The River dealt with. One was in Las Vegas; the other, not surprisingly, was in Cyprus.

The Mohneida had run rudimentary background checks on both men. Born in New Mexico, Douglas had been playing professional poker since he turned twenty-one, when he had moved to Las Vegas. He had been married and divorced twice and had no children. No bankruptcies, no arrests, no drug or alcohol issues. His entire life seemed to revolve around poker. The report noted that, like Maynard, Douglas was well respected by his peers. He had won three World Series of Poker bracelets, but none in recent years. The report also commented that although Douglas's best playing days were probably behind him, his reputation would be an asset in terms of promoting The River.

Jeremy Ashton had been born in Sheffield, England, and attended the University of Leeds, where he graduated from business school. He had worked with Smyth's Investment Bank in London for less than a year, and then he went to New York to work as an analyst at Whiteburn. He'd never married and, like Douglas, he seemed to be free of scandal.

Ashton had met Douglas while he was at Whiteburn; he left the firm to help him start The River. They seem to have raised the money they needed quite quickly, Martin Littlefeather wrote in his email, but competition was fierce and the site struggled.

Ava finished making notes and was about to shut down her computer when she saw that she had a message from an mgonzalez. She paused, and then she remembered the woman Mimi had mentioned and opened it.

Dear Ava,

My name is Maria Gonzalez. Your friend Mimi
suggested I contact you, though I have to confess
I've never done anything like this before. I've been
living in Toronto for only six months. I work at the
Colombian trade consulate. I have found, truthfully,
the transition to the city and the weather and the
culture to be very difficult. Mimi thought we had a
lot in common. I like movies, good food, I'm Roman
Catholic, and I love to salsa. I apologize if you find
this approach not to your liking. But Mimi urged me
on, so I thought I would take a chance. I hope we
can get together, maybe for a coffee or a drink?

My best regards,

Maria Gonzalez

Ava read the email twice before responding.

Hi Maria,

Mimi did mention your name to me. I'm away from
Toronto on business, and I don't know when I'll return. If Mimi thinks we could be friends then I think
it's worth meeting. Let's keep in touch. Oh, and I like
to salsa as well.

Ava

Ava flopped onto the bed and then grimaced. Her body
was beginning to recover and the pain was less severe, but
now and then it couldn't help but remind her it was still
there. She sat up. Her cellphone had been off since she left
Victoria, so she turned it on to retrieve her messages. Her

mother had called again to say she'd heard about Philip Chew and that the aunties were ready to kill Tommy Ordonez. Ava was relieved that no fingers were being pointed in her direction. And Uncle had phoned; he said simply, "Call me when you can." She dialled his number after deleting the message.

"*Wei.*"

"Uncle, it's Ava. I'm in Las Vegas."

"The Mohneida cooperated?"

"They did."

"What did it cost?"

"Nothing. I just guaranteed that we would indemnify them from any legal action and try to shield them from negative publicity."

"That is not nothing," he corrected, and then paused so the words would sink in. "So, they were not involved?" he said finally.

"Not in any way that would matter."

"You probably still promised them too much. We cannot speak for Tommy Ordonez."

"I'm sorry, Uncle, but I needed their cooperation, and that's what it cost. And there was one other complication I had to deal with."

"With the Mohneida?" he asked.

"No, two poker players who lost money the same way as Philip Chew. They helped me figure out what happened and who did it. They demanded we get their money back in exchange for their cooperation. I know we never like to have two clients at once, even if it's one thief we're chasing, but I said we would do what we could for them. I didn't feel I had any choice."

"How much?"

"Seven million."

"Our usual fee?"

"Of course."

"If they helped that much —"

"Without them I wouldn't be in Vegas."

"Who are you in Las Vegas to see?"

"A man named David Douglas. He's a professional poker player."

She could hear barking in the background and the sound of traffic. He was walking the dog. "Do you need any assistance?" he asked.

"I don't know yet. I need to locate him and then figure out how to approach him. There's another man involved, a partner in his business named Jeremy Ashton, but I think Douglas will be my first priority."

"Keep me up to date. Chang has called several times today. Ordonez is acting crazy where his brother is concerned. He thinks Chew's attempted suicide was just another way for him to avoid taking responsibility. Chang is not sure how long he can keep Ordonez from doing something rash. The only thing holding him back is fear of losing face."

"Things won't work on my end if he blows up."

"I have been telling them that."

"And?"

"Chang agrees, but Ordonez is a man who needs to be in control and needs to be doing something. He is not accustomed to being made to wait."

"I need time."

"I will do what I can."

Ava knew he would. Anything more she had to say

would be redundant, if not insulting. "I'll call tomorrow around the same time," she said.

"Just a second," Uncle said. "Jackie Leung — I found out that he is back in Hong Kong. Sonny is looking for him, and knowing Sonny, he will find him soon enough. In the meantime, I have been talking to Guangzhou. They do not want to unilaterally cancel the contract. They feel they have made a pact with Leung that they need to honour."

Ava felt a tiny knot of anxiety in her stomach. "What does that mean, that they don't want to unilaterally cancel the contract?"

"As long as Leung is alive we have to assume they will continue to look for you."

"And if he's dead?"

"No Leung, no contract."

"And in the meantime what am I supposed to do?"

"Be careful. I cannot imagine they will find you before Sonny finds Leung. Leung is in Hong Kong, and not many people know Hong Kong better than Sonny."

"How hard are they looking?"

"They are professional," Uncle said.

Ava shook her head. She didn't need this distraction, not now, not ever. "I'll be careful," she said.

21

BY 9 A.M. AVA WAS RUNNING ALONG LAS VEGAS BOULEVARD.
It was as if she were in a different world than the one she
had arrived in nine hours before. The sidewalks that had
been clogged with tourists and locals the previous night
were now blissfully vacant. She ran south, retracing the
route the limo had taken from McCarran Airport.

The desert air was crisp and clean. The streets had been
washed and cleared of the beer bottles, empty cigarette
packs, and other debris that the drunken revellers left
every night. The casinos, so gaudily lit at night, now looked
almost naked to Ava's eyes.

She ran for close to an hour, starting on the west end
of the Strip, past the Bellagio, with its man-made lake set
before the façade of an Italian village nestled in mountains;
on to the Luxor Hotel, which was shaped like a pyramid;
and past the Paris Las Vegas with its Eiffel Tower and the
Venetian, where gondoliers were now stationed in the canal.
Vegas brought the world to America.

Back at Wynn's she showered, put on a black Giordano
T-shirt and her Adidas training pants, and then made

herself a Starbucks VIA instant coffee. She opened the drapes, sat at the dining table, and turned on her computer. The golf course offered a pleasant view: ribbons of green punctuated by pale white bunkers and man-made ponds.

Ava's plan for the day was low-key. She wanted to find out a bit more about The River, Ashton, and Douglas. Online she found The River's website and its office address, which was on Korval Lane, the first street south of Las Vegas Boulevard. Then, using the information Martin Littlefeather had provided, she located Ashton's residence, a condo near the Hard Rock Hotel, and Douglas's house, in what looked like a ritzy neighbourhood southwest of the city called The Oasis. With time to kill, she decided to take a look at all three.

Ava left her room and took the elevator to the hotel lobby, then walked outside and joined the queue for a taxi. There were ten people ahead of her, but with typical Vegas efficiency she was in a cab in less than five minutes. With the luck of the draw, she got a driver who was Chinese. She spoke English to him at first, but when he answered haltingly, she switched to Cantonese. His Cantonese was as rough as his English, so Ava changed to Mandarin. The driver smiled at her in his rear-view mirror and introduced himself as Au.

"Could you take me to Korval Lane?" she asked.

The River's office was only a few minutes away. They drove a kilometre south from Wynn's to Flamingo Avenue and then turned left and drove towards Korval, which was at the next intersection. Even though they were only a block away from the Strip, the neighbourhood was decidedly plain in contrast. They passed small office complexes, low-rent motels, and several rows of townhouses that rented by the week or the month. The River was in a three-storey brown stucco building whose walls were starting to peel. A sign outside listed two dentists, an accountant, a chiropractor, and a podiatrist. There was no mention of The River. She had Au stop outside, just as he was telling her that he was from Beijing and his wife was from Hong Kong. She got out of the car and walked into the lobby. A tenant board listed the same occupants on the first and second floors and, in smaller letters, The River on the third. *Why such a dumpy building?* Ava thought. *Why so inconspicuous a presence?*

Ava got back in the cab and directed Au to Ashton's condo. They drove west along Harmon, past low-rise apartment buildings, strip malls, and gas stations to Paradise Road, and then turned south. Ashton's condo was close to twenty storeys high and one of several in a row just beside the Hard Rock Hotel. It was set back from the road, with no security at the driveway entrance. Au drove up to the front door and Ava got out.

The door to the building required a code. Through the glass door Ava could see inside, where a security guard sitting behind a desk was eyeing her. Another guard appeared from a side door and glanced in her direction. Ava knew there would be security cameras as well.

"Do you know where The Oasis is?" she asked Au when she got back into the idling taxi.

"It's about a thirty-minute drive beyond the Strip," Au said.

"Take me there, please."

They wormed their way through the suburbs, stopping at nearly every intersection until they reached the desert. Ava knew that distances in the desert were deceptive; the complex came into view at least five minutes before they got to the gated community. The Oasis was essentially in the middle of nowhere, a sprawling mass of houses whose roofs peeked above a ten-foot-tall brick wall crowned with razor wire. Across the entranceway sat a lonely looking service station.

"Drive slowly past the entrance," she said. When they were just past it, she asked him to pull over and park.

Ava noted the double-barrelled security system. First there was a security gate with a barrier activated by a card and a speaker set up for visitors to identify themselves. A car drove past them and into the complex; the driver waved a plastic card in front of the box and the barrier rose. Two guards were manning a security checkpoint about fifty metres past the barrier. When the driver got to the checkpoint, one of the guards came out of the hut to look inside the car. The guard was young, fit, and alert. Ava noticed he carried a gun on his hip in an open holster.

"Let's go back to the hotel," she said.

As they drove back to the Strip, Au continued to chat, but Ava's mind was elsewhere. It wasn't until they were back in the city that she finally tuned in. He had just finished telling her about his arrival in Las Vegas five years before, as an acrobat in a Cirque du Soleil show, when they pulled up in front of Wynn's. "I injured myself, and I've been driving cabs ever since," he said.

A Wynn's doorman knocked on the driver's-side window to tell Au he was blocking traffic. Ava opened her door. "Are there any Chinese restaurants you'd recommend?" she asked him.

"Go to Chinatown, on Spring Mountain Road," Au said.

"Anything closer?"

"There's a noodle bar at the Venetian."

"I'll go there for lunch," she said. "How about dinner? Are there any good Japanese restaurants outside the hotels? I can't stand paying those prices."

"Ichiza," he said.

"Where is it?"

"It's on Spring Mountain Road as well, just past the Chinese mall, on the second floor of a strip mall."

"So far again?"

"It's worth it," he said. "That's where all the Chinese chefs from the hotels go at night when they've finished work. It costs two-thirds less than Japanese on the Strip, and the food is great. You'll save enough on the food to pay for a taxi, and then some."

"I'll try it," she said.

He passed her a business card. "My cellphone number's there. Call me whenever you need a cab. I'm usually no more than ten minutes away from anywhere."

Ava walked back to the Venetian and into the noodle bar. She sat at a Formica table that would have felt at home in any American diner. All the chefs and servers were Chinese but the customer base was nearly all *gweilo*. Ava's waiter fussed over her in English until she responded in Cantonese. He responded in Mandarin. Ava made a mental note that she wasn't in Toronto anymore, where Cantonese was dominant because of the influx of Hong Kong immigrants.

She ordered baby bok choy and har gow noodle soup. When the soup was served, Ava grimaced. Two shrimp dumplings and a sprinkling of chopped green onion floated in cloudy chicken broth. The waiter noticed her reaction.

It's one thing to stick it to the gweilos, she thought, *and another to take advantage of a fellow Chinese.*

When she had finished eating, the server asked her how her meal had been. "Adequate," she said. As he picked up her bowl and plate, she asked if he had heard of a restaurant called Ichiza.

"I go there all the time," he said.

"Good food, good value?"

"Better than here," he whispered.

It was almost two o'clock when she strolled back into Wynn's to wait for Douglas. She leaned against the wall directly across from the room's entrance and took in the action. There were twenty-six tables and fifteen were in play, most of them on the ground level. The upper level, where she assumed Douglas played, had only three active tables. Ava searched for a silver halo but didn't see one.

She had a thing about being prompt, even early. Marian shared the same characteristic; she said it was in reaction to a mother whose idea of being on time was within two hours of a scheduled appointment. Ava was thinking about her mother when she caught her first glimpse of the Disciple. He was taller than she had thought, well over six feet. His belly was particularly prominent and his hair had receded since the photograph, the afro more wispy than wiry. He walked slowly through the casino, greeting patrons who had left their tables to approach him. She watched as he stopped to chat, shake a hand, sign a cocktail napkin. In this place he was a celebrity.

She waited until he was ten yards away from the host's desk before she intercepted him. He looked down at her with eyes that were a watery, washed-out blue. "And what can I do for you?" he asked.

"My name is Ava Lee," she said.

"And what can I do for little Ava?"

"You can talk to me about The River."

"I beg your pardon?"

"I believe you've been involved, perhaps inadvertently, in a fraud perpetrated by some people playing on The River. I would like a chance to talk to you about it."

He twitched, turning his head away from her. "Get away from me," he said.

"Mr. Douglas, that isn't helpful. If you can give me fifteen minutes of your undivided attention I'm sure we can sort this out."

"What's your name again?"

"Ava Lee."

"Get away from me, Ava Lee."

"I'm afraid I can't do that," she said.

He stared down at her. "Don't make me call security," he said, lowering his voice. "I can have you carted off."

"If that's necessary, then do it," she said.

He hesitated and looked up at the ceiling. "Where are you staying?" he finally asked.

"Here."

He looked at the host, who was pretending not to listen. "Is my seat open?"

"Waiting for you, sir."

"Ms. Lee, I play poker for a living, and that's what I'm going to do right now. I'll be finished around midnight. If you're still here, then maybe we can talk."

She thought about her options. "Okay, I'll be here."

"See you then," he said with a nod.

22

AVA WANDERED THE CASINO FLOOR FOR FIFTEEN MINUTES and then found a spot where she could watch the poker room without being seen. Douglas was on the upper level, looking completely relaxed. She left again, this time for half an hour. When she came back, Douglas hadn't moved. She headed for her room.

At six o'clock she came back downstairs and saw that Douglas was still holding court. Ava decided it was safe to leave the hotel. The Disciple, true to his reputation and his word, wasn't going anywhere.

Ichiza was only ten minutes away by cab. Ava hadn't known there was a Chinatown in Las Vegas, and when they drove past it she knew why: it was basically one mall with about thirty restaurants and stores. Ichiza was exactly where Au had said it was, on the second floor of a strip mall next to Chinatown. She climbed the stairs, past a Chinese bakery and a Korean barbecue restaurant, and entered sashimi heaven.

The restaurant was small and unassuming. It held maybe sixteen tables that were strictly mix and match. There were no shoji screens or tatami mats, no pictures of Mount Fuji on the walls, just a poster advertising Kirin beer and colourful notices about special dishes handwritten on oddly shaped pieces of paper. The young Asian servers were in jeans and T-shirts, and the six young chefs wore baseball caps.

One of the servers tossed a menu at her that listed more than a hundred items, and that didn't include the specials. She ordered a glass of Chardonnay, seaweed salad, red snapper carpaccio, and a sashimi platter with yellowfin tuna, surf clams, octopus, and salmon. *That's enough*, she thought, until she saw that chawanmushi was on the menu. She couldn't resist adding the steamed egg custard served with soy sauce, dashi, mirin, boiled shrimp, and shiitake mushrooms.

By seven o'clock she had finished her meal, which was truly exceptional. Ava called Au as she settled the bill; he promised to be there in ten minutes. With time to kill, she went into the Chinese bakery and bought two coconut buns for breakfast. As she descended the stairs she noticed a man wearing a black T-shirt and jeans standing off to one side in the shadows. His large head almost disappeared into his barrel-shaped, muscular chest. *A steroid user*, she thought as she passed.

As she neared the bottom of the stairs, the man began to edge after her. She turned left, towards the parking lot. Sensing that he was following her, Ava turned, just in time to see his right fist heading for her face. She moved her left foot back and swivelled out of the way, his fist gliding harmlessly past her chin. Before he could recoil, she drove the middle knuckle of her right hand into his ear. He screamed, staggered, and lurched sideways. Ava moved closer, the man's nose her next target.

Then she hit the ground. Her legs had been swept from under her by a man wearing a white tracksuit and black boots. She looked up at his pale, fleshy face and manic eyes. He was aiming a kick at her head when she rolled away from him. Ava tried to leap to her feet, but the man caught her on the hip with his second kick, throwing her onto her other side. As she tried to move away, the man she had struck earlier jammed his boot into her ribs. She lifted her arm to protect her face, in the process exposing her ribs to another kick.

She was still struggling to get to her feet when she heard someone yell, "Cut that shit!"

She looked up at the two men standing over her. They were looking up at Gilbert Jackson, and another black man who was at least Jackson's height and maybe fifty pounds heavier. They stood at the top of the stairs, their fists clenched at their sides. Ava's two attackers ran to a car that was idling in the parking lot. She tried to get a read on the licence plate as they drove off, but it was just past dusk and she couldn't make out the numbers.

"What the hell was that about?" Jackson asked when he reached her. "Are you okay? Can you move?"

Her ribs were aching, but Ava's keenest pain was from humiliation. "I'll live," she said as she struggled to her feet.

"What did they want?" Jackson asked, his hand on her arm to steady her.

"I have no idea. They jumped me when I came down the stairs."

"We need to call the police."

"Forget it. It would just be a waste of time."

"You can't let them get away with this!"

"I don't know who they are, and neither do you. What would we tell the police? That two guys with roid rage tried to rob or rape me? That description would fit a quarter of the men in Vegas . . . I'm fine."

"We should get you to a hospital," Jackson said, still holding her arm and looking down at her.

She winced. Her side was sore, but she knew there wasn't much to be done for a bruised or broken rib except tape it. "No, I don't need a hospital."

"We'll take you back to your hotel then. That's the least we can do," he said.

"No, that's not necessary. I'd already called for a taxi," she said. As if on cue, Au drove into the parking lot. "Look, thanks for the help. I really appreciate it, but I want to leave this thing alone. I'm leaving tomorrow anyway. I just want to put it behind me . . . But thank you," she said, and squeezed Jackson's arm.

Ava walked over to the cab. Au was standing beside it with a look of concern on his face. She knew what he was thinking. "Those two guys helped me," she said. "I had a problem with two other men."

Her hip hurt when she sat down. Despite what she had told Jackson, she contemplated going to a hospital or a walk-in clinic. Then she decided again that they wouldn't do much more for her than she could do for herself. "Can you stop at a drugstore?" she asked.

Au drove a block south and then pulled into a strip mall. Ava bought two rolls of medical tape and extra-strength Tylenol. When they got back to Wynn's, she asked Au to wait outside with the meter running and his phone turned on. "I may need you," she said. He nodded.

Ava went directly to the poker room. There was no sign of Douglas. As she stood at the rail peering into the room, the host walked over to her. "David Douglas has left?" she asked.

"No more than five minutes ago. He left this note for you," he said.

She read it as she walked to the elevator. *I hope you enjoyed the visit from my friends. Those are two of the nicer ones. Stay away from me and you won't have to worry about seeing them again.*

She called Au from her room to tell him she'd be down soon. She was packed and checked out of Wynn's in less than fifteen minutes.

"Where are we going? Airport?" Au asked as he threw her bags into the trunk.

"No, I'm staying. I just need to change hotels," she said, easing gingerly into the back seat. "I need one that isn't quite so mainstream."

He peered at her in the rear-view mirror. "Miss, if you have a problem, I don't mind helping. I have a house with a spare bedroom. And my wife won't mind. It would give her a chance to speak Cantonese again."

"That's really kind, but it isn't necessary. Can you suggest a hotel?"

"The Mandalay Bay is at the end of the Strip."

"I don't want to be on the Strip."

"Near the Strip?"

"That would work."

"There's the Hooters Hotel across from the MGM, tucked in behind the Tropicana."

"Take me there, please."

By the time they were about two hundred metres from the hotel, Ava had booked a room for thirty-nine dollars a night under the name Jennie Kwong, one of her backups. She looked at the Hooters logo lit up in brilliant orange. The place advertised itself as Vegas's discount hotel. *That's certainly truth in advertising*, Ava thought as she got out of the cab.

Au got out and went to the trunk to take out her bags.

"I may need you in the morning. Could you keep it free for me?" she asked, slipping him a hundred-dollar bill.

He reached into his pocket for change. "No, that's all for you," she said.

"Okay. And thank you, Ms. Kwong . . . It is Ms. Kwong, right?"

"Call me Jennie," Ava said. "And Au, if anyone asks where I am, you don't know."

23

SHE WALKED INTO THE HOOTERS HOTEL LOBBY AND took in the plain tile floors, the dim overhead lighting, and the small sitting area facing a long wooden reception desk. A small, plump woman with a Spanish accent greeted her warmly.

Ava showed her Jennie Kwong's credit card and driver's licence and was given a room in the Oceanview Tower. "There's no ocean, of course," the woman told her, "but you do have a view of the pool."

When Ava opened the door to her room, Wynn's felt a world away. There was nothing sedate or neutral about Hooters. The bedspread was a print of giant green and orange palm leaves, and the lamps had matching tangerine shades. The furniture was woven rattan, and near the window was a small round table and two stools upholstered in orange vinyl fabric. Ava went to the window and pulled open the orange drapes. A sharp pain shot down her side. She stood looking out the window, waiting for the throbbing to subside. The MGM Grand dominated the view; she carefully closed the curtains to block out the green glare that emanated from the hotel and casino. Then she took two Tylenol, taped her ribs, and went down the hall to fill the ice bucket. When she got back to the room, she filled a towel with ice and lay on the bed, pressing it against her side.

David Douglas hadn't reacted as well as she had hoped, but neither had his lack of cooperation really shocked her. She hadn't expected the goons, though. They had been a bit of a surprise. That was no excuse for not handling them better, she told herself, but even if she had taken them out, she didn't see how that would have helped her get closer to Douglas. *So now what to do?* Ava thought.

There were three obvious options, none of them particularly appealing. She could go to The River's office and broach the subject with Ashton. But he would have to agree to see her, and she knew there wasn't much chance of that, given how his partner had reacted. And given that there were office staff and other tenants, she'd have police or security all over her in no time if she tried to force her way in.

Ashton's condo was the next choice, and if anything that was less appealing than the office. Not only were there twenty-four-hour guards, but it was also likely there was a security camera at the front entrance. That left Douglas's home as her best bet — it was the most isolated of the three. She just had to find a way into the complex and then into the house.

It was time to make some phone calls.

"*Wei.*"

"Uncle, it's Ava."

"How are things?"

"Not so bad."

"Progress?"

She didn't try to soft-pedal it. "I want you to send Carlo and Andy."

Uncle fell silent. She knew she had upset him. "You said not so bad."

"There are still challenges."

He paused. "I am not sure that they are in Hong Kong."

"Do you have them working on a job?"

"No."

"Then they're probably in Hong Kong. Could you get them on a plane today? They can land in Los Angeles, San Francisco, Seattle, it doesn't matter — every major city connects with Las Vegas."

"Are you sure?"

"A couple of things," Ava said, ignoring his question. "Please make sure they wear turtleneck sweaters or shirts with long sleeves. I don't want their tattoos to attract attention. And tell them not to try to bring any of their gadgets with them. I don't want either of them stopped at U.S. Customs or Immigration for a baggage check. Tell them that whatever they need, I'll get it for them here."

"You are sure you want them?" he repeated.

"I want you to email me their schedules. Give them my cellphone number so they can call me when they've landed in the U.S. and have been cleared. Tell them not to call when they're still in the arrivals hall — it's a red flag. Book them a room at the Hooters Casino Hotel, and please make sure they have their itinerary with them in case they're stopped. They're coming to Las Vegas to gamble; that's the story. Get them a return flight for a week later. If we finish sooner I'll put them on an earlier flight out."

"Ava, I do not like this."

"Uncle, it's either them or Derek, and I think this job is better suited to their talents. But if you don't want them to come, I'll call Derek and have him here tomorrow."

"You are so stubborn."

"You taught me well."

"What about the money?"

"I wouldn't be doing this if I didn't think I had a shot at it."

"I will send them."

"Thank you, Uncle. I have some calls to make here, but when I'm done I may have to impose on you again, so please keep your cellphone on."

She closed her phone and reached over to the bedside table, trying to ignore the pain. She opened the drawer to look for a phonebook but found only a Gideon's Bible. Las Vegas — Hooters — Gideon's Bible; she tried to understand the connection but failed. She climbed off the bed and walked over to the bureau, holding the ice-filled towel against her hip. There were both White and Yellow Pages in the top drawer.

She took out the Yellow Pages and found listings for at least fifty private detective agencies. She looked for ones that promised twenty-four-hour service and began calling them alphabetically. On her fourth try she got a live human. After she had explained what she wanted and how quickly she wanted it, she was told it would take two hours and cost two hundred dollars. She put the charge on Jennie Kwong's Visa card and promised a one-hundred-dollar bonus if it could be done inside an hour.

Then she waited, watching television and wondering how this was all going to play out.

The agency called back in forty-five minutes. She authorized the hundred-dollar bonus and then called Hong Kong.

"Uncle, do you have a pen?"

"I will turn on my recording device."

"Even better," she said, and read the list of names she had got from the detective agency, along with the supporting documentation.

"They are all Chinese," he said.

"Yes, they live in a complex called The Oasis. I need you to find out if we're connected to any of them, either directly or through friends. If we are, then I need to know if I can count on one of them to help me. It would be a favour, of course. And it isn't dangerous, I promise you that."

"I will do what I can."

She knew that finding an ally inside The Oasis was a long shot, but the long reach of Uncle's network had never failed to surprise her.

Next Ava flipped through the Yellow Pages to the guns section. She picked a supplier with a half-page ad. The store was located on the Strip closer to downtown Vegas and was open twenty-four hours a day, seven days a week. Shopping made easy.

She called Au and got his voicemail. "This is Jennie. I'd appreciate it if you could pick me up at ten o'clock tomorrow morning. If I don't hear from you I'll assume you'll be here."

Then she sat back on the bed and closed her eyes. She wanted to sleep, but between her aches and her racing mind she knew slumber would come slowly and with some difficulty. She tried to force other thoughts into her head. Often she found visualizing bak mei moves soothing, so she began to picture herself as a leopard. Then Derek intruded.

About a month before, she had walked from her condo to the house where her bak mei instructor, Grandmaster Tang, lived and taught several disciplines of martial arts. The building had no sign, and she was quite sure he was operating without a licence, but no one doing serious martial arts in Toronto didn't know who he was or where to find him. Tang had only two bak mei students, Ava and Derek, and their sessions were always, as was the tradition, one on one.

She remembered that the day had been overcast, with a sluggish, damp wind. She wrapped a scarf tightly around her neck, took a toque from her pocket and jammed it over her head, and walked as fast as she could through the cold air. It was almost noon. The gym was theoretically open from 4 p.m. to 11 p.m., but she rarely made an appointment and always went during off-hours.

There was a large window at the front of the building, and as Ava drew near, her eyes tearing from the wind, she saw that someone else was already inside. She was cursing her luck and about to head home when she recognized the student — Derek. Grandmaster Tang was strict in enforcing his one-on-one code, so Ava felt a touch of guilt at watching her friend. He stood in the low traditional stance, his hands soft and floating. She marvelled at how graceful he was. Then she saw his waist torque, and with a twist of his hips his right fist shot forward. It travelled not much farther than six inches, but it could well have been the most deadly six inches in all of the martial arts.

Bak mei was meant to be fought at close range. Its practitioners never made the first move, but with precise footwork and perfect timing they were always positioned to respond to any attack. Ava had just watched Derek perform the phoenix-eye fist, the trademark strike of bak mei. The knuckle of the index finger of his right hand was extended from a fist, and the entire force of the punch — all the power that could be generated by timing, footwork, and back, chest, and shoulder muscles — was focused in that single knuckle. It could be driven into the target's most sensitive body parts: nose, eyes, ears, the temple and the sternum, where nerve endings gathered. It had taken years of practice for Ava to perfect her phoenix-eye fist. Derek, she saw, was at least her equal.

As she lay on her bed in the Hooters Hotel, she pictured him in her mind's eye, his floating hands beginning to lull her to sleep. She was somewhere between consciousness and the dream world when her phone rang.

"Yes," she said.

"Ava, we had no luck," Uncle said. "Two of them are Taiwanese and have been in the United States for at least twenty years. The other two are American born, one of Malaysian origin, the other from Hong Kong. We tried to find out if any of them had even a cousin we could talk to, but we came up empty."

"Thank you, Uncle. I'm sorry for putting you through all that trouble," she said. "I knew it was not very likely."

"Is it a problem?"

"Not yet."

"Carlo and Andy?"

"I'd still like you to send them."

"They leave in an hour for Los Angeles. They will be in Las Vegas tomorrow night around ten."

"Could you have someone email me the flight schedule? I'll meet them at the airport myself," she said before hanging up.

She checked the time — just past midnight. *I hope Martin Littlefeather's a night owl*, she thought.

He answered on the fifth ring, his voice sleepy and hesitant.

"Martin, this is Ava Lee. I'm really sorry for calling so late."

"That's okay," he said, without any conviction.

"Are you still in Victoria?"

"Yes, and you're in Las Vegas?"

"I am."

"Did you have any luck with Douglas or Ashton?"

"No, not yet, and that's why I'm calling. I need your help."

"Me? How?"

"I need you to fly to Las Vegas, preferably tomorrow."

"That's a strange request."

"There's something I need you to do for me here."

"Ava, I just can't up and leave Chief Francis at such short notice. We have meetings scheduled here tomorrow."

"What I want you to do is probably more important than any meeting you have planned."

"And if the Chief doesn't agree?"

"Don't tell him."

"Ava, you're crazy. You don't know him — he'll kill me."

"He made you responsible for communicating with me."

"But he didn't authorize me to make that kind of decision."

"Then I'll talk to him."

"I think you'll have to."

"Where is he?"

"In his room."

"Do me a favour: go to his room and call me from there. We can talk on speaker phone so there's no misunderstanding."

"It's past midnight."

"Martin, believe me, he won't care about the time after we've finished."

"Okay, I'll do what I can."

Five minutes came and went. Ava was beginning to worry when her phone rang.

"Ms. Lee," Chief Francis said, "I can't say I'm happy to hear from you. I thought we had agreed we'd seen the last of each other."

"And I'm not happy I had to call, but unfortunately things have gone a bit off track."

"What do you want that is so urgent?"

"I want Martin — or you, if you think that's better — to call David Douglas and arrange a meeting for the day after tomorrow. Tell him you don't want to be seen at their offices or anywhere in public. Ask if you can meet at his house."

"Under what pretence?"

"Chief, this company has potentially used the band to commit major fraud. They've put everything you've been working to accomplish at risk. That's why you or Martin wants to talk with them. A phone call from some techie won't cut it — or any phone call, for that matter. You want a face-to-face meeting with Douglas and Ashton. Tell them some nosy Chinese girl has been poking around, asking questions, stirring up trouble. You need their assurance that there's nothing to it."

Francis muttered something to Martin. She was sure it wasn't complimentary. "And if they agree to a meeting?"

"Then I want you to send Martin to Las Vegas to represent you."

"This is a very long way from never hearing from you again." She heard him sigh. "Okay, now we have Martin in Las Vegas for a meeting. How does this help you?"

"I'll go to the meeting with him."

"How will he explain your presence?"

"He won't have to."

"Why not?"

"They won't see me until it's too late."

"Too late for what?"

"To cancel the meeting."

"Why would they cancel a meeting with Martin?"

"He won't be at it. I'll handle the meeting myself."

"This is ridiculous," Francis said.

"No, I'll tell you what's ridiculous," she said. "Two weeks ago, one of The River's clients — one of your clients, by proxy — went to them with the documentation I gave you. Two days later they blew up his car and told him to stay away from your people. Another client made a phone call to them. They broke into his apartment, trashed it, and left a threatening note. A third client — the one whose interests I represent — is lying in a Vancouver hospital close to death after jumping off the roof of his house out of sheer desperation.

"About ten hours ago I had a very polite one-minute chat with David Douglas. Six hours ago I was attacked by two men who threw me to the ground and kicked me hard in the ribs. Thirty minutes after that I was handed a note from

David Douglas saying that they were his men and there was more of the same in store for me if I kept asking questions. Now, all of that is *really* ridiculous."

The line went quiet.

"Ava, is all this really true?" Martin asked finally.

"No, Martin, I'm making it up," she said, more harshly than she intended.

"Who else have you told about this?" Francis asked.

"No one. If I told my people in Hong Kong, all hell would break loose. I'm trying to keep the situation contained because I honestly believe that if I can get face to face with Douglas and Ashton I can resolve this matter in a discreet way."

"You've tried that. What would make it different this time?" Francis said.

"They'll listen to me."

"What if those two men are there?" Martin interrupted.

"I'm going to bring two of my own as a precaution."

"Jesus Christ, I think this is getting out of control," Francis said. "You're talking about some potential for violence here."

Ava shifted on the bed, trying to relieve the pain in her ribs. "You know, Chief, when I read about you in the early days, it seemed that things didn't always go smoothly or peacefully. One newspaper even wrote that the Thousand Islands should be renamed the Wild East. And I read a quote from you that said the occasional run-in with the law was regrettable but the Mohneida were more concerned about the greater good. So please don't talk to me about potential for violence. I'm sitting here on a bed with taped ribs and an icepack on my hip, and the only reason I'm not in the hospital is because a kick that was aimed at my head didn't hit square on. And just to be clear, my objective here isn't revenge. All I want is to get back the money that was stolen from my clients. That is my greater good, Chief Francis."

She could hear Martin speaking in the background but couldn't make out his words.

"Ms. Lee, just who the hell are you?" Chief Francis said.

"I'm an accountant."

"And where would you get two thugs? Accounting school?"

"The firm I work for in Hong Kong has a diverse portfolio."

"Ava," Martin interjected, "if I can arrange a meeting with Douglas and Ashton, how do you expect me to bring you and the two other whatever-you-might-call-them?"

"Martin, I promise you, if you can get a meeting booked I'll find a way to get me and my associates into that house without causing any fuss."

"And assuming you get in, then what?" Francis asked. "Civil war?"

"No, sir. I will persuade them that it is in their best interest to return the money and to keep the Mohneida's and my client's names out of any scandal."

"And if you don't?" Francis said.

"Nothing ventured, nothing gained. The way I see it, the status quo isn't tenable. If I can't get to Douglas, my clients will lose all patience with him and The River and I'll probably be fired . . . And I won't be responsible for whatever happens after I leave."

"You're threatening me again," Francis said.

"No, sir, I'm not, and I'm sorry if it sounded like that. I'm just being completely practical."

"Are you certain you can persuade Douglas and Ashton?" Martin interjected.

"That's my job. And I don't fail very often."

"Chief, I think it's worth a try," Martin said.

A heavy silence set in; Ava guessed they had put the phone on mute. *Let them talk*, she thought. *The more they talk, the better my chances.*

"When do you want Martin in Las Vegas?" Francis asked as the line came alive again.

"Tomorrow — I mean today. It's already past midnight."

"We'll call Douglas now; I'm sure he's still up. There isn't any point in delaying, and besides, a late-night call might emphasize just how important I think it is that he schedule an immediate meeting with us."

"I'd like both Ashton and Douglas at the meeting if possible."

"I understand that."

"You said *us*. Are you coming as well?" she asked.

"No, I'm an elder statesman now — my Wild East days are over. Martin can handle whatever you want done."

She realized he hadn't liked her reference to his smuggling days. "Chief Francis, I'm sorry if I caused offence earlier," she said. "I just wanted you to understand how passionate I feel about my clients."

"Ms. Lee, I think you've said enough. I'm going to make that phone call. If we get a meeting, Martin will be in Las Vegas tomorrow . . . Just make sure he gets back to me in one piece."

24

AFTER SHE HUNG UP, AVA HOBBLED TO THE BATHROOM.
The towel she had been using as an icepack was saturated
and dripping all over the place. She got a fresh towel, filled
it with ice from the bucket, and checked her watch. It was
a bit too soon for more Tylenol, but she took two anyway.

Ava turned on her computer and logged in to her email
account. Uncle's travel agent had sent her Carlo and Andy's
complete itinerary. She scrolled through the balance of the
messages, prioritizing as she did. There wasn't much related
to business; it was mainly personal missives.

Maria Gonzalez had written again and this time had
attached a photo. Ava saw a beautiful young woman
standing against a brick wall and staring directly into the
camera, a tiny smile playing on her full lips. Her brown
eyes looked happy, even teasing, and were framed by long,
curly black hair. She was wearing shorts and a tank top
that showed off her toned arms and full breasts. Mimi
showed me some pictures of you, she wrote. I thought I
would send you one of me. When do you think you'll be
returning to Toronto?

Ava knew she was going to call this girl when she got back. I don't know when I'm coming back. Soon, I hope. I'll be in touch, she wrote.

She sent the email and clicked back to her inbox, where she found a message from Marian. She hesitated before opening it, since complaints about their mother, her husband, or her kids were her sister's usual content. For once, though, Ava was pleasantly surprised. Marian had written to say that she had phoned their father in Hong Kong to discuss his spring trip to Canada. It was a pre-emptive strike, she wrote. Marian had convinced him to book a two-week cruise in the eastern Caribbean — there would be no Las Vegas trip for their mother. She was very pleased with herself, and Ava was pleased for her.

Both Mimi and Derek had written several times, which wasn't unusual. She was about to delve into their messages when her cellphone rang.

"We're on," Martin said. "One o'clock at Douglas's house. He said Ashton should be there as well."

"Thank you."

"No, thank Chief Francis. He was the one who made the call. Douglas gave him a rough time about meeting at the house. He wanted to meet at the office, but the Chief said that with all the rumours flying around, he didn't want to be seen on their premises."

"I'm very grateful. Please tell him that."

"I will . . . Now, I can get into Vegas today around five o'clock. Does that work?"

"Which airline?"

"Air Canada from Vancouver."

"I'll meet you at the airport."

"Okay."

"You need to rent a car."

"Okay."

"A big car, a fancy car. Try to get something like a Mercedes S-Class."

"I'll do the best I can. How about a hotel?"

"I'm staying at Hooters, but you don't have to."

"Hooters?"

"It's a long story."

"What the hell, book me a room there as well."

25

AVA SLEPT SURPRISINGLY WELL, WAKING ONLY ONCE
to replenish the makeshift icepack and to take more Tylenol.
When she finally eased herself out of bed in the morning,
she found that her hip wasn't nearly as sore, though her ribs
still throbbed.

She made herself a cup of Starbucks VIA instant coffee
and turned on her computer. There were no new emails of
any interest. The messages from Derek and Mimi were still
unopened and she decided to leave them that way. The last
thing she needed was distraction, and Mimi specialized
in that.

She left the computer and turned on her cellphone to
check her messages. There was one. She heard a slow intake
of air. "Call me," Ordonez snarled. "I'm not happy." Ava
deleted the message.

She went to the nightstand where she had left the Yellow Pages and found the detective agency she had hired the
night before. She called the number again and got the same
male voice. "Don't you ever sleep?" she asked.

"Twelve-hour shifts. I'm just ending this one."

"I need the blueprints for this house," she said, giving him Douglas's address.

"You aren't planning to rob the place, are you?" he said.

"No, I promise."

"Give me half an hour. Same rate."

"Email the information," she said, giving him the address.

She looked at herself in the mirror before she stepped into the shower. The bruises on her neck and shoulders now looked insignificant compared to the deep blue and yellow mark on her left hip. Fortunately the icepack and Tylenol had numbed the pain. She peeled the tape off her ribs and found similar discolouration on her right side. She tried stretching, but her ribs screamed at her to stop.

When she got out of the shower, Ava went through her Louis Vuitton suitcase to find fresh clothes. She was down to one clean T-shirt and one set of underwear. She called the front desk and arranged for same-day laundry service.

Dressed in her usual black Giordano T-shirt and Adidas track pants, she sat down again at the computer. The detective had come through for her once more, sending a description of Douglas's house and a drawing that outlined the exterior. She had a rough idea of what to expect after having seen the complex, but he had filled in the detail. There were no walls or fences around the house and no apparent external security other than that provided by the complex. A three-car garage was attached to the right side of the house, with the front door set farther back at the end of a small walkway. *Perfect*, she thought.

There was an alarm system in the house, but there would be no reason for it to be on during the day. Even if it was, she expected that Douglas would open the door quite willingly for Martin Littlefeather. The only disquieting note in the document was the fact that Douglas owned three Rott-weilers. Carlo and Andy, like most Hong Kongers, weren't comfortable with dogs. *Too bad for them*, she was thinking, when her cellphone rang.

It was a Vegas number, and she hesitated before answering it. "Jennie Kwong."

"It's Au. I'll be there in five minutes."

Ava turned off her computer and went downstairs to the lobby. It was a gorgeous morning, with a clear sky, a hint of breeze, and the Sierra Nevadas glistening on the horizon. Au's taxi arrived just as she left the hotel.

"My wife says *nee hoi*," he said.

"*Nee hoi* to her."

"Where are we going?"

"To Doug's Nevada Gun Shop. It's at the far end of the Strip, towards the Golden Nugget."

Doug's was in old Vegas, a section of the city that began almost as soon as they had passed Steve Wynn's second deluxe hotel, Encore, on the northern end of Las Vegas Boulevard. It didn't take long for her to notice the difference between the old and the new. The city went immediately from grandiose to grungy. One minute Ava was looking at Encore, shining like a brown jewel framed by lush, mani-cured gardens, and the next she was staring at a series of strip malls selling cheap T-shirts and liquor, the sidewalks cracked and covered with debris. It got worse the closer she got to Doug's. Many stores were boarded up and the streets were populated by the down and out. Two men were rooting through a garbage bin in front of the gun store. Au offered to take her in, but Ava politely declined.

Doug's was a supermarket of weaponry. Ava had been in American gun stores before and thought she had seen just about everything, but Doug's raised the bar. The store was shaped like a horseshoe, lined with guns in glass cases mounted on the walls. They seemed to have every type of gun she had ever heard of, and more brands than she had known existed. For anyone planning a coup, a quick trip to Doug's would be one-stop shopping.

She walked past rifles, shotguns, machine guns, and automatics until she came to the section signed GUNS FOR THE LITTLE LADY. She browsed the cases until she caught the clerk's eye.

"What would you recommend?" she asked.

"What's it for, ma'am?"

"Self-defence."

"A .380 should be just about right. Powerful enough, light, easy to fire, and accurate within about fifteen yards. Take your pick," he said, sweeping his hand across a case.

"So many choices."

"It's a popular weapon."

"Show me a range."

He opened the glass case and took out three guns. "This is the Hi-Point 380. It's heavier than most, about twenty-nine ounces, but it's still easy to shoot and has a reputation for accuracy. It'll set you back about $150," he began. "Then we have the Kel-Tac P-3AT. It's a lighter gun, just over eight ounces, and it's $300. The last gun is the Rolls-Royce of .380s, the Kahr P380. It's probably the most accurate. Shit, you can hardly miss from fifteen yards, and it only weighs ten ounces. Here, feel it," he said, passing her the gun.

She picked them up one by one. The Kahr seemed to

have the best balance. "How much?"

"That's the problem with this gun, ma'am. It comes in at over five hundred dollars."

"What ammunition works best with it?"

"I've been told that the Winchester Ranger ninety-five-grain is good."

"I'll take the gun and a box of ammunition," she said.

He reached for a sales pad. "Now, you do know, ma'am, that you can't take the gun with you today?"

"And why not? I was told that a permit wasn't required here."

"Not for a weapon you intend to carry in the open."

"That's what I would do."

"Sorry, ma'am, there's still a seventy-two-hour cooling period. You can come back in three days for the gun."

"I may not be alive in three days," Ava whispered.

"Sorry, ma'am?"

"You heard me. Look at this," she said, pulling up her T-shirt to show him her battered body. "My boyfriend beat the crap out of me last night. He threw me on the floor and kicked me like I was a dog. Then he took off just before the cops came — a lot of good they'd do anyway. I know he's coming back and he's going to do more of the same. But this time it isn't going to be so easy."

"Ma'am, there are rules —"

"What's more important, the rules or your conscience? Is this Nevada or Massachusetts?"

He stared at her. Ava looked back at him defiantly. "If I don't get it here I'll go somewhere else."

"You got a car outside?" he said.

"Taxi."

"You got cash?"

"Not enough."

"There's an ATM about a block left of here. Get the cab to park there. I'll meet you in ten minutes."

"How much cash?"

"Six hundred will do."

She was about to argue that he had quoted her five hundred for the gun, then caught herself. "See you in ten," she said.

She directed Au to the ATM. She had four hundred dollars on her and took out another five hundred. Then she stood on the street corner and waited. The clerk walked towards her with a brown paper bag in his hand. "Get in the back of the cab, away from the security cameras," he said.

Ava handed him the cash and he stuck the bills into his pants pocket without counting them. She wasn't so trusting. She opened the bag and saw the Kahr .380 and a box of Winchester Ranger ammunition. "Thanks," she said.

"I just don't want to see your photo on the front page of the newspaper tomorrow," he said.

"If you do, it'll be because I shot him, not because he beat me to death."

After the clerk left, Au kept looking at her. She knew he had a lot of questions. "I need to find a Chinese grocery store," she said.

"What do you need to buy?"

"A meat cleaver."

He rolled his eyes. "I'm worried for you," he said.

"And then I need to get some duct tape and smelling salts," she added as Au drove out of the parking lot.

When the car stopped at a red light, he turned around. "I told my wife you were a different kind of lady, but I don't think she'd believe me if I told her about this."

26

TERMINAL TWO AT MCCARRAN INTERNATIONAL WAS smaller and more relaxed than the main terminal. It was a one-minute walk from her cab to the main level, and once there Ava could position herself at the bottom of an escalator that carried a steady stream of new arrivals.

The Air Canada flight from Vancouver was on time, and at ten minutes after five she saw Martin Littlefeather among the throng, an excited gleam in his eye. She smiled and waved. When he got to her, he hesitated as if trying to decide whether to offer his hand or give her a hug. Before he could do anything, Ava thrust out her hand. "No bag?" she asked.

"I had to check it. Remember, I was packed for four days in Victoria."

The baggage area was highly efficient, and Martin retrieved his luggage within a few minutes. *They'll do anything to get you to a casino faster*, Ava thought. "What kind of car did you get?" she said.

"I couldn't get a Mercedes, so I thought a Lincoln Continental would meet your size requirement."

"Perfect."

It was a short drive to Hooters. Ava told Martin to leave the car with the valet service and then waited in the lobby while he checked in and took his bag to his room. When he came back to the lobby, she saw that he had exchanged his Western plaid shirt for a black tee and a buckskin jacket with elaborate beadwork across the chest and leather fringe down the arms. *He's handsome*, she thought as she took in his soft brown eyes, fine features, high cheekbones, and long, silky black hair.

"Do you like Japanese food?" she asked.

"Never really had it. Cooper Island and Kingston are more meat and potatoes, although Kingston does have more variety."

"Well, we'll try Japanese," she said.

They took a cab to Ichiza and were early enough to get a table. When Martin was handed a menu, he looked at Ava and grinned awkwardly. "You'll have to do this," he said.

"Garlic chicken gizzards?"

"You're kidding, right?"

She pointed to it on the menu.

"I can't eat that."

She laughed. "Don't worry, I'll order food you can recognize. Wine? Beer?"

"Wine is good. Red, preferably."

Ava ordered everything in one go. Miso soup, seaweed salad, broiled eggplant, seared black cod, and a sashimi platter with yellowfin, snapper, octopus, and shrimp. She ordered the house wine, a California Pinot.

"Is Chief Francis still angry with me?" she asked.

"He isn't angry; you just confuse him."

"How?"

"He's used to getting his own way and sort of takes that for granted. He's had two meetings with you and both times you got what you wanted. He thinks you manipulated him."

"What did you say?"

"No more than you were manipulating me."

"That was an astute comment."

"He also thinks you have some serious muscle behind you. Is that true?"

"My muscle arrives tonight from Hong Kong. Carlo might weigh 140 pounds, Andy a bit less."

"What kind of names are those for Chinese?"

Their wine arrived. She watched as the waiter filled two glasses almost to the rims. "Cheers," she said. They clinked glasses, his eyes trying to catch hers. *Shit*, she thought.

"Anyway, we were talking about Chinese names," she said. "We're given Chinese names at birth, but when we move into Western society, many of us adopt — or in my case are given — English names. Carlo and Andy chose their own names. Actually, Carlo was Billy for a while and then decided he liked Carlo better."

"What is your Chinese name?"

She shook her head. "Sorry, Martin, that's my secret."

He looked up at the ceiling. "You know, Ava, I'm really attracted to you."

"I know, Martin." She shook her head.

"What does that mean?"

"It means I'm sorry."

"For what?"

"I'm gay."

She saw a hint of shock, and then disappointment spread across his face.

"And besides, I'm way too old for you," she said.

"That's bull."

She smiled. "Well, maybe a bit too old."

"The gay thing?"

She picked up his hand, pulled it towards her, and kissed the back of it. "All very true, since the day I felt my first sexual impulse. Never any doubt, never any regrets."

"God, I feel so clumsy," he said.

"I think you're sweet," Ava said, still holding his hand. "And I think you're smart, really smart. You aren't thirty yet and already you're a CFO. Chief Francis listens to you as well, that's obvious. And I don't blame him. You aren't afraid to give advice, and when you do, it's thoughtful and pragmatic."

He covered her hand with his. "That's because I've told him twice to do what you wanted."

"See what I mean? Sweet and smart." She smiled. "Friends?"

"Yeah, friends — I told you that back in Victoria. Even if this Vegas thing hadn't come up, you would have heard from me again."

The restaurant was full now, people standing at the door and spilling outside. "I hope you like this," she said as the miso soup and broiled eggplant were served.

It was just past eight o'clock when they left the restaurant. "What's the plan?" Martin asked as they went down the stairs to the car.

Ava couldn't help looking around as they walked across the parking lot. "That's up to you. I have to go to the airport to meet my boys."

"Can I come with you?"

"Sure," she said as she climbed into the car.

It was no more than a ten-minute drive to McCarran. They parked the car and jostled their way into the terminal.

"You've obviously worked with these people before," Martin said.

"Once or twice."

"What is it they do exactly?"

"It depends on what's called for."

"That's vague."

"As it should be."

Carlo and Andy came down the escalator side by side. Carlo was about five foot six and 140 pounds. He had shaved his head since she'd seen him last, and added a wispy moustache that only partly hid the scar running down the right side of his nose to his mouth. Andy was an inch shorter and a good ten pounds lighter. His thick black hair was brushed straight back and gelled into place. To her relief they were both wearing long-sleeved shirts buttoned right up to the neck. She could still see the tip of a dragon's tail on Carlo's neck, but she had to search to find it.

Their eyes scanned the arrivals hall, looking for her. She waved and Andy saw her. He nudged his partner and they both waved back.

"They don't speak English," she said to Martin. "So I apologize in advance for the fact that we'll be speaking Cantonese."

They each carried one small bag. Ava knew they always

travelled light, getting by with a toilet kit, a couple of shirts, a pair of jeans, and two sets of underwear for a week. When they reached her, they put down their bags and pressed the palms of their hands together in front of their chests, moving them up and down, their heads bent slightly forward. It was a sign of respect, a greeting to a superior. She wondered what Uncle had said to them before they left Hong Kong.

During the entire ride to Hooters, the two men sat in the back of the car talking to each other. "I'd translate," Ava said to Martin, "but they're just talking rubbish."

She checked them into the hotel using her Jennie Kwong credit card. They were, as was their custom, sharing a room.

"Drop your bags off and then meet us downstairs in the bar," she said to them, pointing towards the Dixie Dam Bar. "We have a lot to go over."

27

AVA SLEPT BADLY, WAKING THREE OR FOUR TIMES DURING
the night, trying to get rid of a dream that clawed its way
back into her head every time she shut her eyes.

She and her father were in a massive hotel. They had a
flight to catch in an hour, so he sent her to get the luggage
from their room while he checked out. She wandered aim-
lessly from floor to floor, searching for their room, poking
her head through open doors to gawk at strangers. Panic
began to set in. She gave up looking for the room and went
to tell her father, but she couldn't find him. She ran outside
to catch a taxi to the airport, where for some reason she
assumed her father had gone. When she looked back, the
hotel had disappeared.

The last time she forced herself awake, she had been sitting in the cab in the middle of a traffic jam, the airport
visible on the horizon, unreachable. She sat up in bed, a
cold sweat on her brow. This was a recurring dream. She
had lost her father in more places than she could count, but
it always unsettled her.

She made herself an instant coffee and sat on the side of

the bed. Then she lowered her head and said a small prayer to St. Jude, asking that the day go well and end with her and her boys safe and secure. Prayer usually calmed her, but she still felt edgy. She took a bottle of vitamin B from her kit bag and swallowed two tablets, then sat on the bed again, drawing deep, slow breaths.

They had gone over the plan the night before. Ava had presented it to the men confidently, but deep down she wondered if it would work. *Sometimes*, she thought, *you just have to have faith.*

She went to the desk, turned on her computer, and typed in DAVID "THE DISCIPLE" DOUGLAS. Ten minutes later she sat back in the chair, frustrated, unable to find anything of substance to add to the information Maynard and Littlefeather had already given her.

Ava turned her attention to Jeremy Ashton. The investment firm he had worked for in New York was the Whiteburn Group. The name sounded familiar to her, and when she accessed its website, she saw why — it was a major player in many Asian markets. She had been going to call Uncle to tell him the boys had arrived; now she had another reason.

"*Wei*," Uncle said.

"Carlo and Andy are here and there weren't any problems."

"Good. And when do you expect to use them?"

"Today."

"I will not say anything to Chang yet. Let's wait to see how things go."

"Yes, I think that's best. But in the meantime, Uncle, I could use some help getting information. His name is Jeremy Ashton. He's English and he worked for the Whiteburn Group in New York. I would like to speak to one of his former bosses or colleagues. Whiteburn has a big presence in Asia. We must know someone who's worked with them, someone who can exert enough influence to find me a contact to talk to."

Uncle paused. "I think I may know someone myself, and if I do not, then Chang might. And if he does not, between us we will find what you need."

It was her turn to hesitate, a question about Jackie Leung on the tip of her tongue. She left it there. If Uncle had any news he'd tell her. "I'll call after we're done. It could be early in the morning your time."

Ava turned off her phone and went back to the computer. She reread the data she'd already dug up on Ashton and then googled a name that was linked to his several times: Lily Simmons. Ava was impressed. Simmons seemed to be something of a party girl, but she attended only the best parties. She had gone to the finest schools — Marlborough and then Cambridge — and she had been a champion show jumper, representing Great Britain internationally, including in one Olympics. Now she worked for Smyth's Bank in London, and Ava assumed that's how she and Ashton had met. Her mother was Scottish, the daughter of a peer whose title was hereditary. Her father, Roger Simmons, had been a successful businessman who manufactured generators and then turned to politics. After being elected to the British House of Commons and serving three years as a backbencher, he had been appointed to the Cabinet and was now minister of industrial development. Ava saw that he was still listed as the major shareholder of the generator company. Given that the British political system operated much like Canada's, she assumed his assets were being administered by a blind trust.

She has great pedigree, Ava thought, and then wondered why Simmons was linked to Ashton. What was the connection? She knew enough about England to know that a man from Sheffield who had attended Leeds University and now ran an online gambling site would hardly be a catch for a woman in her social circle. He'd be strictly downmarket to someone like her.

She drank another coffee and downed two Tylenols. Her hip was feeling better, but the pain in her ribs wouldn't let up. She got up and took a long, hot shower.

When she had dried herself off, Ava put on her bra and panties. Normally for this type of job she would have thrown on a T-shirt and a pair of track pants. Instead she chose her black linen slacks, a white Brooks Brothers shirt, and her black Cole Haan pumps. She dressed slowly, carefully inserting the jade cufflinks, securing her chignon with the ivory pin, slipping her Cartier watch onto her wrist, and finally putting on her gold crucifix pendant. She went to the bathroom and applied black mascara and a light touch of lipstick, and then for good measure a spritz of Annick Goutal perfume. She stood back and looked at herself in the full-length mirror. *I may not feel confident*, she thought, *but I sure as hell look that way.*

She made a fresh coffee and then went over to the table where she'd left the gear. She loaded the gun and put it in a paper bag for Carlo. She put the cleaver in a separate paper bag. Two rolls of duct tape and the vial of smelling salts went into her Chanel purse. Then she retrieved her notebook and sat down next to the computer. Taking out copies of the emails she had received from Jack Maynard, Felix Hunter, and Martin, she started going through them, her focus not on entering the house but on what would happen when she was inside.

Ava knew the money wasn't going to be all in one place — this was not going to be a simple one-time transaction. Douglas and Ashton had the holding company and a controlling interest in The River. Undoubtedly each of them also had personal accounts and assets spread out over various locations. One way or another she had to get at both of them, and she also needed time to execute multiple transactions.

She glanced at her cellphone and saw that she had missed calls; her phone must have rung while she was in the shower. There was a message from her mother telling her about the planned cruise, which she implied had been her idea. *That didn't take long*, Ava thought. Uncle had called to say he had found a contact at Whiteburn and to expect a call. Maggie Chew had left a message saying that her father was out of intensive care but the doctors were worried about his will to get better. Ava deleted the messages and had turned back to her paperwork when the phone rang.

"Ms. Ava Lee?"

"That's me."

"My name is Jeff Galley."

"I'm sorry, I don't know you."

"I was told to call you by Harold Knox."

"And I don't know anyone named Harold Knox."

"Mr. Knox is chairman of the Whiteburn Group."

"Oh, yes," Ava said. "I'm sorry about the confusion."

"Evidently Mr. Knox was speaking with a friend of his in

China, who requested that someone from Whiteburn call you to chat about Jeremy Ashton."

"And that's you?"

"It is."

"Good. So tell me, how do you know him?"

"I worked with him for three years, side by side."

"What kind of work?"

"We were on the investment side, mainly doing analysis — real drone work."

"You've moved on since then, I imagine."

"I'm a senior manager. I handle the energy sector."

"You're American?"

"A New Yorker."

"Jeff, let's talk about Jeremy Ashton. I need to understand him — professionally, personally, it makes no difference."

There was a long pause. "Personally?"

"I'm assuming that Mr. Knox told you to be candid."

"I didn't actually speak to Mr. Knox. George Hall called me — he's my boss. Mr. Knox called him. George didn't say anything about personal. I thought this was more of a professional reference kind of thing."

"So do I need to call my friend in China, so he can call Mr. Knox, so Mr. Knox can call Mr. Hall, and Mr. Hall can call you back to tell you to give me what I want?"

"No, you've made your point."

"Good, and thank you. Now, what was Ashton like to work with?"

"Well, you never really worked *with* Jeremy. He was on a little island, looking after himself. When it came to the job, he was a loner, a one-man band."

"Selfish, self-centred?"

"Yeah."

"Secretive?"

"Absolutely."

"Give me an example."

"The job he ended up with is almost perfect for Jeremy. The guys behind that gaming site came to Whiteburn looking for funding. The first and only guy they talked to was him. He was still kind of junior but he was the first point of contact, and he saw an opportunity to get into something from the ground floor and leapt at it. The only reason we found out they had approached Whiteburn at all was because the IT staff cleaned up his computer after he left. There was a long email trail."

"A conflict of interest, surely."

"Yeah, but so what? In our business that's called taking the initiative. No one cared. Besides, it was a fairly small placement."

"Did he make many friends at Whiteburn?"

Galley snorted. "Hardly. Jeremy thought he was too good for us and he didn't hesitate to let us know. I mean, he had the Oxford education, the fiancée connected to royalty, the big-shot future father-in-law. He was always harping on about how bush-league Whiteburn was. He came from Smyth's Bank in London, and his girlfriend was still working there. Smyth's is, I admit, the penthouse of investment banking but, I mean, we're hardly the fucking basement."

"He said he went to Oxford?" Ava said, looking at her notes that said otherwise.

"Every day."

"And he's engaged to Lily Simmons?"

"He wouldn't shut up about her."

"Mr. Galley, if Ashton was so secretive, tell me, why did he tell you about his fiancée?"

"That was one of the things that was weird about him. As secretive as he was about business, when it came to personal shit he was like the *National Enquirer*."

"Like how?"

"The fiancée."

"What do you mean?"

"He talked about her all the time, about how kinky and what a wack job she was."

"Define kinky."

Galley paused. "You sure you want to hear this?"

"I'm a big girl."

He laughed nervously. It always surprised Ava how uncomfortable Americans were talking about sex. "She lives in London, he's in New York. He went there once a month for a weekend and she came here once a month. On any Monday after a visit, Jeremy used to drag his ass into the office saying he could hardly walk."

"Go on," Ava said.

"He'd say they hardly left the bedroom for the entire weekend. She was like a fucking rabbit. As many times as he could get it up, she could take it. And when he couldn't get it up, she'd find other ways to get off."

"Like how?"

"Ms. Lee, really —"

"It's okay. Tell me."

"She evidently liked being tied up. She liked being spanked. He said she'd play with herself while he was spanking her, and it would always end up giving him a boner. Then she'd suck him to death."

"Did you ever meet her?"

"Once."

"And?"

"She was absolutely crazy about him and kept telling me how fantastic he was and how lucky she was to have him . . . It was a bit bizarre, to tell you the truth. I mean, Jeremy was listening to her go on about him with this big, stupid grin on his face. He was high on something, and she was too, I think."

"High on what?"

"I have no idea. I'm not into pharmaceuticals."

"But, high or not, she was obviously strongly attached to him?"

"Given how ugly she is, it's hard to blame her for being grateful."

"What does she look like?"

"Tall, skinny, frizzy red hair, long, pointy face. No tits and no ass to speak of. She's no beauty, that's for sure."

"What did Ashton think about her looks?"

"He used to joke about them, but he said anyone who could fuck like that had to be forgiven."

"Charming."

"That was Jeremy."

"You said that was one of the things you found strange about him. What else?"

"Like I said, I'm not into pharmaceuticals and I'm not a doctor, but I think he was manic-depressive."

"What made you think that?"

"Well, the normal Jeremy was very contained, a bit slow to react. Not stupid or anything, just deliberate, thoughtful, careful. Then once in a while this other Jeremy would appear in the office. He'd be jumpy, his eyes were off-centre, and he'd talk fast and get angry fast. One of the assistants said he must have gone off his meds. I asked her what she meant, and she said her brother was manic-depressive and that Jeremy had all the classic symptoms."

Ava paused to review her notes.

Galley said, "You still there?"

"I'm here . . . Tell me, where did the money come from to fund The River? Did Ashton have it?"

"Not a fucking chance."

"So from where?"

"I think the fiancée talked Smyth's into putting up some of it. The rest, I heard, came from her family."

"I saw the shareholder register, and Smyth's isn't listed."

"That's not unusual. They get into start-ups, and if they don't work out real fast, they bail."

"The family isn't listed either."

"They put their money in through a holding company."

"How do you know that?"

"I heard it from a reliable source."

"Who?"

He paused. "A Whiteburn girl he was fucking when the fiancée wasn't around."

"Nice."

"You gotta do what you gotta do."

"One of life's essential guidelines."

"Ms. Lee, are we done?"

"I think so," Ava said.

"Would you do me a small favour?"

"What do you have in mind?"

"Could you let your Chinese friend know that I was helpful —"

"Of course," Ava said, cutting off the rest of the sequence.

She sat quietly at the desk, then pulled up a photo of Lily Simmons and Jeremy Ashton on her computer. She tried to imagine Simmons naked, being spanked, Ashton's thin, ferrety face hovering over her, his penis heading for her mouth. Ava shuddered. Likeable or not, Ashton was turning out to be a lot more interesting than she'd thought he would be.

HER THREE BOYS WERE WAITING ANXIOUSLY IN THE
lobby. Ava strode up to them confidently and nodded.
"Let's go," she said.

As they drove out of Las Vegas and into the desert, she
kept up a steady stream of questions. How did Martin do at
the craps table? Did the boys play baccarat? What time did
they go to sleep? What time did they wake up? What did they
have for breakfast? Back and forth she went in English and
Cantonese, trying to keep their minds off what lay ahead,
trying to make the day as normal as any other.

When they were five minutes from The Oasis, she told
Martin to pull over. They sat on the shoulder as cars passed
from either direction. Finally the road was clear. "Open the
trunk," she said.

She gave Carlo the paper bag with the gun. "It's loaded
but the safety is on."

She gave Andy the bag with the meat cleaver. He looked
inside and smiled.

"Andy, you get in the trunk first, and then you, Carlo.
Now listen, if by some fluke security stops Martin and

forces him to open it, don't react. Carlo, no gunplay, do you understand?"

"Nothing?"

"You roll over and play dead."

"Okay, boss."

"Cellphones off?"

They nodded.

"Fine, get in."

Andy got in first. He lay on his side, his face turned towards them. Carlo joined him, his position identical. Ava kissed Martin on both cheeks. "I thought about this last night, and I'm convinced it will be smooth sailing. So no worrying, okay?"

"I'm ready."

She squeezed into the trunk, her ribs protesting. She lay on her good side, her face pressed again the wall. Martin closed the lid gently. The last thing she saw was his eyes, full of concern but not fear.

The air inside the trunk was stale, and Ava had trouble breathing. *It's just my imagination*, she told herself. *There's no danger of running out of air*. Behind her, Carlo and Andy lay absolutely still. They smelled like baby powder.

The car stopped, and Ava guessed they were at the first security gate. It started forward again almost immediately, turning left, and she remembered there was a stoplight at the off-ramp to the road leading into The Oasis.

The car stopped again. She counted. At fifteen it crept back into motion.

I hope the guards wave Martin through, Ava thought, but they stopped again. It was quiet; she imagined that Martin's ID was being examined. *Don't say too much*, she thought. *Keep it simple.* She waited for the car to move, but instead she heard the door open. Behind her, Carlo stiffened. "*Momentai,*" she whispered, but there was a lump in her chest and sweat was beading on her forehead.

The car door closed. Silence. Ava closed her eyes, convinced that the next time she opened them a strange face would be staring down at her. Then she heard Martin's voice and heard the door open again, then slam shut. The car moved forward. She could feel Carlo relax behind her. "I told you, no problem," she said.

Ava began to count again. At thirty-six the car came to a halt. At forty-two it reversed. At fifty-five the trunk popped open. She raised herself on one elbow and peeked out. Nothing. No one. Ignoring the pain in her body, she climbed out and stood beside Douglas's garage door. Andy and Carlo were right behind her.

Martin was standing beside the car. When they were all out, he closed the trunk. "I don't see anyone at a window or the door," he said quietly.

"What happened with the guard?" she asked.

"He took my ID into the security office and then made me get out of the car to get it back."

"Lazy."

"Whatever. I wasn't going to argue with him."

Ava scanned the street. There wasn't a soul in sight. She wasn't surprised; it was hardly the kind of neighbourhood where people went for strolls or lounged on their front porches.

"Okay, walk to the door. We'll be behind you. When you get to the door, we'll get on either side of it so they can't see us through the door window or the peephole. Then you give it a good knock. When they open the door, take two steps back. We'll take it from there."

"And you want me to stay in the car?"

"I think that's best, unless you want to head back to Vegas. I could phone you when we need you to come back."

He looked doubtful. "This is nerve-wracking. Let's get this over with and then I'll decide."

"You're doing just fine," Ava said.

Martin shrugged, took a deep breath, and turned the corner onto the walkway leading to the house. Ava tucked in behind him and the boys followed, clutching their paper bags. They separated at the door, Ava going to the left, Carlo and Andy standing with their backs pressed against the garage wall on the right.

"Do it," she said.

Martin lifted the metal knocker and rapped. Then he stood back and waited. He was reaching for the knocker again when the door swung open. "You're early," a voice said.

Martin took two steps back and Ava slipped in front of him. She looked up to see the pale, fleshy face of the man in the white tracksuit who had attacked her in the parking lot. He stared at her, puzzled. *He doesn't recognize me*, she thought, as she drove the phoenix-eye fist into his stomach, just below the ribs. He yelled in pain, then spun backwards and gagged. Ava pivoted to his right side, twisted her hips, and drove the toe of her Cole Haan pump into his ear. *That's how you kick someone in the head*, she thought. He stumbled into the house and collapsed onto a white shag carpet.

She moved past him, Carlo and Andy flanking her, their weapons now in plain sight. Ava scanned the ground floor.

It was one large room set up as separate areas. On the right was the den, which had a black leather couch, a La-Z-Boy recliner, and an enormous home entertainment centre. On her immediate left was a sitting area with two upholstered loveseats covered in plastic and a wooden coffee table. There were three doors in front of her. Two were closed but one was open; she could see a refrigerator.

Then a new player stepped into the kitchen doorway. The man was at least six foot six and as heavy as Ava, Carlo, and Andy combined. His long blond hair was tied back in a ponytail and his tanned face was dotted with pockmarks. He stared at Ava, a mixture of anger and curiosity in his blue eyes. "What the fuck do you think you're doing?" he said.

Right behind the man she could see David Douglas and Jeremy Ashton, peering around him into the room.

"I said, what the fuck are you doing here?" the man repeated, and then he started to charge.

Carlo had been holding the gun against his hip. Quickly he aimed it and shot Douglas's bodyguard, the bullet ripping into the giant's right thigh. He lurched forward and then collapsed onto the floor. He grabbed his leg, but blood spread quickly onto the carpet. Then the man Ava had taken out threw up. The white shag was now covered with viscous yellow vomit and fresh blood.

"Holy shit," Douglas exclaimed.

"Stay exactly where you are," Ava said to Ashton and Douglas, who were still standing in the kitchen doorway.

"Holy shit," Martin said.

Ava turned around. Martin was still standing at the front door.

"Holy shit," he repeated.

"Keep everyone covered," Ava said to Carlo, then went over to Martin. "That's it — the worst is over," she said to him. "Now please get in the car and stay there. You won't hear any more gunshots, so don't worry about that. Things are under control now."

"Holy shit, Ava."

She took him by the elbow and moved him outside, half closing the door behind her. "I need you to get in the car," she said gently. "I also need you to stay here for a while. If you see anyone approaching the house, call me on my cell. But please, don't wander into the house."

When Martin didn't move or acknowledge Ava's words, she gripped his elbow a little tighter and steered him to the car. "I need you to keep calm," she said.

"I'm all right," he said as he climbed in.

"I know you are. And as I said, the worst is over."

29

AVA WALKED BACK TO THE HOUSE, PUSHING MARTIN
further out of her mind with every step. When she opened
the door, Douglas's man was throwing up again. His partner was bleeding badly, the leg of his blue jeans completely
soaked from the thigh down.

"Where are the dogs?" she said to Douglas, who stood
paralyzed.

He looked at her blankly, his mouth hanging open, a
streak of saliva on his chin. His eyes flickered from her to
Carlo, to Andy, to his two men on the floor.

"Where are your dogs?" she said.

"Out back."

Ava walked over to the sliding glass door leading to the
backyard. There were three Rottweilers, as the detective
had said, each in its own steel cage secured by a padlock.
"Do I need keys for the locks?" she asked.

"Yeah."

"Where are they?"

"In the kitchen, on the counter by the toaster."

"The two of you, sit over here," she said, pointing to a

loveseat. "Don't move and don't speak unless I tell you to."
Then she said to Carlo, "Keep an eye on them."

She retrieved the keys and came back into the living
room.

"What are we going to do with these guys?" Carlo asked,
pointing at Douglas's men.

"How badly is that one bleeding?"

"We should tie it off," Carlo said.

"Andy, go to the bathroom and get what we need."

Ava turned to the bleeding man. "What we're going to
do is put a tourniquet on your leg to help stop the bleeding.
If you and your friend here behave yourselves, this should
be over soon and you can go to a hospital. If you give us any
trouble . . . well, these two won't care what happens to you.
Understand?"

"You fucking —"

"That is exactly the wrong attitude," Ava said, stepping
on the hand he was holding over the gunshot wound. He
screamed in pain as his partner nodded.

Andy brought towels, gauze, and two ACE bandages
from the bathroom. Without a word he split the blood-
soaked jeans with the cleaver and then went to work on
the leg.

Ava took the duct tape from her bag and taped the other
man's hands and ankles together. She felt him tense when
he saw Andy standing over him with the cleaver. She turned
to the man with the gunshot wound to do the same.

"You don't have to do that to me," he said. "I can't move
anyway."

"Sorry, but I can't play favourites," Ava said, as she wound
the tape around his wrists and then his ankles.

She got up and tossed the keys to Andy. "Take them to the backyard and put them in the cages with the dogs."

"What did you tell him?" the pasty-faced man asked nervously.

"You're going to stay with the dogs for a while."

"What the fuck, are you crazy?" he yelled.

Ava looked at Douglas. "Have the dogs eaten today?" she asked.

"This morning."

"When next?"

"Around five."

"You'll be okay for a while," she said to the two men.

Carlo gave Ava the gun and went to help his partner. They took the smaller one first, making him hop. Then they each grabbed an arm of the other man and dragged him to the cages. She could hear the dogs barking when the men came into view. Ava walked towards the kitchen, still pointing the gun at Douglas and Ashton, and looked through the glass door. Each man had his back pressed against the bars of the cage and the dogs were sniffing at their feet. Andy was smiling nervously; even on the other side of the bars the dogs made him nervous.

Ava turned her attention back to Douglas and Ashton. "Now, Mr. Ashton, I think it's your turn."

"Who the hell are you and what the fuck do you want?" he said, his eyes jerking back and forth between Douglas and the door leading to the backyard.

Ashton's hair was gelled and spiked. He was heavier than she had thought, and his five-foot-six frame didn't carry the weight well. He wore a black silk shirt that hung loosely over his stomach and a pair of fashionably ripped blue jeans.

"I'm the woman your partner met at Wynn's two days ago, the woman you sent two goons to beat up."

"I don't know what the fuck you're talking about," he said, his eyes flickering towards Douglas. Douglas just nodded as if to say, *That's her.*

"That doesn't matter right now. You'll know soon enough. But first I need to talk to Mr. Douglas, and while I do I'm going to put you in the third dog cage."

"No!" he snapped.

"You can either walk out there on your own or I'll have the boys take you."

"Fuck no!"

Ava walked to the kitchen and opened the glass door, still pointing the gun at the two men. "Come and get the small one and put him in the last cage," she shouted at Carlo and Andy.

Ashton tensed, his teeth gnawing at his bottom lip. His eyes flicked in the direction of the front door. *Don't be stupid*, Ava thought. Carlo and Andy came back in and grabbed Ashton's arms. "There's no need to tape him," Ava said in English. "He's no threat."

Ashton stood and glared at her. Then he spat in Ava's direction. "Fuck you," he said.

Carlo looked at Ava to see whether she wanted him to sort out the Englishman. She shook her head.

When they had left the room, she turned to Douglas. "Well, Mr. Douglas, I guess it's just you and me for a while," she said. "You should have met with me at Wynn's and saved us all this trouble."

30

DAVID DOUGLAS'S LIPS WERE TIGHTLY SET. HE WIPED his mouth, staring hard at Ava as if he was trying to commit her to memory.

"You do remember me, don't you?" she asked.

"Yeah."

"And you do remember why I wanted to talk to you?"

He shook his head. "You can't get away with this. This is the United States, not some fucking Asian backwater. We have laws and we have people who enforce them."

"You seem to be selective about which laws you want enforced. For example, you don't seem to be overly concerned about a massive case of fraud."

"You're going to talk about that shit again?"

"That's the only reason I'm here."

"Those guys who hired you, they're nothing but a bunch of sore losers. They think because they're online, knowing how to really play poker doesn't matter. I've been playing the game my whole life and I've forgotten more than they know. Losing to me is no upset. Beating me would be," he said, still looking hard at her.

"You don't even know who hired me."

"I can guess."

"Well, just so we're clear, the people I work for represent Chinaclipper — Philip Chew. So your Asian remark was at least partially apt."

He started to get up. Ava held out a hand, palm facing him. "I took out the one who wasn't shot, so don't even think about it," she said.

The door to the backyard opened. Carlo and Andy had returned from depositing Ashton in the dog cage. "Get two chairs from the kitchen," she told Carlo, and then turned to Douglas. "They don't understand English, so I have to speak to them in Cantonese. I just asked for two chairs to be brought in here. I'm going to have them tape your arms and legs to one, so basically you're not going anywhere unless you take the chair with you."

"This is such shit."

Carlo and Andy came back into the room, each carrying a chair. Ava watched Carlo tape Douglas's hands behind his chair back and his ankles to the chair legs. She handed the gun to Carlo, positioned the second chair directly across from Douglas, and sat down. She opened her bag and took out the paperwork she had been reviewing that morning. "This is what we're here to resolve," she said. "Over the past six months or so you stole more than sixty million dollars from Chinaclipper, Brrrrr, and Felix the Cat."

"I won, not stole. And it was nowhere near that much money."

She noticed that his hair was beginning to rise. It was very fine, and thinning on top. Her guess was that he got it permed. From a distance it might look angelic; up close it looked absurd. "You used your own name some of the time, but mainly you played under the names Kaybar and Buckshot," she said. "I have all the play data here. I also have a letter from the Cooper Island Gaming Commission confirming that you used both those names. Do you want to see it?"

"No. What's the difference? Using a different name didn't diminish my talent."

"Mr. Douglas, we can do this the easy way or the hard way. Right now you're headed for the hard way. I would prefer that you cooperate and make this as easy on all of us as possible."

He hesitated. "What do you want?"

"I want, as a start, for you to admit that you were all those people."

"You have the letter."

"I want to hear it."

"Fine."

"Fine what?"

"I played as Kaybar and Buckshot."

"There, that wasn't so difficult," she said. "Now I want you to admit that the money you won playing under those two names was stolen."

"No, and you and your little friends can go fuck yourselves," he said.

"Let's not get emotional," Ava said, holding the report that Felix had prepared in front of Douglas's face. "Look at this. It's an analysis of the hands you played against my client and others, and it says that the numbers are statistically anomalous."

"What's that supposed to mean?"

"They don't make sense. The report says you won all that money in the face of all logical probability. That means you cheated. And we think we know how you did it — you breached security and manipulated your own software. We're convinced that you could see all the cards at the table. The Gaming Commission is running cross-checks on this analysis as we speak and will confirm it all. When they do, you will be exposed as a cheat, a liar, and a fraud and the River website will be ruined."

"Is that your threat — that I'll be exposed?"

"Perhaps."

"What if I don't care?"

"You'd throw away a lifetime of building a reputation so easily?"

"I'm a poker player, not a priest. Moral expectations are low to begin with."

"And your website?"

"We're losing money."

"The money you stole didn't help?"

"I've never believed in throwing good money after bad."

Ava took a deep breath. "Mr. Douglas, are you right-handed or left-handed?"

"Right. Why?"

She turned away from him and spoke to Andy, who looked at Douglas, nodding. When she had finished, he went into the kitchen. "Mr. Douglas, I've just asked my colleague to cut off your left thumb," she said. "He's gone to turn on one of the elements on your stove. After he's cut off your thumb he'll press the open wound against the element until it stops bleeding. When he comes back, you will have exactly five minutes to start cooperating with me. If you don't, the thumb comes off. Now, I can't stand to watch, so I'll stay here until he's done. He'll bring you back to me afterwards. Do you understand?"

He blinked, his eyes uncomprehending. She saw beads of sweat form on his upper lip.

"This is nuts. You wouldn't dare do that."

"You won't feel much pain at first," she said. "Shock will set in, adrenalin will be pumping like mad. The thing is, there will be a lot of blood, and I don't want you to lose too much. That's why we need to cauterize the wound. Now, that you will feel. You might pass out and you'll probably mess yourself. You don't have any adult diapers, do you?"

Douglas shook his head. "You aren't going to do this."

Ava reached for his chin and pulled his head in her direction. His eyes were darting around the room in panic. "What you need to understand is that it won't end with your left thumb. Five minutes after you lose that thumb, he'll take off the right. Five minutes later you'll lose the big toe on your left foot, and then the big toe on your right foot. And he'll just keep going until you won't be able to count to one on either your hands or your feet."

"Fuck off," he said.

She let go of his chin. "I'm sorry," she said, standing up. She spoke quietly to Andy. Carlo tucked the gun into his jeans, moved in behind Douglas, and dragged him in the chair to the kitchen. Andy followed with the cleaver. "Five minutes, starting from now," Ava said.

She stood still, waiting. Logic dictated that he would cooperate. If he were Asian he would no doubt understand the thumb would come off, and that more pain would follow until he capitulated.

After four minutes Ava walked into the kitchen and stood in front of him. He stared at her defiantly. She looked down at him and, without a word, grabbed the duct tape, cut off a strip, and sealed his mouth. She nodded at Carlo, who ripped off the tape binding Douglas's hands, and then nodded at Andy before walking back into the living room.

Even with the tape on his mouth, she still heard Douglas scream.

She heard another scream, and guessed that the stub of Douglas's thumb was being pressed onto the red-hot element. She had watched it done only once, and that was enough for a lifetime. She was sure he had convulsed and emptied his bowels and bladder.

Andy and Carlo were talking to each other, their manner calm and professional. The tap was running and she knew they were cleaning up Douglas before bringing him back to her.

Carlo dragged him into the living room and Andy followed, holding the thumb by the nail. Douglas's eyes were rolled back in his head, and she was afraid for a second that he had had a heart attack or a stroke. His pants and underwear were gone, exposing scrawny thighs and thin, meagre calves. She tried to pull his shirttail down over his genitals, but his round, hard belly was too large. If there was anything uglier than a man's shrivelled penis, she didn't know what it was. Carlo and Andy, she noted, had done a decent job of washing him; there was only a light streak of feces on the inside of each thigh.

"Andy," Ava said, motioning at the thumb, "throw that in the garbage or give it to the dogs."

She turned her attention back to the Disciple. "So, Mr.

Douglas, here we are again." His head lolled back and his pupils were dilated. She reached into her kit bag, took out the smelling salts she'd bought the day before, and held the bottle under his nose. "The clock is ticking," Ava said as Douglas came back to life. "You have four minutes before the other thumb comes off. I'm going to take the tape off your mouth now, in case you want to speak."

He grunted. She ripped off the tape and he roared at the pain. He then sat still, breathing heavily. When he looked up at her, his glare was defiant.

She was about to tape his mouth shut again when he whispered, "What do you want?"

"I've already told you."

"You're crazy."

"That could be, but it's only going to get crazier until you decide to be honest."

"Why are you doing this?"

"Your minutes are passing."

"Fuck you," he said without any passion.

"We can forget about the time that is left, if you want. I'll turn Andy loose with his cleaver right now if this is how you're going to act."

"What do you want from me?"

"Straight answers."

"To what?"

"Did you cheat my people?"

"We toyed a bit with the software," he said, his voice devoid of energy.

"No, I want to hear it my way. Did you cheat my people?"

His head sagged to his chest. Ava put her hand under his chin and lifted his face. "Did you cheat my people?" she said.

"Yeah."

She held the smelling salts to his nose. His head snapped back, his eyes took on more life.

"Why did you do it?"

He groaned, but his voice was clear enough. "The company was in the hole, big time. And when we saw how easy it was to make that kind of money, we kept going."

"Why did you stop?"

He closed his eyes. "A couple of players began to complain. Ashton thought they'd picked up on what we were doing. We decided it was time to stop, to not press our luck."

Barking erupted in the backyard. Ava went to the back door and looked out. Ashton had moved to the front of his cage, probably to test the padlock, and the dog had him pinned against the front bars. Ava opened the door. "I'd stay still if I were you," she shouted, "because if that dog decides it wants to have you for dinner, we won't interfere."

When she came back to the living room, Douglas seemed to have passed out again. Another dose of smelling salts revived him. She tapped his naked knee. "Now, Mr. Douglas, we have to talk about how you and Jeremy Ashton are going to give that money back."

"I don't —"

"If we can make that happen," Ava said, "then you get to keep your reputation — even though it doesn't seem to mean that much to you — and your various body parts. That's the deal."

"What do you want me to do?" he asked.

"You can start by telling me where the money is."

He shook his head as if trying to clear it of some bad memory. "My thumb is killing me," he said, his voice cracking.

"First you tell me where the money is and then I'll see if we can do something about your thumb."

He shook his head again. "You'll need Ashton."

"He's next on my list. Where's the money?"

"Most of it is in Cyprus. We moved it to the holding company. That's where it banks."

"You moved all of it?"

"Yeah, most of it anyway."

"And it's still there?"

"Yeah."

"So a bank transfer is doable, I would assume."

"Sure."

"See how easy that was? If you'd taken this approach half an hour ago you'd still have that thumb."

"That's not funny, and it also ain't that easy." He closed his eyes and licked his lips with the tip of his tongue.

"Explain to me why it isn't easy," she said.

"To take any money out of that account needs three signatures."

Ava blinked. "You and Ashton."

"Yeah."

"Who is the third?"

"His woman."

"Lily Simmons?"

Douglas peered at her through hooded eyes. "You've done your homework."

"How does she come into this?"

"Her father put up nearly all the money for The River."

"And left you and Ashton to manage it?"

"No — are you kidding? Jeremy was running off to London every month to report in."

"And this Lily, she is his what — girlfriend, fiancée, wife?"

"They're engaged, he says."

"But no wedding plans?"

Douglas shrugged. "What does that have to do with anything?"

"Did Ashton meet with her father during any of those trips?"

"How would I know?"

"How about this Lily Simmons — did you ever meet her?"

"Once, in New York."

"What was she like?"

"Tall, skinny, no tits, no ass, red hair."

"Doesn't sound like the kind of girl who would attract a man like Ashton. Maybe he has a thing for red hair."

"Yeah, as long as it comes with money attached to it."

"Okay, let's get back to the money. Tell me, how do things get signed around here? I mean, how do you move money in and out?"

He twisted his neck and rolled his shoulders as if trying to gather strength. "We have a bank account in Vegas that we use for day-to-day operations. Either of us can sign for it. To get money from Cyprus, Ashton and I sign a wire or transfer request here and then he flies over to London and gets her to sign."

"Not very efficient."

"It's the way they wanted it, and it was their money. Besides, we don't do it very often, maybe once a quarter."

"How much did they invest?"

"Forty million."

"That's a lot of money. You said earlier you were in the hole. For exactly how much?"

"Up until about six months ago the losses came to more than thirty million."

"That's hard to believe."

"Believe it."

"So the money you stole, it all went to Cyprus?"

"I said that already."

"And it covered the losses and then some?"

"Yeah."

"How much is in the account today?"

"Just over seventy million."

"The rest of what they put in, plus what you stole?"

"Yeah, more or less."

"And no one thought to take money out? Your investors didn't want to claw back their funds?"

"We were waiting until the fiscal year-end."

"Lucky for me," Ava said. "Tell me, does Lily Simmons know how you came by your recent windfall?"

Douglas shrugged. "I have no idea. I don't know what Ashton said to her."

Ava stood. "Andy, get Mr. Douglas a glass of water and then bring in an extra chair from the kitchen." She turned to Carlo. "Bring in the little one. I need to talk to him."

31

AVA HEARD JEREMY ASHTON BEFORE SHE SAW HIM,
a stream of "fucking Chinese" preceding his return to the
house. Carlo was walking behind him, the gun pressed
into his back. It was true that Carlo didn't speak English
and understood very little of it, but "fucking Chinese" was
something he did comprehend. Ava could tell that he was
barely controlling himself.

When Ashton emerged from the kitchen, his eyes locked
on Ava and he yelled, "You fucking bitch," and spat in her
direction. The spit had hardly left his mouth before Carlo's
arm shot out, smashing Ashton across the forehead with
the barrel of the gun. He reeled back, his hand reaching
for his head as blood trickled between his eyebrows and
down both sides of his nose. He started to say something
and then looked at Douglas for the first time.

Ashton gasped. "What have you done to him?" he cried.
Whatever bravado he had left was ebbing away at the sight
of his partner's pain and humiliation.

Ava also turned to look at Douglas. He had sipped half
a glass of water and some colour was returning to his face.

The stump of his thumb was wrapped in cloth but blood had seeped through; he was still naked from the waist down.

"It's worse than it looks," Ava said, following Ashton's gaze to the dried feces on Douglas's thighs.

Carlo pushed Ashton towards her and motioned for him to sit in the chair next to Douglas. As he passed her, Ava smelled urine. "What happened? Did he pee himself?" she asked Carlo.

"No, it was the dog. It splashed him, I guess."

She turned to Andy. "Tape him."

Carlo held the gun trained on both men while Andy taped Ashton's hands together and his legs to the chair. "Now, Mr. Ashton, just so we're clear, I'm not going to waste my time trying to persuade you to tell me things I already know. Your partner has already confirmed that you manipulated the software and cheated various high-stakes players out of more than sixty million dollars. Some statistical analysis has already been done. The Mohneida are now cross-referencing and confirming the information they've been given, but they obviously believe us already. Why else do you think they were prepared to work with us? So you cheated. And you got caught. The only thing up for discussion now is how quickly you'll return the money to the people you stole it from — my clients."

"If they and you are so sure we cheated anyone — and I'm not admitting we did — then sue us," Ashton said. Ava noted his accent. It wasn't exactly working class but it was rough around the edges.

"Lawyers are very expensive and very slow. We prefer a more direct approach. Mr. Douglas has already experienced it. Maybe you would like to try it yourself?"

"You wouldn't dare."

"Mr. Douglas, would you care to talk to your partner?" Ava said.

"Don't be an idiot," Douglas said to Ashton.

"They can't just do this," Ashton said.

"I promise you, we can and we will," Ava said. "We want our money back, and we want it back now."

Ashton went silent. Ava noticed that sweat was mingling with the blood on his face, and his eyelids were flickering. She turned to Douglas. "Do you have a home office, a computer, a printer?" she asked.

"Yeah, it's through the door on the left."

"And when you make a transfer from the Cyprus account, do you use a specific form?"

"No, most times we just write a letter on company letterhead addressed to the bank, asking them to do the transaction. I sign it here, and Jeremy and Lily sign it in London and then send it off to Cyprus."

At the mention of his fiancée's name, Ashton's head spun towards Douglas. "Why did you bring her into it?" he shouted.

"They knew about her already, and if they hadn't, they would have soon enough."

"Where is she, by the way?" Ava asked. "I'm assuming she's in London."

Ashton was silent.

"That was a question, and I'd like an answer," Ava said.

"She's there," he said.

She turned back to Douglas. "Did you keep copies of previous transfer requests?"

"In the bottom right drawer of my desk there's a file."

"Thank you."

Ava looked at Ashton. He was sweating more profusely now. "Do you need your meds?" she asked.

"Fuck off, you Chinese cunt," he said.

Ava drew a deep breath. "You really are beginning to irritate me, Mr. Ashton, and I'm not going to waste much more time being nice to you. So let me tell you what's going to happen now. I'm going to go along to the office and I'm going to prepare a confession that both of you will sign, and a request to transfer $65 million from the account in Cyprus to a bank account in Hong Kong, which the two of you will also sign."

"That —" Ashton began.

"Hit him," Ava said to Carlo, and averted her head as the gun raked across Ashton's face.

She waited until his scream became a moan. "I won't ask him to be that gentle again," she said. "The next time you choose not to cooperate, you're going to lose a body part." Ava leaned in closer. "Look at me," she said.

Ashton tried to avoid her eyes, but Ava kept staring until he gave in. "You are going to do exactly what I want," she said. "You aren't going to argue, you aren't going to negotiate, and you are going to stop telling me to fuck off. There's no other option. I've lost my patience with you, and on top of that, I don't like you. Whatever hurt you decide to bring upon yourself by being less than totally obedient is of absolutely no worry to me, because in the end you will do what I want anyway."

His eyelids were flickering wildly, but Ava held his attention. "Say 'Yes, Ms. Lee, I understand.'"

"Yes, I understand," he said.

Ava turned away from him. "Where do you bank in Las Vegas?" she asked Douglas.

"Tri-State."

"Can you bank online?"

"Yeah."

"Is there a file in your office with an account number?"

"Yeah."

"What password do you use?"

"Disciple."

"Do you need any special codes? Do both of you have to sign on?"

"No."

"Great. Now how about your personal bank and investment accounts?"

"Do you really have to —"

"Yes, I do."

Douglas looked nervously at Carlo and Andy, who were edging towards him. "The information is in the bottom left desk drawer. The password is the same for everything."

Ava looked at Ashton, whose eyes were closed. "Carlo, take his wallet out of his jeans," she said.

Ashton jumped at Carlo's touch and looked at Douglas in alarm. Carlo went through Ashton's pockets and passed the wallet to Ava, who took out three bank cards. One was for Tri-State. She held the other two in front of his face. "Can you bank online with these cards?"

He closed his eyes and lowered his chin to his chest.

"Is that a yes?" Ava demanded.

He was silent, and Ava wondered if his meds had indeed worn off. "Yes," he finally said.

"Password?"

"Sheffield."

Ava stood. "I'm going to be gone for a while. Before I leave I'll ask the boys to see if they can do something about your thumb, Mr. Douglas. Maybe they can find ointment and some bandages. They can get both of you some water as well."

Douglas nodded. Ashton didn't acknowledge that she had spoken.

Ava explained to Carlo and Andy what she wanted them to do. She had started walking towards the door to the office when she remembered Martin.

He was still in the car, his eyes closed and his head resting against the back of the seat. When she knocked on the glass, he jumped, then lowered the window.

"Things have gone very well," Ava said, "but I still have at least an hour's worth of work, maybe more."

"I'm sorry if I was a bit difficult earlier," he said.

"No reason to be; it was more my fault than yours. I should have explained things more clearly so you knew what to expect."

"Ava, I've been thinking," he said carefully. "When we leave here, what's going to happen? I mean, what if they call in the police? They know who we are."

"They won't," Ava said.

"How can you be so sure?"

"Trust me."

32

AVA WAS SITTING AT DOUGLAS'S COMPUTER, LOOKING through his bank and investment accounts, and for once she was pleasantly surprised. There was almost five million dollars in The River's Las Vegas bank account. She transferred four and a half million to Hong Kong.

In Douglas's drawer she found records from three banks and a brokerage firm. The bank accounts held collectively more than two million dollars. She left a thousand in each account. His stock portfolio's most recent valuation pegged it at a million and a half. She put in sell orders for everything. When the stock was turned into cash, she'd move it to Hong Kong as well. Ashton wasn't as flush as his partner, but she still found just under a million dollars in his two accounts. Again she left a thousand in each.

Of all the things that had made her job easier, nothing came close to the advent of electronic banking. *It's too bad Cyprus wasn't set up that way,* she thought. *It's too bad I probably have to go to London.*

She listed all the account numbers and transaction records in her notebook, then searched for flights to London.

There was a Virgin Airlines direct flight from McCarran to Gatwick leaving at nine that evening. It would land in London at three thirty. Ava booked a business-class seat.

When she returned to the living room, Carlo was watching Douglas and Ashton. Andy was at the window, looking out at the two men in the dog cages.

Douglas was slumped in his chair. The stub of his thumb had been taped, but Ava knew the pain wouldn't have eased and that it would keep draining him of energy. Ashton was alert, and he flinched when she came towards them. His eyelids were still twitching, and Ava hoped it was from nervousness and not from lack of medication. She needed him to act as normal as possible when talking to Lily Simmons.

"We're just about finished," she said to Carlo. "Once we get this group sorted we can get out of here. I'm going to leave them tied up. Hopefully no one will discover they're missing or come looking for them until we're out of town."

"What do you want to do with the guys in the dog cages?"

"We should bring them in," Ava said. "Noise carries at night, and we don't want either them or the dogs attracting attention."

"Then we need to feed the dogs."

"Bring the two guys in first. Put them in separate rooms and leave them on the floor. Tape their wrists and ankles again — make sure they can't get out of it — and I'd tape their mouths too."

"Okay, boss."

"When I'm finished talking to these two," she said, motioning to Douglas and Ashton, "we'll take them off the chairs, tape them again, and leave them on the floor as well. Put one in the kitchen and the other one can stay here."

She heard a groan. Douglas was awake, watching their conversation. She smiled at him. "Mr. Douglas, I just told Carlo to bring your men inside in a little while. There's no point in scaring the dogs anymore."

He grimaced. "Did you get what you wanted? Did you do what you said you had to do?"

"Yes. I emptied your personal bank accounts and moved most of the money from The River's account overseas."

"Shit," Ashton said.

"So now you'll leave?" Douglas asked.

"Soon enough. First I need to get your signatures on this transfer request and this admission of guilt," she said, placing three copies of each of the documents she'd prepared on the table. "The transfer is for $65 million. That's what I've been told you stole from the three players I mentioned earlier."

She placed the paperwork on the coffee table and slid the table close to their chairs. "Are you right- or left-handed?" she asked Ashton.

"Right."

"Carlo, untape both their right hands."

As he did, she held out the pen to Douglas. "Sign these," she said.

He hesitated, and she saw that he was trying to read the confession. "These are for signing, not reading," she said.

He took the pen, his hand trembling slightly. Suddenly he looked at her. "That's why you asked me if I was right- or left-handed, wasn't it?"

"What do you mean?"

"You didn't want to cut off the thumb on my signature hand."

"Obviously not."

"That was smart."

"Just sign," Ava said.

The signatures were shaky but passable. "Now you," she said to Ashton.

Carlo hovered, and Ava knew he was looking for any excuse to have another go at the Englishman. Ashton sensed it too, and signed all six documents without a pause.

"Great. Now the next thing that needs to happen is for Mr. Ashton to call Lily Simmons."

"I'm not sure —" he began to say, and then stopped when Ava put a finger to her lips.

"You said she was in London."

"Yes."

"It's around midnight there now. Will she be at home?"

"Probably."

"Good. So now you're going to call her and you're going to tell her that a Ms. Ava Lee, who represents some substantial Asian business interests, is going to be in London tomorrow and wants to meet with her. You're going to tell her that this could be very good for Smyth's and very good for you, because the people she represents have expressed an interest in buying into The River, at a very healthy premium. She would be interested, I assume, in selling some shares at a premium?"

"Keep talking," Ashton said.

"I land in London in the late afternoon, so I won't be able to meet with her until around five at the earliest."

"She works late."

"Good. Now, you need to emphasize that I have to meet with her tomorrow. Tell her I'll call her at the office or on her cellphone as soon as I arrive. Tell her you've given me those numbers. If she has a problem with tomorrow, tell her it's all the time I have available. How does that sound?"

Ashton's eyelids were twitching so quickly she could barely see his eyes. "Why does it matter what I think?" he yelled.

Ava didn't like his reaction. She turned to Carlo. "Pull down his pants. Hold the gun against his balls," she said.

When Carlo reached for his pants, Ashton threw himself back against the chair so forcefully it almost tipped over.

"Listen to me," Ava said. "Carlo is going to hold the gun against your genitals while you're talking to Ms. Simmons. He will fire if I say the word *fire* in Cantonese. And believe me, he won't hesitate to do it. So if I were you, I would follow our script exactly. I want to meet with Lily Simmons tomorrow. Your only priority is to make that happen."

As Carlo pulled down Ashton's pants, Ava went into the kitchen and brought back a portable phone. She sat across from Ashton, who was now as naked as Douglas. Carlo kneeled to one side, the gun pressed against Ashton's testicles. "What's her number?" she asked.

The shock of cold steel against his skin made Ashton jump. He rattled off the phone number. Ava dialled, and when the phone rang, she put it on speaker and held it under Ashton's mouth.

Simmons answered on the third ring, her voice throaty, full of sleep. "Hello?"

"Lily, this is Jeremy."

"Hello?"

"Stop saying that, for Christ's sake. This is Jeremy."

"Jeremy?"

She takes pills to help her sleep, he mouthed to Ava.

"There isn't any rush. Take your time," Ava whispered.

"Yes, it's me," Ashton said.

"It's so late. Is everything all right?" Simmons asked hesitantly.

"Yeah, it's fine, just fine," he said, his voice trembling just a touch. Ava hoped Simmons was too sleepy to notice.

"Then why are you calling so late?"

"I met this woman today, Ava Lee, who's arriving in London tomorrow," he said. "I want you to meet with her."

Ava encouraged him with a nod. Ashton plunged ahead, sticking to the story she had laid out. His confidence seemed to grow and he began to get a little too excited. Carlo pressed the gun harder against Ashton's testicles as Ava motioned for him to wrap up the conversation.

"I've given her your phone numbers. She'll call you when she lands," Ashton said.

"Okay, baby."

Ava covered the mouthpiece. "How out of it is she?" she asked.

"No more than usual," Ashton said.

"Will she remember what you said tomorrow morning?"

"She normally does."

"That's not reassuring."

"Let me talk to her," he said. Ava took her hand off the phone.

"Lily, what's the name of the woman coming to see you tomorrow?"

"Ava Lee."

"And when will that be?"

"Late in the afternoon."

"And how will she contact you?"

"By phone."

Ashton looked at Ava and shrugged.

Say goodbye, Ava mouthed.

"I have to go now. You sleep tight."

"Thanks, baby, you too."

Ava shut off the phone. "Well done." She took a business card and a pen from her bag. "Give me her office, home, and mobile numbers." Then she said, "Tell me, does she know how you got that money?"

"No," Ashton said, handing her back the card.

"What does she think?"

"I told her that we finally became profitable."

"To that degree?"

"The money we've made over the past six months isn't much more than what we forecast when we started the business."

"And she bought that?"

"Is that a problem?" Douglas asked.

Ava shook her head. "No, not really. She'll know the truth soon enough." She turned to Carlo. "Okay, bring in the guys and get them bundled away. Then feed the dogs. I want to get out of here in the next half-hour."

"Now what?" Douglas asked as he watched Carlo and Andy leave the room.

"We're going to be getting out of here soon. We're bringing in your thugs. We'll put them in separate rooms."

"You're going to leave us taped like this?"

"We need to have a serious discussion. Are both of you up for it?" she asked.

Douglas nodded. Ashton said, "I'm listening."

"This part of your ordeal is over. How the rest of it plays out is entirely up to you," she said slowly. "I'm going to give you two clear choices, and I know ahead of time which one you're going to choose. The thing is, you need to understand that by choosing it, you're making a commitment to me and my people that you cannot go back on. You may think you can, you may even be convinced that you can, but I'm telling you it would be the worst thing you could ever do. Understand?"

Douglas said, "Two choices."

"Fine, choice one is that you decide not to cooperate. The consequence: you both die and the two guys with the dogs die," she said. "So I know you're going to take choice two, and that is to tell me you will cooperate. In that case, the boys and I will leave the way we came and I will go and see Lily Simmons and retrieve the rest of the money you stole. Now, the key to all this is, what do I mean by cooperation?"

"I think you're going to tell us," Douglas said.

"Of course I am," Ava said. "Your thugs will be bound and left in the bedrooms. You'll be taped and left in other rooms. It's best if you don't struggle to get free. And if by some fluke you do, you don't contact security. Later this evening, someone will call them and arrange for you to be released. When you are released, you will tell security that this was a home invasion by three men in masks with eastern European accents. You will tell your buddies to stick to that story and you will make sure they do. If security calls in the local police, you'll tell them the same story.

"Neither of you will make any effort to contact Lily Simmons. None. If she phones, don't take the call. No emails, no texts. Nothing." She shot a glance at Ashton.

"I get it," he said.

"Okay, now let me make it clear that my leaving doesn't make your position any easier. If by some chance you decided to gamble and did speak to Lily Simmons, or — just as bad — told the authorities what actually happened here and maybe even managed somehow to get me and the boys arrested, it would not make any difference to your position. In fact, as I said before, it would probably worsen it. For certain my people would go public with the news that The River is nothing but a front for fraud and that you are the primary perpetrators. Your reputations would be destroyed. They'd come after all the money and then, of course, they'd kill you. And it wouldn't be any quick bullet to the head. They'd send guys like Carlo and Andy, who are experts in prolonged agony. Understand?"

"Yeah."

"And neither of you would be able to hide. These people would find you. They always find who they're after, and they would take it out on you for making them hunt you down."

"I understand," Douglas said, sweat coating his face.

"Now, if you do cooperate, what's the upside? You stay alive. You keep the rest of your appendages. Your reputations remain intact. The River can keep rolling as long as it operates above board. And — if I can get Lily Simmons to sign over the $65 million I want from the holding company's accounts, I will return all the money that I just removed from your personal accounts and from The River's operating account."

"You would really do that?" Douglas asked.

"I would."

"And what if you can't get her to sign? Does our cooperation still have some value?"

She admired his nerve. "Do you have any reason to think I won't be able to get her to sign?"

Douglas looked at Ashton, who said, "It's not her that might be a problem. It's her father."

Ava stared at him. "Explain that to me."

"I hardly know where to begin."

"That's not a good start."

Ashton shook his head. "He's a self-made man, or, as he prefers to say, 'a fucking self-made man.' He has a working-class background. His father was a coal miner and he was the first of his family to go to university. He took engineering, and when he left school, he joined a small company that made generators. Within five years he was running it, and five years later he owned it. Ten years after that it was one of the largest generator manufacturers in the world. It's a success story he never tires of telling, and he's always at the centre of it. In his own mind there aren't many people smarter or tougher than Roger Simmons."

"So he obviously made some serious money as well." Ava said.

"That's his second favourite subject — how much he's made and how hard it was to make it. It's how he puts a value on himself. It separates him from the riff-raff he grew up with. It brings him at least close to a level playing field with the blueblood crowd he loves to hang around with now, the crowd he married into." Ashton looked up at Ava. "He loves his money. He was mouthing off to Lily about how much money we had lost, and she thought he was close to shutting us down until we turned things around. Now that he has the money back, he isn't the kind of man to give it up that easily."

"I read that he's in politics now."

"Yeah, that's his latest ego trip. It's a toss-up which he feels the most puffed up about, his business success and his money or his fucking political status."

"I read that he's a cabinet minister in the U.K."

"He is, and when he gets a few drinks in him and he's with friends or family, he doesn't mind telling you he's only one step away from becoming prime minister and saving the country from ruin."

"His assets must be in a blind trust or something like that, no?"

"That's true."

"So his daughter is obviously empowered to manage the money."

"In theory."

"What do you mean?"

"It's still his money. He keeps his eye on every pound. Lily may officially administer the trust and sign all the documents, but nothing happens until she clears it with him. He jokes about it. He says just because his money is in a blind trust, it doesn't mean he's also deaf. They're careful, I give them that. Nothing is ever in writing, not even an email. It's strictly verbal."

"But she has the authority. She doesn't actually need his approval."

"She won't do anything that might upset Daddy, and not many things in life upset Roger Simmons more than losing money."

"He doesn't have to know."

"You aren't listening to me. She won't do it without him, and I'm trying to tell you he'll be a hard man to convince."

Lily Simmons seems to have issues with men, Ava thought. "I appreciate your candour. I assume this is your way of making sure that if she won't sign, it won't come back to bite you."

"She's an only child and she's her father's daughter. The bonds are incredibly tight," Ashton said.

"I didn't want you to have unrealistic expectations," Douglas added.

"I see that, and I appreciate it," she said.

"So how about the deal you mentioned? Is it still on?" Douglas asked. Then, for the first time since she had entered the house, he stared directly into her eyes. It was a hard, questioning look, the kind she imagined he had perfected at the poker table when trying to decide if his opponent was bluffing. She stared back, unwavering, until he turned away.

"If Lily Simmons refuses to sign and I believe you haven't interfered in the process, then I will return half of your personal money, but none of The River's."

Now Ashton looked at her with something other than hatred. "If Lily signs, you'll return our personal money and all of The River's. If she doesn't, we get half of our own money."

"That's what I just said." The offer to return the money both bought her time and acted as a sweetener. It was a lesson she had learned from her father, and one that had been reinforced time and again by Uncle. If you push people into a corner and give them no way out, they attack. It's human nature. She wanted them to cooperate — for her sake, not theirs — and offering them some of their own money back gave them a positive and compelling reason to do so. She had figured out that both cared more about their money than their reputations, and the interest her offer had sparked was proving her right. She knew she had an agreement.

"This isn't so hard, gentlemen," Ava said, holding out her hands, palms up. "Choice one: don't cooperate or pretend to cooperate, and lose your reputation, your business, your money, and your lives. Choice two: do as I say and keep them all."

"You have a deal," Douglas said.

"How about you?" she asked Ashton.

"I'm in," he said quickly.

"I thought you might be," Ava said. "Now, I do need to stress one thing — there's no time limit on our agreement. It doesn't expire in a month, a year, or ten years."

"That's clear," Douglas said.

A noise erupted from the kitchen. Carlo and Andy were hauling in the man who had been shot in the leg. They stood on either side of him, holding his arms, as he hopped in. Douglas looked at him with disgust.

It took fifteen minutes to get everyone double-taped and lying in separate rooms. When they were settled, she said to Carlo and Andy, "Take their wallets and go through the drawers. Make it look like a robbery. You can keep whatever you find; just don't use their credit cards. When you're done, come outside to the car."

As Carlo and Andy started going through Douglas's things, Ava went outside to join Martin. "We're just finishing up," she told him as she slid into the passenger seat.

"And?"

"Here is a confession signed by both of them," she said,

passing him a copy. "It could be useful if the Chief ever has an issue with them."

"What are you going to do with it?" Martin asked.

"It's a bargaining chip."

"Why do you need one?"

"I only got back a little of the money they stole. The bulk is sitting in an account in Cyprus and it takes three signatures to release it. I have only two."

"Who is the third?"

"Ashton's fiancée, and she's in London. I'm going there tonight."

"What about them?" he asked, pointing to the house.

"They're tied up and will stay that way until I can get Carlo and Andy and you out of Las Vegas."

"And they'll stay quiet?"

"Yes, I think they will. Neither of them is stupid."

The front door opened and Carlo and Andy emerged, each of them carrying his paper bag.

"You can open the trunk," Ava said. "We should leave the same way we came in."

They climbed back into the trunk in the same order. The smell of baby powder was gone, replaced by a faint odour of sweat.

They drove out of the complex without any complications, and two minutes later Martin pulled the car over to the side of the road. He popped the trunk, held out his hand to Ava, and pulled her out. She felt stiff, and the right side of her torso was throbbing. The boys climbed out after her.

"Wipe your prints off the cleaver and the gun and then toss them," she said.

As she watched them walk out into the desert to get rid of the weapons, she muttered, "Ninety-five."

"What?" Martin said.

"I'm ninety-five percent of the way to getting that money back."

"That's amazing."

"No, unfortunately, it isn't. Unless I can close, it doesn't mean a thing," Ava said. Half of her brain was making a list of all the things she had to do before she left Las Vegas; the other half was already in London.

33

AVA STRIPPED AS SOON AS SHE GOT TO HER HOTEL
room. She could smell sweat, car trunk, and dog urine. She
packed the clothes she had been wearing in a plastic laundry bag and tied it tight. Then she went into the bathroom
and showered.

When she came out a half-hour later, she put on a clean
black Giordano T-shirt and track pants, then packed the
rest of her clothes for the trip. She buried the laundry
bag in the bottom of her Louis Vuitton suitcase and put
a powder-blue Brooks Brothers shirt and a clean pair of
slacks in her "Double Happiness" bag. If she went directly
from Gatwick to Lily Simmons's office, she would need to
change on the plane.

She sat down near the window with her Moleskine notebook in her lap and began to organize her thoughts. With
the money she'd moved that day, her worst-case scenario
was that they would recoup a bit more than six million
dollars, and that factored in what she had promised to
give back to Douglas and Ashton even if she failed with
Simmons. It was lot of money — more than what they went

after on many jobs. But compared to the sixty-five million that was sitting in Cyprus, it was insignificant. All she had to do to get that jackpot was convince Lily Simmons to sign a piece of paper.

Ava checked the time. It was almost five o'clock — eight o'clock in the morning in Hong Kong. She needed to call Uncle.

"*Wei.*"

"We're back and it went well."

He listened without interruption as she described how the afternoon had gone. When she finished, his first question was, "How soon can you see this Simmons woman?"

"Late tomorrow. I'm flying to London tonight."

"And the woman doesn't know that Ashton and Douglas stole the money?"

"No."

"Could that be a problem?"

"The opposite, I would think. It has a certain shock value that I can embellish. Although, you know, that doesn't mean she'll react the way we want."

"If anyone can manage that, you can," Uncle said. "Now I need to call Chang. It is as I thought. Now that Ordonez knows for sure his brother was swindled, he is becoming fanatical about getting the money back. Chang says he can barely get him to focus on anything else. This news might calm him, but I will tell him only about your success in Las Vegas. I will leave the rest of it as vaguely promising. We do not want to raise expectations that we cannot guarantee will be met."

"Thank you."

"Now, how about Carlo and Andy?"

"I'm sending them to Los Angeles tonight. They'll be on a plane back to Hong Kong tomorrow."

"Ava, do you want to keep them closer?"

"Jackie Leung?"

"Yes. He has not been cornered yet. We have found out that he was talking to Sammy Wing, and I have sent Sonny to see Sammy."

"Wing is a friend."

"Wing was a friend. He is in the process of becoming one again."

"Uncle, I can't take Carlo and Andy to England with me. I have enough on my mind as it is."

"I am just being cautious."

"I know, and I appreciate the offer, but they would just slow me down. Now, when will you call Manila?"

"Not for a while. Chang is as old as me but he still likes to sleep."

"Good luck with him."

"He is not the problem."

"I know. Ordonez left a message on my phone last night. I didn't call him back."

"That is his nature: he feels compelled to manage everything. You would think that with an empire as big as his, he would have learned to let go. And this situation with his brother has probably only made things worse."

"I'm not going to call him and I'm not going to take his calls."

"I will handle it. Call me as soon as you have met that woman."

Ava put down the phone. *Let Uncle work his magic*, she thought. *I'll look after London. Let him handle Hong Kong and Manila.*

She turned on her computer and logged into her email account. She had received a new batch of messages, and almost without thinking she opened the most recent one from Mimi.

Hey sister,
Just wanted you to know that Derek's moved out of your place and into mine for a while. God, girl, why did you keep him from me? He can't stop playing with my tits, and I can't stop playing with his cock. I thought you said Chinese guys had small dicks. Liar.
Love,
Mimi

Ava almost threw her computer against the wall. It took her five minutes to collect herself. *I love them both*, she thought. *Maybe, just maybe, it will work*. But why did Mimi have to share so freely about their sex life?

Dear Mimi, Ava wrote. I'm happy for you if it works out, but I'm nervous that it won't. Either way, I don't want to read or hear any more about your tits or his cock. Love, Ava.

She closed the computer and opened her Moleskine notebook. Across the top of a blank page she wrote *Lily Simmons* and started piecing together a strategy for dealing with her. All she had to do, she reminded herself, was get the woman to sign a single piece of paper. The fact that it was worth $65 million was only a detail.

34

CARLO AND ANDY WERE IN THE LOBBY WHEN AVA CAME down with her bags at six thirty. Through the glass front door she saw Martin sitting outside in the Lincoln. "Let's go," she said to the boys. "I spoke with Uncle and he knows you're heading back."

They grinned, and she knew they'd had more than one beer in the hotel bar.

Martin opened the trunk of the car and helped Ava with her bags. "Thanks for doing this," Ava said.

"No problem."

The boys got into the back seat and Ava sat in the front beside Martin.

"I spoke to Chief Francis," Martin said as they headed south on Tropicana. "He called to find out how things went. I gave him a general description."

"Did you mention the gun, the shooting?"

"No, I thought it was best to leave that bit out."

"I think that's wise. There's no sense in alarming him."

"The fact that you have to go to London alarmed him enough."

"Why?"

"I think he was hoping that Las Vegas would be the end of this affair. The longer it goes on, the more concerned he is that it will go public."

"Douglas and Ashton won't say anything."

"He's more worried about your side."

"Martin, I gave him and you my word. I won't go back on it."

"How about the people you're working for?"

"I speak for them," she said, but his question touched a sore spot. Just how much control did she have over Tommy Ordonez? *Only as much influence as Uncle and Chang can exert*, she thought. The only way to make sure that never happened was to get the money — all of the money.

"That's what I told him."

"Thank you."

"One more thing about this afternoon, Ava. The Chief wanted to know what made you so sure Douglas and Ashton wouldn't go to the authorities and file some kind of complaint against you, against me."

Ava thought about her last conversation with the gambler and his partner, and then she put it aside. "I told them I would have them killed. And they believed me."

"The Chief thought it might be something like that."

They turned south and the airport came immediately into view. Hooters couldn't have been more than five minutes away. "I need you to do something for me before you leave tonight," Ava said.

"What's that?"

"You're the last one out. Just before you board, use a pay phone and call the security office at The Oasis. Tell them there was a home invasion and they need to go to Douglas's house."

"Okay."

Ava turned to Carlo and Andy. "Here you are, you two. I've written out your flight information for tonight and tomorrow, including confirmation numbers. I've also written down your hotel name, address, phone number, and reservation number, in Chinese and English."

"Thanks," Carlo said.

"But do me a favour — stay in your hotel tonight. Don't go wandering. Not many people in Los Angeles speak Cantonese, and I don't want to worry about the two of you getting lost. Uncle would never forgive me."

"*Momentai*," Andy said.

They were flying out of Terminal One, Ava out of Terminal Two. The airport road took Martin past her terminal first. He pulled up at the curb and got out of the car.

"See you soon," she said to the boys as she opened the door.

They each placed their right hand over their left fist, lowered their heads, and moved their hands up and down, the same sign of respect they had shown her when they landed.

Martin took Ava's bags out of the trunk and brought them to her. "I was going to say this was fun, but it was too stressful to qualify as fun. Anyway, I'm glad I met you."

She stepped forward and leaned towards him. He looked down shyly as she kissed him gently on both cheeks. "I'd like to keep in touch, maybe visit the Mohneida Nation one day. You're only a few hours down the road from Toronto."

"Anytime."

"Tell the Chief I'll call him when I've concluded my business in London — however it turns out."

"Actually, Ava, he'd rather you call me. He says every time he talks to you, he ends up doing something he doesn't want to."

She smiled, then turned and walked into the airport. She was halfway through a glass of wine in the first-class lounge when her cellphone rang. She checked the screen, which simply read PRIVATE NUMBER. "Ava Lee," she said.

"You didn't call me back."

She looked at her phone. It was one thing not to answer; it was another to hang up. "I was busy," she said.

She heard the now familiar wheeze as Ordonez drew in air. "I know. Uncle just called Chang with the news."

"Yes."

"It is a start."

"Yes, it is."

"But just a start. I want the rest of it back."

"That's something we all want to happen. Me, Uncle, Chang Wang, and, I'm sure — perhaps more than anyone — your brother."

"My brother has nothing to do with this anymore. They didn't steal from him; they stole from me. It was my money, the company's money, not his money."

A boarding announcement for another flight was being broadcast in the lounge. "They're boarding my plane, Mr. Ordonez," she lied. "I have to go."

"Where are you going?"

"I don't want to discuss that."

He hesitated. "Get the money," he said. "Get it all."

35

THE PLANE LANDED AT GATWICK FIVE MINUTES EARLY.
Ava cleared Immigration and Customs in less than twenty
minutes, then phoned Lily Simmons from the station platform while she waited for the express train to Victoria.
Simmons's mobile went directly to voicemail. Ava hung up
and then tried the office line, expecting to get an automated
receptionist. Instead she heard, "This is Lily Simmons."

Her voice was full of cheer. Ava noticed that her accent
was soft and rounded, the S's prolonged like a hiss.

"And this is Ava Lee."

"Ms. Lee, you are in London?"

Thank God she remembers, Ava thought. "I'm at Gatwick,
waiting for the express train to Victoria Station."

"From Victoria, you know, you can catch the Jubilee line
directly to Canary Wharf."

"Yes, I saw that."

"Your intention is to do that, to come directly to me?"

"It is."

"Excellent. Our offices are in One Canada Square; it's
the tallest building in the complex. Come to the forty-fifth

floor. I'll let our receptionist know you're expected."

"That's perfect."

"Well, I'll see you then. Looking forward to it."

"Me too," Ava said, as the train arrived.

She got off at Victoria Station, where she jostled her way through a crush of people to the subway platform. When she arrived at Canary Wharf, she placed her luggage in a locker and exited the station, her Chanel bag slung over her shoulder.

The air was cool and damp, and the sky was the colour of steel. She shivered, wishing she had a jacket with her. She was grateful that it wasn't windy and hoped that the rain would hold off. She had never been to Canary Wharf, but she knew that Toronto's Reichmann brothers had conceived it as Europe's financial epicentre. Although they had gone broke turning the barren and deserted West India Docks into a massive complex of office towers, others had realized the dream. Ten skyscrapers within immediate view housed more than a hundred thousand workers. One Canada Square was the tallest, with fifty storeys of office space topped by a pyramid-shaped roof.

At ten to five Ava entered the cavernous marble lobby. During the elevator ride to the forty-fifth floor, she checked herself in the full-length mirror on its back wall. At first glance she thought she looked graceful and elegant in her powder-blue shirt and tailored black slacks. At second glance she saw a woman dressed for battle, an avenging angel come to rain misery on Lily Simmons's life.

The reception area was small, not much larger than her room at Hooters. A young man wearing a white dress shirt and matching white tie was sitting at the front desk, focused on his computer screen. The only other furniture in the area was three chairs off to one side. Ava guessed that Smyth's occupied more than one floor, and that the forty-fifth was not the corporate floor.

Ava introduced herself to the receptionist. He turned away from his computer and greeted her with an annoyed look. She glanced at the screen and saw that he was playing Hearts. "Oh yes, Ms. Simmons has booked a conference room for you." He stood up abruptly. "Come with me."

She followed him down a narrow corridor in which every door was closed. Near the end of the hall he stopped, swung open a door, and showed her in. "I'll tell Ms. Simmons you're here," he said.

The conference room was as plain as the reception area, furnished with just a round wooden table, four chairs, and a small credenza with a phone on it. The walls were bare and the room had only one small window. Ava had thought Smyth's Investment Bank would be swankier.

At five o'clock on the dot, Lily Simmons walked into the room. Ava stood to meet her and was immediately overwhelmed by the woman's size. She was long and lanky, her height accentuated by her bony frame. She wore a plaid skirt that fell just below the knee, and Ava could see a smattering of freckles on her shins. Her white silk blouse was buttoned to the neck; her chest was almost completely flat. Her face was gaunt, full of hard lines, and her auburn hair, streaked with shots of ruby red, fell to her jawline in a mass of wild curls. *She is striking*, Ava thought.

"Hello, I'm Lily Simmons," she said, offering her hand.

Ava looked into green eyes that were friendly, if not entirely engaged. "I'm Ava Lee."

"Let's sit, shall we," Simmons said, and then looked at the

table. "Oh, they haven't offered you anything, have they? How rude. Coffee, tea, water?"

"Nothing, thank you."

"I come empty-handed, as you can see," Simmons said. "I normally bring paperwork with me to a meeting, but frankly I had no idea what it was you wanted to discuss. You are quite the mystery woman, you know."

"I beg your pardon."

"When my fiancé called last night to pass on your name, I was asleep. Rather neglectfully, I didn't take the time to ask him more about you. This morning I reached out to our offices in Asia — we're everywhere — and inquired if any of them knew of a woman named Ava Lee attached to what Jeremy described as a substantial Asian interest. None of them did. I called Jeremy several times today, hoping he could fill me in a bit more, but I haven't been able to connect with him. So there you are, Ms. Lee — I come unprepared, and I apologize for that."

"I'm representing the Ordonez Group in the Philippines."

"Yes, I have heard of them," Simmons said, shifting in her chair. "Cigarettes and beer, correct?"

"Among other things."

"At the most economical end of the market?"

"That's one way to put it."

"And they — what? They think there might be a market for those products in the U.K.?"

"My reason for being here has absolutely nothing to do with the normal business of the Ordonez Group," Ava said, opening her Chanel bag.

"Jeremy did mention that you might have an interest in investing in The River."

"No, we have no interest whatsoever in doing that."

"The mystery continues," Simmons said with a slight smile.

"Although The River is why I'm here," Ava said, taking the transfer request from her bag. She turned the document around and slid it across the table. "I would like you to sign this."

In Las Vegas, and then on the plane, Ava had mentally tested various strategies for broaching the topic with Lily Simmons. She had kept returning to this one. Uncle called it starting at the end: make it clear what you want up front and then work your way back. He thought the strategy saved time, eliminated questions and doubts, and softened resistance.

Simmons picked up the paper. Ava watched her green eyes shift from mild curiosity to utter confusion. "Just who are you, and what kind of game is this?" she said, throwing the request back onto the table.

Ava took out the confession. "This may explain things."

"I'm not sure I have any interest in reading anything else, or continuing this discussion. You're obviously here under some kind of false pretense. I think you should leave the premises," Simmons said, standing.

"Ms. Simmons, I understand that this is difficult — and truthfully, it isn't going to get any easier — but you do need to read this document. It's signed by both your fiancé and his partner, David Douglas. It's an admission of their guilt in orchestrating a scheme that defrauded my client, the Ordonez Group, and others of the $65 million I'm asking to be returned. This transfer request will allow that to happen."

Simmons looked down at Ava, who was holding out the confession for her to take. She reached for it, read the first few lines, and then sat down. She read to the end of the page, glanced at Ava, and then read it again. "This is absurd," she said.

"You don't say that with much conviction."

Simmons rose to her feet again. Holding the confession in her right hand, she crumpled it into a ball. Ava saw that her left hand was shaking and her cheeks had turned crimson. "Is this enough conviction for you?" Simmons shouted. Then she threw the ball of paper, which sailed past Ava onto the floor. Ava spun around to retrieve it, and when she looked up, Simmons was gone, the door slammed shut behind her.

Ava straightened out the paper, smoothing it with the palm of her hand, and put it on top of the transfer request. She sat back in her chair, her eyes on the door. In a matter of a few minutes she had lost control of the meeting. *What misjudgement*, she thought. *What a mess.*

Five minutes passed, and then five more. Ava tried to stay calm. She had been escorted from buildings before; there were worse kinds of exits. It was closing in on fifteen minutes when the door finally opened.

"I've just tried to call Jeremy. I can't reach him," Simmons said from the doorway.

"He won't speak with you," Ava said, trying not to show relief.

"What have you done to him . . . with him?" Simmons asked, taking two steps into the room.

Something's changed, Ava thought. Simmons seemed more confident, or maybe just less fearful, than when she had left. There was an edge to her voice, and her body thrust aggressively forward as if she was ready to charge at Ava. Before she had been reluctant to make eye contact; now her green eyes bore into Ava's, the colour heightened and glinting.

"Not a thing. We have an understanding, nothing more than that," Ava said. "Both he and Douglas have agreed to return the money they put into the holding company's account in Cyprus. In exchange, we won't pursue legal action against them and we will permit The River to keep functioning as a business. I asked Jeremy, as a courtesy, not to communicate with you until matters were resolved at this end. Now, you can try to call again if you wish, but I don't think you'll reach him."

"I'm not sure I want to talk to him anyway," Simmons said, picking up the confession, her eyes darting between the paper in her hands and Ava. When she had finished reading it again, she held it against her hip and closed her eyes. When she opened them, they were full of rage. Simmons raised the paper in front of her chest and, with her eyes locked on Ava's, ripped it into shreds.

She's on something, Ava thought. "That won't make it go away," she said.

"I don't believe anything you're telling me."

Ava reached into her bag and pulled out the paperwork that Jack Maynard and Felix Hunter had prepared for her. "Jeremy and David Douglas, as the confession states, manip-ulated the site's software so they could see all the cards at the table — so they could cheat. These are statistical anal-yses that detail the process and prove that it was indeed done," she said as softly as she could while still being sure she was heard. "The Cooper Island Gaming Commission, which regulates and administers your site, has this same data and agrees that it's proof positive. You can call them if you wish. They'll confirm it."

"Then why is the site still running? Why haven't they shut it down?"

"The Gaming Commission, like the Ordonez Group — and, I'm sure, like you — don't want the firestorm of negative publicity this information would generate if it was broadly known. The Commission has agreed to let us pursue our own course of action first. Mind you, if we're not successful, then both they and the Ordonez Group will be forced to seek other avenues."

"Such as?"

"Well, the Gaming Commission would certainly shut down your site, and the Ordonez Group would take legal action."

"The site hasn't been profitable until —"

"Until your fiancé and his partner started stealing," Ava said.

"If it isn't profitable, why should we care if they shut it down?" Simmons said.

She's not listening, Ava thought. "Shut down or not, if the money isn't returned there would still be legal action."

Simmons took another step forward. The only thing separating her from Ava was the small table. "That's rather a stupid threat to make. You know as well as I do how long and complicated a process that would be. God, with all the jurisdictions involved, who would know where to begin? It could take years to sort things out."

Whatever she's taken, it hasn't dulled her mind, Ava thought, and then tried to switch gears again. "True enough, at least from the civil side. But the Americans move more quickly when criminality is involved, and believe me, we would be seeking to have criminal charges brought against Douglas and Ashton. And you must know, Ms. Simmons, how harsh the American courts have been lately on white-collar crime. If Jeremy went to jail for less than five years I'd be surprised."

Simmons closed her eyes, and Ava sensed she was finally beginning to get through to her. "I thought it was too good to be true," Simmons muttered.

"What was too good?"

"The profits."

"They weren't profits."

"We'd been losing money for years until . . . until this started," Simmons said, slapping her hand on the transfer request still lying on the table.

"I have another copy of the confession if you need it. In fact, I have copies of everything," Ava said. "The only thing I want back is the transfer request with your signature on it."

Simmons shook her head. "That's not going to happen."

"You do have signing authority?"

"You obviously know that I do."

"So sign. Pick up a pen and write your name."

"It isn't that easy."

"Ms. Simmons, you don't seem to be grasping the consequences."

Simmons glared at Ava. "You don't have any idea about consequences," she said, saliva flying from her mouth.

Ava saw her hand tremble. "You're prepared to send your fiancé to jail?"

"Well, he is a thief, isn't he."

"Yes, he is."

"And he's betrayed the faith I put in him."

I'm losing her again, Ava thought. "You're angry with him, and no one can blame you for that," she said. "But let's be rational. Sign that piece of paper and then you and he can sort out your differences without all the legal baggage."

Simmons spun away from the table. In two steps she was at the window looking out at the Isle of Dogs. "I talked my father into financing this business," she said. "He was reluctant. I used every bit of persuasion I could. In the end he did it because I virtually begged him to."

"Yes, Jeremy told me that your father's money was behind it."

"Did he also tell you that my father detests him?"

"No."

"He's so self-absorbed he may not even realize it."

Ava felt another layer of leverage being stripped away. "I see" was all she could say.

"All he cares about is himself and his needs. He thinks that because I've never had much luck with men he can do with me as he wants. But there are limits to what I will do for him," she said, and turned to look at Ava. "He has no idea what he and that partner of his have put me through."

"I know this must be difficult —"

Simmons waved Ava to silence. "The River has been losing money from the day it started, and every fiscal quarter I've had to go to my father and give him the numbers, and whatever explanations I can come up with for them. More than once he'd had enough and told me to get out. I'd go to Jeremy and he'd tell me they were just around the corner from turning a profit. Always just around the corner.

And I believed him . . . At least, I wanted to believe him, because if I didn't and I told my father, the business would have been shut down in a heartbeat and Jeremy would have left me.

"Then, six months ago, Jeremy comes to me with a profit, a real profit. And every week, every month after that, the profits keep rolling in. I waited until the first full quarter was over before I gave my father the numbers. He was relieved, and when he got the second-quarter numbers, he was ecstatic. Quite suddenly Jeremy wasn't such an idiot and I wasn't such a fool for standing by him. In fact, I'd carried the day — he even said that. My father, I mean. He would have cut and run ages ago, he said. It was my judgement that got us out of the red . . ."

It was dark outside, and the interior light had turned the window into a murky mirror in which Ava watched Simmons speak. She was partially in shadow but Ava could see the intensity in her face and hear a growing determination in her voice. She knew where Simmons was heading, and there was nothing she could say to stop her from going there.

"There's no way you could be held responsible for any of this," Ava said.

"You don't know my father."

"I'm sorry."

"No, you're not. All you care about is your bloody money."

"It's my job. I take no pleasure in some of the things I have to do."

Simmons turned from the window and lunged towards the table. She moved so quickly that Ava jumped in surprise. The other woman stopped just short of physical contact, both hands resting on the table, her head thrust forward. "Well, you'll take no pleasure from what I have to say, because there's no way I'm going to sign that piece of paper."

"Ashton?"

"What about him?"

"You'd let him go to jail?"

"Do what you want with him," Simmons said. "I can defend a badly thought-out and badly run business, but I can't explain away a liar and a thief. Oh God, when I think about the things I said to my father about him, and how pleased my father was."

"Speaking of your father," Ava said gently, "Ashton or no Ashton, if you don't settle with us there will be legal proceedings against the company — against you, in all likelihood — and your father's name will be dragged into it."

"My father knew nothing. His assets are in a blind trust. I was responsible for administering it."

"That's not what you said earlier. And it isn't what Ashton told me."

"Not that anyone can ever prove it."

"But he did know."

Simmons shrugged. "You won't be able to discredit my father with this fiasco. I won't let you. I'll take full responsibility. So sue me, sue the company — I don't care. Put Jeremy in prison. I don't care about that either, and I won't raise a hand to help him. But when it comes to the money, I'll fight you every inch of the way. I have enough of a bank-roll in Cyprus to keep this going for years."

Ava glanced down at her notebook, at the talking points

she'd crafted in Las Vegas and on the plane. They had looked good on paper but were ineffective in practice. She felt a lump return to her chest, the same one she'd felt when Maggie Chew first told her about her father. "This won't go away," she said, closing her notebook and slipping it into her purse.

"Here, take this too," Simmons said, throwing the transfer request across the table.

"No, you keep it. You still might decide to sign it."

"There's no chance of that," Simmons said. She stood to one side. "Now, if you don't mind, I would like you to leave. And if there's anything else you want to communicate, please use your legal representatives."

Ava didn't move.

"I will call security if I have to."

"I have sex tapes," Ava said.

"What?"

"You heard me," Ava said, her eyes locked on Simmons.

The woman tried to hold Ava's gaze but gave way. "That's not true," she said, her voice breaking ever so slightly.

In that second Ava knew that Simmons wasn't sure. "I got them from Ashton."

Simmons blinked and then threw her head back. "That's not true. There are no such tapes."

"I didn't know anyone could enjoy a spanking quite so much. Jeremy filmed you over and over again. You hear about these things, of course, but until you actually see it — and all the peripheral sex play that goes along with it . . . Well, I found it rather lurid and upsetting. It didn't do anything for me, though I'm sure there are people who enjoy watching that kind of thing."

Simmons stared at Ava, her eyes wide and darting. Her face had collapsed. Her right hand reached for the table and she leaned on it for support.

"I'd be sorry if it had to come to that," Ava said.

"To what?"

"There's no need for me to say it, is there?"

"What are you trying to do?" Simmons demanded.

"Get my client's money back. Nothing more than that."

"With sex tapes?"

"Why not?"

"You'd release them?"

"Could there be a more receptive market for them than the British media? I mean, the daughter of a cabinet minister, a trusted senior officer at one of the country's most respected private banks? A former Olympian? They would eat it up, no?"

Simmons sat down. "You bitch," she said.

"Sign the request."

Simmons didn't respond.

"I've given you all the right reasons to do this and none of them seem to matter to you. So it comes down to this unfortunate one. Sign the transfer request and the tapes will disappear. Your fiancé will not go to jail and we can all be spared years of legal wrangling. Ms. Simmons, that money was stolen. This is the right thing for you to do under any circumstances. Tell yourself that and it might seem more palatable."

"I need to think."

"Yes, you do."

"I need time."

"I don't have a lot of time to give you."

"Tomorrow. Give me until tomorrow."

Ava hesitated. "This can't drag on."

"I need to talk to someone."

"What difference —"

"Please."

"Does his approval mean that much to you?"

Simmons turned her head away.

"Tomorrow. I'll give you until noon tomorrow, but if I don't hear from you by then —"

"How do I reach you?"

Ava slid a business card across the table. "My mobile number is the best way."

Simmons looked at the card, her eyes glazed and watery. "I'll call you," she said.

"Yes, you will."

"Now I would very much like you to leave."

Ava stood and walked towards the door. Stopping an inch away from Simmons, she said in a low voice, "Tomorrow, by noon."

36

IT WAS DARK WHEN SHE LEFT ONE CANADA SQUARE, and a light drizzle was falling. Ava's shirt and hair were damp by the time she got to the Canary Wharf tube station. The weather matched her mood. She had nearly lost Lily Simmons, and the way she had had to claw her way back depressed her. There were times when she came close to hating her job, and this was one of them. *Well, I did what I had to do*, she thought.

She reclaimed her bags and then debated whether to hail a taxi or take the subway to her hotel in Kensington. She checked the route map on the station wall. Kensington was just a few kilometres west of the very heart of Greater London, so she took the tube.

The drizzle had let up as she walked up the steps of High Street station and into Kensington. She had been to London before, and although she didn't know the hotel, she did know the area. On the north side of High Street was Kensington Gardens, and contiguous to the gardens on the east was Hyde Park. The south side was filled with trendy restaurants and upscale boutiques that extended to

Knightsbridge and the famed department store Harrods. Ava's hotel, the Fletcher, was on the south side of the street, directly across from Kensington Gardens. She could see the entrance from the station, its sign lit up red and wrapped around a curved glass overhang.

She checked in and found her way to the eighth floor. Her room was furnished with a king-size bed with a massive wooden headboard built into the wall. There was plenty of space for the fully equipped workstation, settee, easy chair, coffee table, armoire, and flat-screen television attached to the wall facing the bed.

Ava unpacked. She felt like a shower, for more reasons than one, but she had been out of touch for close to fifteen hours and felt the need to reconnect. It was one o'clock in the morning in Hong Kong, normally too late to call Uncle, but she knew he was probably waiting up to hear from her.

"I met the girl," Ava said after the familiar "*Wei*."

"How did it go?"

"I don't know yet."

"So she did not sign," Uncle said.

"No, she told me she needed some time to think about it. Actually, what I think she needs is talk it over with someone."

"Who?"

"Her father."

"You have not mentioned him before."

"It's his money that financed The River."

"Then why is it not his signature that we need?"

"It's complicated, Uncle. He's a politician, and his business assets, of which this is one, are in a blind trust. He's supposed to have nothing to do with how they're managed."

"Except?"

"She is his only child and quite devoted to him, and from what I've seen she's also afraid of him. She keeps him updated on everything."

"And does nothing without his approval?"

"Yes."

"And do you think he will approve?"

"I don't know that either."

"You thought you had some compelling arguments to make."

"Most of those had no effect."

"So, what makes you think there is any chance she will sign?"

"I finally found an argument that did impress her."

Uncle paused. "When do you talk to her next?"

"Tomorrow," Ava said, relieved that he hadn't asked about her leverage.

"That is reasonable."

"I thought so."

"What is your feeling?"

"I don't know with any certainty. I think she might sign. It's too much in her best interest for her to do anything else. But I've been wrong before."

"If she does not sign, I do not know how much longer I want us to pursue this. Your last telephone conversation with Ordonez upset him."

"He caught me by surprise by calling from an unidentified number."

"He thinks you were being deliberately rude to him, and certainly not as cooperative as he expects. Of course, he thinks we should all be kowtowing to him. Now he feels he has earned the right to berate me. The sooner we are finished with him, the better."

"I wasn't rude," Ava said, upset that Ordonez had been disrespectful to Uncle.

"I did not say that you were."

"I'm sorry, Uncle, I wasn't implying that you did."

"The man is ignorant and arrogant, and that is a terrible combination."

"I should have things settled one way or another by tomorrow."

Uncle went quiet, and she wondered if Tommy Ordonez had said more. "There have also been some developments in Hong Kong today."

"Jackie Leung?"

"Yes. Sonny met with Sammy Wing and they have agreed to pursue him together."

"But they haven't found him yet?"

"Not yet, but soon. I talked to Guangzhou tonight. They still will not cancel the contract. The two men who have been tracking you will not back off until we eliminate Leung."

"Tracking?"

"They have been using your credit card transactions to locate you. They went to Las Vegas but they thought you were at Wynn's."

"Where are they now?"

"Guangzhou did not know."

"Do I need to worry?"

"No, no. We will get Leung."

Ava had booked her flight to London using one of her credit cards. She tried to remember if she had seen any suspicious-looking Chinese men at the airport, on the plane, at Gatwick, on the train, in the tube. It was all a blank. "Then I won't worry," she said.

"That is best. Just focus on the woman. Call me as soon as you hear from her."

Ava closed her phone. She still felt a lingering disquiet from the way her meeting with Simmons had ended. Now it was joined by an intense dislike of Tommy Ordonez and the looming threat of Jackie Leung. *This job*, she thought, *is hard enough without all the side complications.* However quickly Uncle wanted to end it, it wouldn't be quick enough for her.

37

AVA GOT OUT OF THE SHOWER AND GENTLY TOWELLED off her damp body, which was still healing from the altercation in Las Vegas. She put on a clean black Giordano T-shirt and her Adidas track pants, then thought about dinner. The hotel was surrounded by restaurants, none of which she knew anything about. She called the concierge and asked for the best Italian restaurant in the area. He recommended Cibo, which was only a short walk from the hotel, in Russell Gardens.

When she got to the lobby, she saw that it was raining again. The concierge loaned her an umbrella and gave her directions to the restaurant. She crossed Kensington High Street, turned left, and walked north on Russell Road. About four hundred metres along she turned into the mews that was Russell Gardens.

Cibo was small and unassuming, its name simply written on a cloth awning that overhung a double window. When she stepped inside, she was quickly charmed by its intimate ambiance. The overwhelming aroma of garlic and olive oil washed over her and spiked her hunger.

She was led to a table near the back of the restaurant. The walls were covered with artwork, all of it original, the host said, and none of it traditional or stereotypically Italian. It looked to Ava as if the pieces had been chosen for their depth and wild colour. They were jarring and, it turned out, a suitable prelude to the meal.

She ordered *fricco*, wild mushrooms sautéed with potato and melted Asiago cheese, and a small plate of swordfish, tuna, and octopus marinated in thyme and olive oil. The waiter recommended Petrussa Pinot Bianco to accompany her food. She finished the first glass with the mushrooms and ordered a second with the fish. The food and wine were so good she thought a small plate of *linguine aglio olio* with one last glass of wine would be the perfect way to end her meal. But when she had finished the pasta, she noticed the man at the table next to hers eating some fish that looked succulent and smelled divine. He told her that it was monkfish baked with saffron. Ava ordered that as well, and finished a fourth glass of wine.

It was just past eight o'clock when she left the restaurant. The area was bustling; Ava was reminded that most Europeans ate dinner late, like the Chinese. The thought had barely crossed her mind when she spotted two Chinese men standing a few store windows ahead of her. They were glancing sideways in her direction.

Two couples were walking directly in front of Ava and two men were behind her. She moved closer to the couples and as close to the curb as she could get without stepping onto the street. The Chinese men were pretending to look in the window of an Indian restaurant. One of them was about six feet tall and looked beefy beneath a badly fitting raincoat. He had two earrings in his left ear. The other one was only slightly shorter and his hair was shaved into a mohawk, a style Ava knew was popular with some of the Chinese gangs. He wore a raincoat that hung loosely over jeans and designer running shoes.

As Ava drew near they turned away from the window and looked in her direction. She tipped her umbrella to the left to hide her face and pushed closer to the people in front of her. Just then the door to the Indian restaurant opened and a large group spilled out onto the sidewalk between Ava and the Chinese men. She quickened her pace, got in front of the couples she'd been following, and then slowed slightly so they covered her back.

It wasn't until she reached Kensington High Street that she turned and looked back up Russell Road. There was no sign of the Chinese men. When she got to the hotel entrance, she stopped just inside the door and waited for five minutes, surveying the street. When she was convinced they weren't following her, Ava returned the umbrella to the concierge, thanked him for his restaurant recommendation, and went directly to her room.

It was three o'clock in the morning in Hong Kong. She thought about calling Uncle and then dismissed the idea. What was she going to tell him? That she had seen two Chinese men on a street in London?

She flopped onto the bed and turned on the television. She thought about ordering another glass of wine from room service but decided she'd had enough. She made it through only fifteen minutes of *Antiques Roadshow* before falling asleep.

She dreamt about her father again. This time they were

on a Caribbean island, having arrived on a cruise ship that had docked for the day. They disembarked and then separated to go shopping. When Ava returned to the wharf, there were six ships in the harbour and she couldn't remember which one was hers. She raced from one to the next, begging the staff to let her board. No one would. Ava was left standing on the pier searching for her father, trying to find his face among the crowds gathered at the railings as the ships slowly pulled away.

She woke with a start, the sense of panic still clutching at her chest. Her cellphone was ringing. She looked at the bedside clock and saw that it was just past nine o'clock.

"Ava Lee," she said.

"This is Roger Simmons."

Ava sat upright. "Yes."

"You do know who I am?"

"Of course."

"We need to talk."

"I was expecting your daughter to call me."

"You have me instead."

"Did she tell you —"

"I don't want to discuss any of this on the phone. I want to meet with you. Tonight, if possible. I don't see any reason for putting it off."

"I don't either."

"Where are you staying?"

"The Fletcher Hotel," Ava said without thinking.

"I live close to there, on Praed Street. Ten minutes away, no more than that. There's a bar downstairs in your hotel called Alfie's. Meet me there in fifteen minutes."

"Yes, I can do that. Will Lily be with you?"

"No, but a man named Hawkins will. He is my executive assistant."

"Do I need to bring anything with me?"

"I don't think that's necessary. My daughter described to me the material you have."

"How will I recognize you?"

"I have red hair."

"And I —"

"My daughter described you. No need to add anything further."

"Fifteen minutes, then."

"Yes," he said, and hung up the phone.

I should have insisted that Lily be there, Ava thought too late, her head still partially lost in sleep.

She sat on the side of the bed, gathering herself together. She was dressed in her most casual clothes, and that wouldn't do for a meeting with a cabinet minister. She went into the bathroom, drank two glasses of water, and took some Tylenol. The clothes she'd worn that day were hanging on a hook on the back of the door. They didn't look too wrinkled, and all she could smell was a lingering trace of her Annick Goutal perfume. She dressed quickly, put on a touch of mascara and lipstick, fixed her hair with the ivory chignon pin, and left the room.

38

AVA STOOD AT THE ENTRANCE OF ALFIE'S SCANNING the bar for a head of red hair. When she couldn't find one, she asked for a table for three and was led to a secluded booth at the rear of the bar. She ordered a soda water with lime, sipping it while keeping her eyes locked on the front door. They arrived five minutes later. The man Ava assumed was Hawkins spotted her first and tapped Simmons on the arm; they walked towards her.

Lily Simmons was definitely her father's daughter, at least physically. The minister's hair was also red, almost ginger. He wore it parted down the middle and swept back on either side, the curls held in place by gel. He had a large face and his eye sockets receded like hers. His sharp cheekbones were accentuated by a long, pointed nose and a massive square jaw. He was a big man, easily six foot two, and he wasn't carrying any excess weight. The belt around his waist was tightly cinched and his broad shoulders strained his grey suit jacket. He sauntered like an athlete, a man who had spent his youth playing rugby instead of tennis.

Hawkins skittered behind Simmons. He was at least six inches shorter and twenty years younger than his boss. He had copied Simmons's distinctive hairstyle, though his sandy hair flopped onto his thin, pale face as he walked. Ava had seen his type before. They always seemed to trail in the wake of successful men.

When Simmons was a couple of steps away, Ava stood and offered her hand. He took it and then cast it aside, establishing only the slightest contact. She looked up into his eyes. They were smaller than his daughter's, shifty and alert.

"Do you see anyone we know?" he asked Hawkins.

"No, Minister."

"Then we'll sit."

Ava resumed her seat on the right side of the booth. Simmons slid in beside her, keeping a few feet away. Hawkins sat on the minister's far left, physically removed from both of them but still within earshot.

The waiter came and Simmons waved him away. "We won't be here that long, thank you."

"Mr. Simmons —" Ava began.

"The proper term of address is Minister, Mr. Minister, or sir," Hawkins said.

"That's no matter," Simmons said, and then turned to Ava. "You do understand that I am a minister of the Crown?"

"I do."

"But I am not here in that capacity."

"I see."

"I'm here as a father."

"So Lily obviously discussed our chat with you. I'm sorry that it —"

"Spare me your nonsense."

"I beg your pardon."

"You heard me."

Ava looked at him. His face was turned away from her, his eyes fixed on the bar. "I thought we were going to talk about our mutual problem," she said.

"I would prefer it if I talked and you listened," he said.

His jaw was set firmly and his body was stiff. Ava knew he was struggling to contain himself. "That's fine," she said.

"Lily said you were clever, so I assume I won't have to repeat any of this. In case there is any misunderstanding, Hawkins here will act as a witness."

"A witness to what?"

"A witness to my outright refusal to allow you to blackmail my daughter, and to my promise that if you release so much as a single foot of those tapes you say you have, I will pursue you legally to the full extent of British law and beyond."

Ava drew a deep breath and detected the smell of Scotch. "Mr. Simmons, I met with your daughter today to try to resolve a business dispute in an amicable way. A company, one that you have invested in, has orchestrated a large-scale theft. The two partners in that company have already admitted to culpability. All we want is the return of the money that was stolen. The offer we made to the partners, and to your daughter, is, we believe, fair in the extreme. Return the money and we will forego any civil or criminal legal remedies. We will make sure the entire affair is kept private. And The River can continue to operate."

"I know nothing about any such problem, and I have barely any familiarity with the investment," Simmons said.

"Sir, you can deny it all you want —"

Simmons banged his fist on the table so hard that Ava's glass jumped and she had to grab it to stop it from spilling. "Are you calling me a liar?" he demanded.

"Sir, people can hear you," Hawkins said.

"Let them. I won't sit and listen to this tripe."

"Ms. Lee, the Minister is obviously upset," Hawkins said, leaning towards her. "His daughter came to him earlier this evening and relayed the content of your meeting this afternoon. She was very emotional. She wondered if she should go to the police, but the Minister prevailed upon her to wait until he had had a chance to speak with you."

"I don't mean to be impolite, and I'm certainly not in the blackmail business," Ava said to both of them, "but I don't know how else to say that two partners in a business financed by the minister — directly or indirectly — and of which his daughter is a director and signing officer, stole more than sixty million dollars from my clients."

"You need to prove that," Simmons said.

"I have documentation. I gave it to your daughter. And in our earlier phone conversation you said you were aware of it."

"Don't tell me what I said or didn't say."

"Then let me be clear, for the record," Ava said. "We have proof positive that Jeremy Ashton and David Douglas orchestrated a fraud that netted The River more than sixty million dollars. I met with your daughter to ask for the money back. Ashton and Douglas have already signed the transfer request; all I need is her signature. When she refused to give it to me, I explained that we would sue the company and its officers. I also told her that we would seek criminal charges against Ashton and Douglas."

"According to my daughter you have allegations, not proof, and when she pointed that out to you, the blackmail attempt ensued," Simmons said.

"I can give you whatever documentation you require," Ava said.

"I can't look at it, can I, Hawkins."

"No, sir."

They might be taping this conversation, Ava thought. It was all too careful, and Hawkins's presence was too contrived. "So why are you here?" Ava asked.

"I told you at the outset. I want you to leave my daughter alone."

"If we can't settle this dispute, that's impossible. We will sue the company and we will file criminal charges."

"Sue away. I've been in business my entire life; I understand that process. It will take years to drag through the courts, assuming you can find a court to hear the case."

"And your daughter's fiancé? You have no concerns about him, about how all this might affect her?"

"Jeremy Ashton is an ass. I never understood what my daughter saw in him. But I'm realistic. She isn't any prize catch, and she did seem to love him, so I supported her choice until now. But that's over — I want him out of her life. If he did wrong and you can put him in jail, as you told my daughter you would when you were attempting to intimidate her, then I say, 'More power to you.' You have my blessing, and she won't interfere."

Ava sipped her soda water. She knew where the conversation was headed but she had no idea how to stop it. "Would you care for a drink now?" she asked.

Simmons shook his head. Then he turned to Hawkins. "I've changed my mind. Get me a single malt, neat."

"Yes, Minister."

"And bring me another soda with lime," Ava said.

Hawkins looked at Simmons. "What are you waiting for?" Simmons snapped.

When he was gone, Ava moved closer to Simmons and said quietly, "We won't let go of this. We'll do whatever we have to do. You have to understand that. You can pretend that you know nothing, but it doesn't change a thing."

"You fucking chink," he murmured.

Ava froze. "Pardon?"

"You heard me. You and the other fucking chinks you work with can go to hell. You think you can come here and operate the way you do at home. I've done business with the Chinese; I know how it works. If it isn't bribery, it's extortion."

"I'm Canadian, and my client is in the Philippines," Ava said, struggling to maintain control.

"Makes no difference which flag you wave. You're all Chinese at heart, aren't you."

"My client, the Ordonez Group, is based in Manila and is a respected multinational corporation."

"You can say that with a straight face?"

"Yes."

"What, with the same sincerity you show when you talk about lawsuits and criminal charges, when all the time you're holding sex tapes over my daughter's head?"

"Our claims are legitimate," Ava said.

"Then take them to fucking court."

"As you said, that takes time."

"And you people never want to take the time, do you."

Ava sipped the last of her soda water. She saw that Hawkins was still standing at the bar trying to get the bartender's attention. "We will release the tapes, you know," she said.

Simmons leaned back. "Go ahead," he said.

"What?"

"You heard me. Go ahead."

"Your daughter —"

"It will be media fodder for a couple of days, maybe a week. Her mother will be embarrassed and her friends will probably find it amusing. It will pass."

"She'll be humiliated."

He shrugged. "She'll get over it."

"How about your reputation?"

He gave her a half-smile. "I'll put on a brave face and stand by my daughter. I have a reputation for being a hard-ass, you know. This could show my softer side, earn me some sympathy."

"I don't understand how you could —"

"How I could what? Let that happen? This is the United Kingdom, not some jacked-up Third World country where extortion always wins out because people are worried about their precious fucking face. Right now sixty million dollars is worth more to me than my daughter's face."

Hawkins was approaching the table. Simmons saw him first and slid away from Ava. "Ms. Lee was just telling me that she might release those sex tapes my daughter spoke about," he said. "What do you think of that?"

"You are very good," Ava said quietly.

"Thank you," Simmons said.

Hawkins set their drinks on the table. "Surely there is another solution," he said.

"Give us back the money that was stolen," Ava said.

"You'll need to take that up with my daughter," Simmons said, downing the Scotch in one gulp. "And that might not be easy. She's meeting with a lawyer tonight, and I suspect they will advise her to avoid any further contact with you."

"I have to say, Mr. Simmons, that I don't think our chairman, Tommy Ordonez, is going to be happy when I relay this conversation to him. Up until now he hasn't been aware of your involvement, directly or indirectly, in this matter. But when I tell him, I know he'll be surprised by your refusal to pay back money that was so obviously stolen. He will also be rather dismayed by some of the attitudes you've expressed."

"Ms. Lee, I know who Tommy Ordonez is. I know he's a Chinese hiding behind a Filipino name. I also know that he built his business on cheap beer and cigarettes, and I can only imagine how many people he paid off in the Philippines and China along the way. So I'm not going to be offended by any poor opinion he may have of me."

"Minister," Hawkins said, caution in his voice.

"I'll let Mr. Ordonez know how you feel," Ava said.

"Do that," Simmons said. "I actually met him once, you know. In Singapore at a dinner, when I was still running my generator business. He had a strange voice, like a monkey's. Don't you think he squeaks like a monkey?"

"Minister, I think we should be leaving now," Hawkins said, sliding from the booth.

Simmons also stood, then looked down at Ava. "Our dinner host pulled me aside and apologized for seating me next to him. He told me where Ordonez was from and explained how, despite having hardly any education and not an ounce of class, he'd built his business. He said he thought Ordonez was worth maybe a billion dollars, but it didn't matter how much money he had, you still can't shine shit . . . *You still can't shine shit.*"

Ava blinked, scarcely believing his crudeness. Even Hawkins seemed disturbed by it. "Minister, we must leave," he said.

"Of course," Simmons said, smirking at Ava.

Ava sat rooted, her eyes on her soda and lime. When she looked up again, they were walking towards the exit. Her palms felt clammy. Her mind had trouble focusing on where she was. She guessed that was how it felt to lose $65 million.

39

AVA SAT AT THE DESK IN HER ROOM UNTIL ONE IN THE morning, her notebook open, forcing herself to review the strategy that had gone so wrong.

She had bought a bottle of white Burgundy in the hotel bar and brought it up to her room. She had finished half of it, which meant that she'd drunk a bottle and a half of wine that night. It had little impact, however — her mind and her senses were as sharp as ever. And no matter how she rearranged her notes and reworked the strategy, both were telling her she was in big, big trouble.

She was going to have to call Uncle, and he'd call Chang, and Chang would talk to Ordonez, and then what? Would he blow the whole thing up? Would he go public? Would the accusations and the lawsuits start flying? And if they did, how could she keep the Mohneida out of it? Even as she asked herself these questions she knew the answers. Ordonez would sue The River, and if his lawyers were any good — and she was sure they were — they would sue the Mohneida as well. The letter of indemnification she'd given Chief Francis would be brushed aside as a useless piece of paper signed by someone not authorized to act on behalf of the Ordonez Group. As much as she cared about the money, the idea of Chief Francis's thinking she had lied to him and betrayed him bothered her more.

It was eight in the morning in Hong Kong. She knew she should make the phone call, but she went back to her notebook one more time. The only chance she had to resolve this was to get Roger Simmons to change his position. Everyone else was irrelevant.

She went online and began to read everything she could find on him. There was hardly anything of a personal nature. The first part of his life was all about business; his interest in politics had emerged once he became a rich man. In his earliest political days he had served two terms as president of the local Conservative constituency association. The media had identified him early on as a major financial backer of the national party and a potential parliamentary candidate. But about ten years ago he had gone public with his disenchantment about some Conservative Party policies, specifically those related to immigration. He had left the party briefly and attached himself to a right-wing movement that wanted to repeal immigration laws that gave preferential treatment to citizens of many of Britain's former colonies. The colonies cited were in the Caribbean, Africa, and Asia. *Now why isn't that a surprise?* Ava thought.

Simmons's public flirtation with the far right hadn't lasted long. He was wooed back to the Conservative Party and made a successful run for a seat in Parliament. His success in business had resonated with serious newspapers such as the *Times* and the *Guardian*, which earmarked him for a future Cabinet post. The party elite obviously thought highly of him; he was rewarded with a position as parliamentary secretary two years after the election and had become a full-fledged cabinet minister the year before. There was already talk of him as one of a handful of high fliers in the party, and that a more senior Cabinet posting, such as the Exchequer or maybe even the Foreign Office, wasn't beyond his reach. The *Daily Standard* had even gone so far as to say that the "local lad" had the brains and the toughness to become prime minister; that story had a link to a BBC television interview, which Ava clicked on.

The questions were general and gentle in nature. Simmons downplayed his business achievements, spoke glowingly about the prime minister and his Cabinet, and when asked about his own ambitions said he was happy to serve in whatever capacity his leader saw fit for him. The interviewer then asked if he had any interest in heading the party, in leading the country. Simmons laughed off the question, saying that his only ambition was to do his job as well as he could, every day of the week.

Ava remembered Jeremy Ashton's words about politics being Simmons's latest ego trip, and the remark he'd made about Simmons believing he was only one step away from the Prime Minister's Office. It brought to mind a Canadian client she and Uncle had worked with, a man who had a hand in both the business and political spheres. Ava had asked him how the two cultures differed.

"In business," the client had said, "sooner or later most people find out where they fit best. The sales and marketing guy wants to do sales and marketing; he doesn't dream about becoming the chief financial officer. And the CFO, well, he's got no interest in product development. People find their level of competence and are normally content about where they fit in the structure.

"Politics," he went on, "is a completely different animal. Everyone who's in the game has — whether they admit it or not — an oversized ego. The system fawns over them until most members of Parliament lose all sense of perspective. There isn't a single backbencher in the House who doesn't believe he or she belongs in Cabinet and could manage any portfolio. And there isn't a single cabinet minister who doesn't secretly believe he or she would make a terrific prime minister. That kind of ambition is the nature of the beast. Status and stature within the peer group becomes the most important thing in their lives. It's the only way the score is kept."

Ava wondered aloud, "What in life matters most to Roger Simmons?" She stopped watching the BBC interview and saw that it was now past nine o'clock in Hong Kong. She knew she couldn't put off making the call to Uncle any longer.

"Uncle, it's Ava," she said when he answered.

"Have you heard from the girl?"

"No, but I met with her father last night."

"Will the girl sign?"

"Not unless he tells her to."

"And will he?"

"Not as things stand."

He paused. "That is unfortunate."

"She is not her own woman."

"Is there any way to persuade him?"

"I've tried to come up with something, and I have at least

a sliver of an idea," Ava said. She paused, taking a deep breath. "I need to speak to Tommy Ordonez. I'm not sure how he'll react to what I have to say, so I thought I would run it past you first."

They spoke for fifteen minutes, Uncle listening quietly at first, then interjecting questions, anger steadily creeping into his voice. When Ava had finished, he asked, "Do you have Ordonez's phone number?"

"I have the number he used to call me."

"That will work," Uncle said. "But wait about half an hour. I want to call Chang first. He needs to know what you want to do. His support will be invaluable."

"Thank you. I'm sorry I have to use this route."

"What choice is left?"

"None that I can think of," she said. "Uncle, one more thing. I'm going to be aggressive with Ordonez."

He paused. "You have that right."

Ava closed her cellphone. The notebook was still open in front of her, and she noticed the phone numbers for Lily Simmons. *I'm not entirely finished with you*, she thought.

She called the home number first, and after four rings it went to voicemail. Simmons's mobile did the same. Ava redialled the home number, and when Lily Simmons's voice prompted a message she said, "Ms. Simmons, this is Ava Lee calling. Please don't hang up until you've listened to my message. First, and perhaps most important to you, I am not going to release the tapes. I repeat, I am not going to release the tapes. But you should know that when I met with your father tonight, he told me to go ahead and do exactly that. I must say I was appalled by his attitude. He said he thought it was something you would get over fast enough, and that on the political side it might actually do him some good. I can't understand the logic of that, but then I'm not English, I'm not a man, and I'm not a politician. Anyway, your father's attitude is something you have to bear, and I can only say that I feel some sympathy for you in that regard.

"That's the good news. The bad news is that we will be pursuing The River and all its officers and directors for the $65 million. We will also have criminal charges brought against your fiancé and David Douglas in the United States. As far as the lawsuits are concerned, I can only tell you that I know we will eventually win. I don't know how long it will take or how much it will cost, but we will not stop until we get our money back."

Nothing may come of it, Ava thought, *but it's never unwise to plant seeds of doubt.*

She pushed her chair back from the desk and went into the bathroom, took off her slacks and shirt, and brushed her teeth and washed her face. Then she threw on a T-shirt and crawled into bed with her cellphone by her side. She waited until the full half-hour had elapsed and then waited another five minutes for good measure before picking up the phone.

"Ordonez."

"This is Ava Lee."

He breathed rapidly, as if, Ava thought, he was struggling for air. "Chang spoke to me and then the two of us spoke to Uncle. This man Simmons, he said I squeak like a monkey?"

"He did."

"He said, 'You can't shine shit'?"

"Yes."

"And I'm the piece of shit that can't be shined?"

"Yes."

"And he said I built my business using bribes and extortion?"

"He did."

"And he called me a fucking chink?"

"You and others."

"And he is a cabinet minister in the British government?"

"Yes, he is."

"Where am I supposed to have met him?"

"Singapore."

Ordonez's breathing slowed as he took deeper and deeper breaths. "I want you to get that fucker! I don't care what you have to do!" he screamed.

"No!" Ava yelled back. "This is on you, not me!"

He hesitated. Ava waited, determined to remain quiet until he asked the question.

"What do you mean?" he snapped.

"This has got to be about the money," she said.

"What?"

"I've found the money, all of it, but I can't get it until Simmons's daughter signs off on the transfer. And she won't do that unless he tells her to. So this is about getting him to do exactly that, and the only person who can make that happen is you. So it's on you. What I don't know is whether you're up to it."

"Up to what? I'd kill him myself if I could get in front of him," Ordonez said.

"Listen to me. Simmons is a man who loves money more than his family, a man with an outsized ego, an inflated sense of his position in the world, and huge expectations for his future," Ava said, conscious that she could be describing Ordonez himself. "The best way to hurt him is by getting your money back and at the same time threatening what he sees as that future."

"What do you want me to do?" he said slowly.

"How powerful are you?"

"What?"

"I know what Chang Wang and Uncle say, but is it real?"

He paused, and Ava thought, *This is where I lose him.*

"Do you doubt them? Do you doubt me?" he snapped.

"I need to know what's real."

"Tell me what you want me to do," he said.

"We need political pressure applied — serious and heavy political pressure. Can you deliver that?"

"You have to be more specific."

"Your contacts need to put pressure on the highest levels of the U.K. government. Our story is that Simmons is a racist with a particular bias against the Chinese and that he has caused you personal harm. They need to know what he said and they need to be told that fences must be mended — especially the fences around Tommy Ordonez. Explain to them about the missing money and make sure they know that I'm here in London to collect it. Tell them that Simmons is the key to getting it back. Don't say he stole it; just emphasize that he has to play a major role if the money is to be returned. Your contacts need to get the Brits to understand that if the money is returned, Tommy Ordonez will be willing to forget some of the things that were said. If it isn't returned, they must make it very clear that there will be widespread repercussions."

"I'll call Arellano," Ordonez said.

Ava searched her memory. "The president of the Philippines?"

"Yes."

"He'll cooperate?"

"I own him. At least, I own the biggest part of him."

"That's good."

"And I'll call Tong in Beijing."

"The vice-premier?"

"His oldest son runs our Shanghai office."

"Mr. Ordonez," Ava said carefully, "those are big guns. Can you control them?"

"I said I'd call them!" he shouted. "They'll take my calls."

"But can you control them?"

"Why do you keep asking that?"

"Because we can't have them running off half-cocked. We need to make sure the focus is on the money and an apology to Tommy Ordonez. We can't have them demanding Simmons's head. If he loses his Cabinet post, then he doesn't have any reason to cut a deal."

Ordonez went quiet. All she could hear was his deep, heavy breathing, and she began to wonder if she had offended him again. Then he said, "You aren't the only one who understands how things work."

"Of course not."

"I'll make the calls."

"Thank you."

"You'll hear from someone," he said, and slammed down the phone.

Ava closed her cellphone and rolled off the bed. She retrieved her half-full bottle of wine from the work station and poured a glass. "Cheers," she said, raising the glass in the air. She took a long swallow.

She turned on the television and tried to focus, but her mind was in overdrive, imagining the conversation Tommy Ordonez was having with Felipe Arellano at that very moment. She finished off the wine, filled her glass with the balance of the bottle, and downed it quickly. She turned off the television and lay on her back.

Her last thought before falling asleep was that she had forgotten to tell Uncle about the two Chinese men she'd seen on the street.

40

AVA'S CELLPHONE RANG AT FOUR THIRTY IN THE MORNING.

"I know it is probably too early to call," Uncle said, "but I thought you would like to know that Felipe Arellano just left Ordonez's office."

"His office?"

"Yes. After he spoke to you he called Arellano. According to Chang, he went ballistic over the phone. Chang is not sure how much of it was acting and how much was real. Whatever, it was effective. Arellano, along with his full team, went to Ordonez's office, and by the time Ordonez was finished with him, the President could hardly wait to contact London."

"I thought he might be exaggerating about that relationship," Ava said.

"Ordonez owns him."

"So he said."

"And what about Vice-Premier Tong?"

"That is a far more delicate arrangement. Even with all his money and investments, Ordonez is a minnow to Tong. Any help Ordonez wants from China will have to be carefully phrased and presented as a request for a favour. The good thing is that Tong loves his son more than anything, and he knows that his son's success is tied to Ordonez. So he will listen to what Ordonez has to say, and if he can do anything to help — without putting himself at risk — he will probably do it."

"So they haven't spoken yet?"

"Yes, they have, but Chang was not there when they did, and he says Ordonez was not forthcoming with details."

"Was he worried by that?"

"Not particularly."

"So now we wait," Ava said.

"Chang said that the British are to contact you directly if they need more information. He gave them your cell number, so keep it on."

"I will."

"Call me the moment you hear anything. I will keep my phone on as well," Uncle said. "Ava, my instinct is that this thing will either move quickly or not at all. If you do not hear from anyone by mid- to late afternoon, you should start planning your trip home. We have exhausted our options. There is not much to be gained by spending time and money just spinning our wheels. We have the money you got from the men in Las Vegas. Everyone will have to be satisfied with that."

"I agree."

Ava tried to fall asleep again but her mind was racing. At five o'clock she heard a noise at the door and knew the newspapers had been delivered. She slid out of bed and dropped to her knees. For five minutes she prayed, asking St. Jude to look after her for one more day.

She got up and collected the *Times* and the *Wall Street Journal* at the door, made herself a Starbucks VIA Ready Brew, and pushed a chair towards the window. She opened the curtains and looked out onto High Street. The sidewalk and roads were wet, but the streetlights were now illuminating only a fine mist.

She read both papers from cover to cover, made herself two more coffees, and at six thirty turned on her computer. She returned to the web pages she'd been reading about Roger Simmons and watched the BBC interview one more time. *He's a man with ambition*, she thought. The more she listened to him, the more hypocritical he sounded.

Ava stretched her arms over her head, yawned, and then yelped as pain coursed through her ribcage. She was still dressed only in panties and a T-shirt, and her legs felt chilled. She stood up and looked outside. The sun had finally emerged, the sidewalk was dry, and Kensington Gardens was lit up so brightly it looked as if the leaves on the trees had been polished. Ava went to the bathroom, washed, brushed her teeth and hair, and put on her running gear. She debated about putting her mobile in her pocket but decided not to.

She left the hotel, crossed Kensington High Street, and entered Hyde Park at the Alexandra Gate. She ran north across the Serpentine Bridge and continued to North Carriage Drive, where she turned east. She thought about Roger Simmons as she ran. A good run usually cleared her head, but the pathways were busy and she couldn't get to full speed as she dodged in-line skaters and groups of walkers. Negative thoughts began to intrude. She became convinced that no one would call her, that Roger Simmons was going to get a free pass. In the light of day her late-night inspiration seemed more wishful thinking than cunning strategy. She sped along to Stanhope Palace Gate and then south through the heart of the park, to the pathway that ran along the south bank of the Serpentine. She ran as fast as she could, trying to burn off the negativity that gnawed at her.

She checked her cellphone as soon as she got back to the room. Nothing. She sat down at the computer and emailed her travel agent in Toronto, asking her to hold a seat on the day's last flight from Heathrow to Pearson. *I'll give it the entire day*, she thought as she headed for the bathroom and a shower.

Ava stripped and had just turned on the water when she thought she heard her phone ring. She considered running to the bedroom to answer it, but the sound died. Perhaps she had just imagined it.

When she came out of the bathroom, she put on a clean T-shirt and track pants and began thinking about where to have lunch. Moving towards the room phone to call the concierge, she noticed the message light blinking on her cellphone. A man named Anderson had left a number, asking her to call him back.

"Prime Minister's Office," a receptionist answered.

Ava drew a deep breath. *God bless Tommy Ordonez*, she thought. "My name is Ava Lee. Someone named Anderson left me a message and asked me to call him back."

"That would be Daniel Anderson. I'll put you through." The line went silent for a few seconds.

"Ms. Lee, thank you for calling back."

Ava heard paper rustling in the background. "Are you Daniel Anderson?"

"I am."

"And am I on speaker phone?"

"Yes, you are."

"And are there other people with you?"

"No, I was sorting through some papers, but I'm done now. Just a second," he said. Ava heard him pick up the receiver. "So, thank you for calling back."

"You're welcome, although I'm not sure why you phoned me in the first place."

"We understand you're here in the U.K. on business."

"Yes."

"Has it been going well?"

"No, it hasn't."

"Ah. We were told the same thing — that there were some issues."

"Mr. Anderson, who is *we*?"

"Ms. Lee, I think you should expect a phone call from Roger Simmons at some point during the day," Anderson said, sliding around her question.

"I wish I shared your confidence."

He hesitated. "Look, I don't want to go into this any further than I already have. What I would like to do, sometime later today, is give you a bell to see how your day has progressed. Would you be amenable to that?"

"I don't see why not."

"Excellent. Well, good luck to you then," Anderson said and hung up.

It was close to midnight in Hong Kong. Ava phoned Uncle.

"I've just received a call from the British prime minister's office and was told to expect Roger Simmons to contact me," she blurted.

"We were told something like that might happen," he said over the noise of dishes clattering in the background.

"By whom?"

"Arellano, and then by Tong as well. They both told Ordonez they had spoken to the Prime Minister, or at least someone senior in his office — you can never be sure with these people. In any event, the message got delivered."

"And it seems that the Prime Minister, or someone in his office, has spoken to Simmons."

"It seems that way."

"That still doesn't mean he's going to give us what we want," Ava said.

"No, but at least the door is open again. And we will find out what matters most to Simmons — his reputation and position as a minister of the Crown, or fighting lawsuits and negative publicity as a private citizen trying to hang on to stolen money."

"Would they have made the choice that clear-cut?"

"Let's hope it is in his mind, although I am sure that Arellano and Tong did not make it that blatant, and I am sure the Prime Minister did not make any promises. But they know each other and understand each other's needs. Some things do not have to be said between men in high positions."

"I was planning to fly to Toronto late tonight. I'm going to cancel."

"Yes, you need to wait."

Ava went over to the window. The sky was cloud-free, the sun shining brightly. As she looked down at the street she spotted the two men from the day before. They were standing on the sidewalk in front of Kensington Gardens, directly across the street from the hotel. Even from that distance she could make out the one with the mohawk.

"Uncle, I think Jackie Leung's men are here," she said quietly.

"What?"

"I saw two men last night, and now they're back. They're outside my hotel, facing the entrance."

"The contract has been cancelled," Uncle said.

It was Ava's turn to be surprised. "What?"

"Jackie Leung is dead."

"When?"

"Sonny caught up with him tonight. Leung fell into Victoria Harbour. It turns out he could not swim."

"And the contract?"

"Cancelled as of fifteen minutes ago. I had just finished talking to Guangzhou when you called."

"No one seems to have told the two guys outside my hotel."

"There has not been much time."

"What do you want me to do?"

Uncle paused. "Describe the men to me."

She did, emphasizing the mohawk and the earrings.

"It sounds like it could be them. I will call Guangzhou on my other phone to confirm."

She tried to listen but his conversation was muffled. When he came back on the phone, the first thing Ava heard was a heavy sigh. "It is definitely them. The one with the earrings is the leader; his name is Ko. Guangzhou has been trying to contact them. They tell me their mobile phones are off."

"So what am I supposed to do?"

"Write down this phone number," he said. "It is the number of the boss in Guangzhou. His name is Li. He is waiting by his phone now and will not leave until he hears from them. He suggests that you go outside and talk to them. Tell them the contract is cancelled and they need to talk to Li."

She was still standing by the window looking down at them. Their raincoats were buttoned, and she knew that beneath the folds, probably tucked into their belts, they were carrying weapons. She could only hope they were knives or machetes and not guns.

"Okay, I guess I can't stay in my room all day waiting for them to turn on their phones," she said. "I'll go downstairs and talk to them."

"Call me back as soon as you are finished," he said.

41

AVA STOOD BY THE WINDOW, STARING DOWN AT THE two Chinese men. They were smoking, their backs pressed against the wrought-iron fence that fronted the Gardens. The one called Ko was talking to his partner, a small smile on his face. They looked relaxed and comfortable, but Ava noticed that their eyes never wandered from the hotel entrance.

She grabbed her phone and put the piece of paper with Li's number on it into her pocket. She debated putting her jacket on and decided it was warm enough for just her tee. *Besides, I shouldn't be outside that long*, she thought. She took the elevator to the lobby and walked out the front door, stopping when she got to the entrance so that she was framed by it and clearly visible.

Ko was talking to his partner, but he glanced across the street and saw her. His eyes locked on to Ava and, without turning, he elbowed his partner. Ava raised a hand to acknowledge them, just as the sightline between the hotel and the opposite sidewalk was blocked by several large trucks waiting for the light to change.

Ava waited for the traffic to shift, reluctant to get closer until she could see them again. It was a long light, and it seemed like several minutes before the trucks moved on and her sightline was clear. When she looked across the street, Ko and his partner were gone.

She scanned the length of the sidewalk in front of the Gardens and saw no one she recognized. There was nothing to her left but the intersection and traffic moving along High Street. She looked to her right. The sidewalk ran for about fifty metres to the next light, and standing alone beside it was Ko. There was no other person between him and her.

Ava started to walk towards him, the phone in her hand hanging loosely by her side. She kept her eyes fixed on him. Ko was as focused on her, his expression, even from a distance, intense and determined.

Halfway towards him, she passed a narrow alley on her right. A sign screwed into the wall read DELIVERY ENTRANCE. She was almost beyond the alley when she sensed movement.

She instinctively pulled back to her left and caught the glimmer of steel. The man with the mohawk had removed his coat and wrapped it around his wrist, covering everything but the knife blade. He lunged, aiming at her side. Her backwards motion had shifted her body out of its path; the blade swept past, catching the underside of her left arm. Her cellphone fell to the ground. Ava's right hand shot down to grab his arm at the wrist, immobilizing it.

He stepped back into the alley, trying to wrest his arm free, pulling her in with him. "You have to call Li!" she yelled, still hanging on.

Ko appeared at the alley entrance, only four or five paces away. He reached into his raincoat pocket and pulled out a knife handle, pressed it, and a nine-inch stiletto blade hissed into view.

Ava was trying to keep an eye on Ko while still holding on to his partner's wrist. The man was lashing out at her with his free hand, so she twisted the wrist with as much force as she could. The snap was audible. He screeched, dropping the blade, and she felt the fight go out of him. She shoved him at Ko, who was now only three paces away. She kneeled to pick up the stiletto he had dropped, her eyes never leaving them.

The two men exchanged some words. Then Ko reached under his raincoat, took out another knife, and gave it to his partner. She watched in disbelief as the man with the mohawk clutched it in his good hand. The men separated and moved to either side of her, still keeping some distance. Ava moved backwards towards a wall so she could keep both of them in front of her.

"The contract is cancelled! You have to call Li!" she yelled again.

The man with the mohawk took up a position on her left. She could see the pain on his face, the arm she had broken dangling uselessly at his side. Ko was taking small steps to the right and then the left, inching forward all the time. The knife hung loosely by his side. She could feel him measuring the distance between them. She was doing the same, while keeping an eye on his partner.

Ko crept closer, his eyes fixed on Ava, the knife now poised to strike. She focused on his feet, knowing they would tell her where to move when he began his attack.

"Talk to me, Ko," she said.

He stopped, a glint of recognition in his eyes. *He doesn't understand*, she thought — she'd been speaking Cantonese. "Ko, you need to phone Li," she said in Mandarin. "The contract has been cancelled. Li is waiting for your call."

Ko held his ground, the knife pressed against his thigh, but she could see the first sign of understanding in his eyes. "There's no need to do this now," she said. "And if you take one more step in my direction I'm going to defend myself." She raised the knife she held. "I know how to use this. I'll cut your heart out if I have to."

"The contract is cancelled?" he said.

"Yes. Li has been trying to reach you."

"Our phones don't work here," he said

"Li said they were off." Ava gestured towards the alley entrance. "Call him on mine. It's on the sidewalk back there."

He hesitated.

"Call him," Ava said. She took the piece of paper from her pocket. "I have his number. Do you need it?"

"No."

"Then do it," she said.

Ko backed up carefully to the alley entrance, found the phone, and slid it across the pavement with his foot. He bent over to pick it up, his eyes still on Ava. "Come here," he said to his partner.

The man with the mohawk sidled back to Ko, who guided him to a place against the wall about six metres from Ava. The two men spoke briefly, then Ko opened Ava's phone and punched in the numbers.

Ava noticed a middle-aged couple standing at the

entrance to the alley, looks of shock and fear on their faces. "This was a family squabble," Ava said. "It's over now. There's no need to be concerned. There's no need to involve yourselves or anyone else in this. It's over."

"But you're bleeding," the woman said.

Ava looked down at the gash on her arm. It was about ten centimetres long but not very deep. Still, blood was running down her arm and hand, and a few drops had trickled onto the pavement. "It looks worse than it is," she said, wiping at the wound with the bottom of her T-shirt.

"We should call someone," the woman said.

"No, please. I'm okay."

They hesitated, then the man took the woman by the arm. "You people shouldn't bring your ways to this country," he said as they turned to walk away.

Ava shook her head and looked back at Ko and his partner. Ko was talking on the phone, nodding his head. He listened for another minute before closing the phone, and then he whispered in his partner's ear.

"Li says I'm to tell you it was just business," Ko said.

"I understand."

"It was just business."

"I know — just business."

Ko held out Ava's phone. "Here."

"No, slide it to me," she said.

He shrugged, then tossed it at her feet.

Ko's partner, leaning against the wall, groaned.

"You'd better look after him," she said.

Ko spat on the ground and reached for his partner's good arm. "I would have taken you," he said. "Next time."

AVA DROPPED THE KNIFE AND WITH A SWIPE OF HER FOOT
kicked it against the wall. Her arm was bleeding badly. She
lifted the hem of her T-shirt, wrapped it around the gash as
best she could, and pressed her arm against her side. Then
she walked out of the alley and onto High Street. The hotel
entrance was only twenty metres away; she could see the
doorman helping a couple out of a taxi. As Ava walked past
him, he smiled at her and tipped his cap.

She was almost across the lobby, her arm throbbing and
blood seeping through her T-shirt, when her cellphone
rang. *Why now?* she thought.

"Ms. Lee, this is Andrew Hawkins, Minister Simmons's
executive assistant. We met last night."

Ava stopped walking. "I know who you are."

"I've been asked to call you."

"Why?"

"It's about the subject you discussed with the Minister
last night."

"We discussed a lot of things. Can you please get to the
point? I'm rather busy right now," Ava said.

He hesitated, and Ava wondered if Simmons was listening to their conversation. "I'm calling to see if you would be available for a meeting this afternoon."

"With the Minister?"

"No, actually, it would be with his daughter, Lily, and her lawyer, George McIntyre."

"And why would I agree to that?"

"I'm not privy to all the details, and neither, I assure you, is the Minister. I am told that Ms. Simmons and Mr. McIntyre have reviewed the material you left with her yesterday and have decided, upon second thought, that you have made a strong and compelling case for return of the money that was represented to her as company profits."

"The stolen money?"

"As I said, I'm not privy to the details, so I'm not in a position to say yea or nay to your characterization."

"What are you in a position to say?"

"Ms. Simmons has indicated that she is prepared to meet with you and to execute the document that you wanted signed."

Ava was standing by the elevator, blood now dripping on the marble floor of the lobby. She noticed the concierge staring at her in shock. "Can you get me a towel, please?" Ava asked. "I had an accident outside."

"I beg your pardon?" Hawkins said.

"I wasn't speaking to you."

"Oh."

"Give me a moment."

The concierge walked quickly towards her, holding a small towel he had taken from a drawer in his desk. She took it from him and, seeing the panic in his face, said, "It's not that serious. I'll be okay. Now please excuse me, I have to finish this phone call."

"I can get a doctor here in minutes."

She waved off the offer and put the phone back to her ear. "Mr. Hawkins, you were telling me that Ms. Simmons is going to sign my transfer request."

"Those weren't my exact words," he said cautiously. "I said she was *prepared* to do that."

"It sounds as if there are conditions attached."

"Well, there is one complication that I've been advised about. The request you mentioned — the paper you evidently left with her yesterday — she doesn't have it anymore."

"She lost it?"

"She tore it up."

At least he's honest, Ava thought. "That isn't a problem. I have another copy."

"I am sure she will be relieved to hear that."

"Is that all, then?" Ava asked.

"No, there is one more thing."

"I'm listening."

"It's in regard to the conversation you had with Minister Simmons last night."

"Yes?"

"You expressed the opinion at one point that he may have violated the integrity of his blind trust."

"Yes, I did imply that was possible."

"And then things may have been said or implied that could be construed as inappropriate, in terms of his experiences doing business in Asia or with certain Asians."

"Yes, he did express some opinions that I thought were out of place."

"Ms. Lee, that was simply a case of his emotions getting the better of him. He was obviously upset about his daughter. Surely you can understand that."

"Where is this leading, Mr. Hawkins?" Ava asked.

"Would you be prepared to attest, in writing, that the Minister did not directly discuss any issues, financial or otherwise, connected to The River?"

"Are you asking if I would swear that he didn't breach the integrity of the blind trust?"

"Yes, I am."

"I can do that."

"That's wonderful."

"Is there anything else?" Ava said.

"Yes, there is one last thing. Can you also, again in writing, attest to the fact that the Minister did not disparage Asian business culture in general or specifically anyone who works in that culture?"

"And if I can't, is Ms. Simmons still prepared to sign the transfer?"

"I really don't know," he stumbled. "I was asked to make the request, and I have."

"So it isn't a condition?"

"You'll have to take that up with Ms. Simmons."

"Mr. Hawkins, tell whomever you are reporting to that I am prepared to forget both the Minister's views on how business is conducted in Asia and the issue about the blind trust."

"It is being requested that you put something in writing."

"If something short and to the point is acceptable, I'll consider it."

"Thank you."

"Is that it?"

"No, I have also been asked to inquire whether you need time to consult with anyone overseas or if you need to involve legal representatives from your side."

"No."

He paused, and she knew he hadn't expected that answer.

"When do I meet with Lily Simmons?" Ava asked.

"I believe that may be possible today. Mr. McIntyre's office is in Knightsbridge, just down the road from you."

"What time?"

"I believe the plan is that, after I pass along my report of our conversation, either Ms. Simmons or Mr. McIntyre will call you directly."

"I'll be waiting."

"Ms. Lee, I'd like to know . . ." Hawkins began awkwardly, and then stopped.

"Know what?"

"Actually . . . I'd like to know who you are."

"What do you mean?"

"I spent close to an hour with Daniel Anderson this morning. He's a friend of my older brother, and it was Daniel who arranged for my appointment to Minister Simmons's staff. He grilled me about your meeting with the Minister last night. I was honest with him — I'd like you to know that. I found the Minister's comments about Mr. Ordonez to be completely inappropriate, and I confirmed to Daniel that they had indeed been uttered. He told me that the Prime Minister had a personal interest in the matter. I was taken aback. Who are you, to bring this about?"

"Is that Daniel Anderson asking or you?"

"Me. Daniel seemed to know."

"Then you ask him," Ava said, and then cut off the line.

43

AVA WENT DIRECTLY TO HER BATHROOM TO LOOK AT THE
cut. It was longer than she'd thought, maybe fifteen centimetres, but the wound was shallow. She washed her arm in
cold water, smeared some Polysporin on it, and wrapped it
tightly in gauze.

She walked back into the room and sat on the bed to
phone Uncle.

"Did Ko call Li?"

Andrew Hawkins had driven Leung's hired killers from
her mind. "Eventually," she said.

"Eventually? Did you have problems with them?"

"None worth mentioning."

"Good. I am glad it is over."

"Li conveyed his apologies."

"I will thank him from my end. He is a useful man to
keep close."

"You'll be happy to know that Lily Simmons has decided
she wants to keep close as well. They used her father's executive assistant as the middle man. He says she's prepared to
execute the transfer."

"That is good news."

"But it isn't done yet. I came to London needing just one signature, and after everything I've gone through, I still need that one signature. I'm not taking it for granted."

"Still, we see movement in the proper direction," Uncle said, blunting his optimism.

"I'm told we're probably going to meet sometime later today at her lawyer's office. They'll want me to sign for our side. Will Ordonez have a problem with that?"

"I cannot see him objecting."

"Well, let's make sure of that. Before I go to the lawyer's office I'd like something in writing from Manila that authorizes me to sign on behalf of the Ordonez Group, and that binds them to honour whatever I do sign with regard to this debt."

"What is involved?"

"For starters, Roger Simmons wants me to say that I misinterpreted our conversation last night. That nothing was said that violated the terms of the blind trust. And that I invented the remarks he made about Asian businessmen."

"And he never said Tommy Ordonez was a piece of shit that cannot be shined?"

"I guess I made that up too."

"What do you want me to get from Manila?"

"You'd better make it a blanket authorization. Have them fax it to me here at the hotel. And then have someone on standby in Manila in case Simmons's lawyer wants to call to confirm its authenticity."

"I will call Chang. He will be pleased."

"I'll call you when everything's wrapped up, Uncle." Ava hung up the phone, then leaned back on the bed and closed her eyes. She was trying to calm herself by taking deep breaths and visualizing bak mai moves when her phone rang. An incoming call — MCINTYRE CULLEN appeared on the screen.

"Ava Lee."

"This is Loretta Michaels, from McIntyre and Cullen. Is four thirty a suitable time for you to meet with Mr. McIntyre and Ms. Simmons?"

"Yes."

"Our offices are just off Knightsbridge Road. The eighth floor, 88 Ford Street."

"Tell them I'll be there."

Ava called her travel agent and asked her to book a seat on the eight-o'clock Air Canada flight from Heathrow to Pearson. One way or another, she had a feeling she was going to be on it.

44

AT FOUR FIFTEEN AVA WAS DOWNSTAIRS WITH HER luggage. As she was checking out, the concierge handed her a fax from Manila. She reviewed the document on the limo ride to Knightsbridge and then slipped it into her Chanel purse.

She arrived five minutes early and was debating waiting in the car when she saw Lily Simmons approach the front doors of 88 Ford Street. She was wearing a black wool suit and carried a small black leather briefcase. Her hair was tangled and her shoulders slumped. Ava waited a few minutes before following her in.

"Wait for me," she said to the driver as she was getting out of the car. "I shouldn't be long."

The lobby of McIntyre and Cullen was expansive. The white marble floor was complemented by a six-metre-long Persian rug. The dark wood-panelled walls showcased the rich forest green of the leather couches and chairs.

"You must be Ms. Lee," the receptionist said, not unkindly.

"I am."

"They're expecting you," she said. "Let me take you in."

The boardroom was massive, its size accentuated by a nine-metre-long table with twenty red leather chairs. Sitting alone at the far end was Lily Simmons. She looked up at Ava. "They should be along in a minute," she said.

"Is your father coming?" Ava asked, taking a seat halfway between Simmons and the door.

"No. Why would he?"

Ava could see black shadows under her eyes, and her lips were chapped, or bitten. Her hands were on the table, the thumb of the right hand rubbing the palm of the left. "I'm sorry if this is uncomfortable for you," Ava said.

Simmons shrugged. "I just want to get this over with."

"Me too."

There was an awkward silence. Ava took a copy of the transfer request from her Chanel bag, and then, for good measure, a copy of Douglas and Ashton's confession and the paperwork from Jack Maynard and Felix Hunter. *They're going to get their money back too*, she thought as they came to mind for the first time since she had last talked to Maynard. How long ago had that been? Three days? A week? It felt like a month. It felt like another world away.

Simmons was leafing through her own papers. *A convenient distraction*, Ava thought. Suddenly the woman raised her head and said, "There is something I'd like to say to you before the others arrive."

Ava twisted in her chair so she could face Simmons. "Go ahead."

"I listened to the message you left on my phone this morning."

"Yes."

"I have to say I found it completely perverted and twisted."

"I'm sorry if you think that."

"No, you're not. You're not sorry about anything. First you try to drive a wedge between me and my fiancé, and then you attempt to discredit my father and damage our relationship by suggesting he would do something so venal."

"Do you seriously think I was making it up?"

"You've proven yourself capable of doing absolutely anything to get your way."

"Not to that extent."

"I don't believe a word you say."

"You shouldn't be so naive about the men in your life."

Simmons slammed her palm on the table. "You thought I'd sign that damn transfer if you could convince me that my father didn't care whether or not you released those tapes. Well, here we are, and I'm going to sign it, all right, but only because he wants me to."

And for what reason? Ava wanted to ask, but bit back the question. Nothing positive could come from telling Lily Simmons something she didn't want to hear.

The boardroom door opened and a middle-aged man walked in with a young woman. He was tall and slim, and his silver mane contrasted nicely with his classic navy-blue pinstriped suit. The woman wore a soft cream suit that enhanced her dark skin and fashionably cut hair. "My name is McIntyre, and this is my associate Monique Hutton," he said.

Ava stood and shook hands with them. Simmons stayed seated. The lawyers sat next to Ava, McIntyre to her immediate left and Hutton next him. He took two files from his assistant and then said, "Lily, could you come closer, please."

Simmons sat stone-faced, grinding her teeth. Then she

picked up the papers in front of her, and seated herself next to Hutton.

McIntyre opened the first file. "I hope this is what you're expecting to see, Ms. Lee," he said. "We prepared it under the direction of Ms. Simmons, and she thinks it fairly reflects a discussion you had with Andrew Hawkins earlier today." He passed her a three-page document. "Do you need some time alone with this?"

"No," Ava said, scanning the page.

"And Ms. Simmons said that you see no need to employ legal counsel from your side."

"That's correct."

"And that you have the authority to bind the Ordonez Group."

"I do," Ava said, opening her purse and taking out the fax she had received from Manila. "Here — this should be satisfactory. If you need to speak to a representative of the law firm in Manila, I have them on standby."

He scanned the fax. "No, this seems perfectly straightforward and clear. Have them courier the original for my records, if you don't mind."

"Certainly," Ava said, and continued reading.

The document laid out the details for transfer of the $65 million. The deal bound the Ordonez Group: its representatives could not so much as utter the words *The River*, *Simmons*, *Ashton*, or *Douglas*, let alone contemplate taking legal action against any of them. If they did, The River and its investors would be entitled to damages that far exceeded $65 million. It was familiar posturing, full of bluster that amounted to very little.

Ava paused when she got to the last page of the document.

She looked up at Simmons and her lawyers. "I didn't discuss this with Mr. Hawkins," she said.

McIntyre cast an anxious look at Lily.

"But it is what I discussed with Ms. Simmons when I first proposed a settlement, so it isn't entirely unexpected or unreasonable," Ava said slowly. She signed the document.

"Excellent. And now this one," McIntyre said, handing her a single piece of paper.

She read the paper and then leaned forward so she could speak directly to Lily. "You're pushing me to the limit with this."

Simmons turned her head towards Ava but didn't look her in the eye. "We think it's necessary."

"I don't object to admitting that I may have misinterpreted your father's remarks, but I have trouble signing a piece of paper that says I deliberately lied about what he said for my own selfish motives."

A heavy silence settled in the room. McIntyre tapped his pen against the back of his hand while his assistant stared at the wall.

"Mr. McIntyre," Simmons said, "you know my father. What do you think he would say about making changes to this document?"

"He would be quite adamant about leaving the wording intact," McIntyre said.

Ava pushed it aside and handed a paper from her stack to McIntyre. "This is another copy of the letter authorizing transfer of the money from Cyprus to a Hong Kong bank account. I want it signed before I sign anything."

McIntyre took it from her, read it, and passed it to Simmons. "Ms. Lee, before Ms. Simmons signs, I have to ask you to confirm your intention to sign both documents that we've presented to you."

"I'll sign."

"Then I will sign immediately after," Simmons said.

Simmons and Ava took turns signing five copies each of McIntyre's documents, and then both McIntyre and Hutton witnessed them. Ava had them make three copies of the money transfer and then witness that the copies were of an original signed document. It was five o'clock when they finished.

Ava took two sets of each document and slipped them into her bag. "The transfer request will be couriered to the bank in Cyprus tonight," she said. "I hope no one will think they can interfere with the process."

"We have an agreement that benefits both parties, Ms. Lee," McIntyre said. "It would be foolish, not to mention damaging, for anyone to do anything contrary to it."

Ava stood and extended her hand. As she did, her phone rang. She was about to turn it off when she saw the incoming number. "It's the Prime Minister's Office calling," she said. "I'm afraid I have to take this."

McIntyre looked at Simmons. Her mouth was fixed in a tight smile.

"Yes, I've had a much better day than yesterday," Ava said, "and I want to thank you for your concern . . . No, Mr. Anderson, Mr. Simmons didn't call, but Mr. Hawkins did and he was very helpful . . . Yes, we have resolved the issues between us, and I don't think you'll be hearing any more about this from our side . . . I'll be sure to pass that along to President Arellano . . . Yes, I won't hesitate to call you if the need arises."

She closed the phone and slipped it back into her Chanel purse. "Well, thanks for this."

Simmons looked at her lawyer. "Ms. Lee, just a reminder," McIntyre said. "You've just signed a binding agreement. I'm not sure that conversations with the Prime Minister's Office, however casual or uninitiated, are in anyone's best interest."

"I agree completely. I think that might be worth reiterating to your clients as well, particularly the one who isn't in this room."

AT TEN AFTER FIVE AVA LEFT THE FORD STREET OFFICE and climbed into the waiting limo. "Can you take me to Heathrow?" she asked.

When they got to the international departures drop-off, Ava got her bags from the trunk, gave the driver a hundred-pound tip, and went directly to the Federal Express office to send the transfer request to the bank in Cyprus. As soon as she had the tracking number she called Hong Kong. It was just past one o'clock in the morning there, but she knew Uncle would be waiting.

"It's done."

"She signed?"

"Yes."

"Any complications?"

"I almost lost my temper when they asked me to sign a document stating that I'd lied about what Simmons said about Ordonez."

"Did they change it?"

"No. I signed it."

"You did not have to," Uncle said.

She knew he meant it. He never second-guessed her. That was part of the burden she carried — no matter how expedient she had to be, no matter what it cost them, even if she recovered nothing, he didn't second-guess her.

"Yes, I did have to. It was the cost of doing business. He's probably sent it to the Prime Minister's Office already."

"Not that that will do him any good; he already has a black mark next to his name. They may leave him where he is, but he is not going any further up the political ladder."

"I can only hope that's the case."

"Where are you now?"

"I'm at Heathrow. I've just sent the transfer request via FedEx to the bank in Cyprus. I'll give you the tracking number to pass along to our bank. Have them follow it from their end; they should call the Cypriot bank to make sure the money is moved as quickly as possible."

"I will look after it."

"Thank you. I leave here at eight o'clock. I'm looking forward to getting home."

"Ava, I know this was hard on you, doing two jobs back to back and then having Jackie Leung to deal with."

"Uncle, I really don't want to talk about it right now. I just want to get home."

"There are times when you push yourself too hard."

Ava had already begun to feel the truth of that statement on the limo ride from Ford Street to Heathrow. At first she had felt a sense of relief that it was over and that she'd recovered her client's money. But that feeling was quickly overtaken by bone-aching exhaustion. The adrenalin that had driven her from Hong Kong to the Philippines to San Francisco, Vancouver, Victoria, Las Vegas, and London now gave in to too many flights, too many time zones, too much stress. She hadn't thought about those things when she was on the hunt because she wouldn't let herself. The focus was on getting from A to B, connecting the dots, pushing and driving, putting together the pieces until the final one fell into place.

"I did what I had to do," she said.

"I should call Chang," Uncle said. "He will want to tell Ordonez about your success."

"Yes, you do that. I need to check in and make some calls too. Bye, Uncle."

She sat in the Star Alliance lounge with her notebook open on her lap. It was eleven o'clock in the morning in Las Vegas and Vancouver and two in the afternoon in Virginia and Cooper Island. She thought about calling David Douglas, Maggie Chew, Jack Maynard, Martin Littlefeather, and Chief Francis. She thought about it, but she didn't. *Tomorrow*, she said to herself. *Or maybe the day after.*

She went to the ladies' washroom to change her clothes for the flight. In a cubicle with a full-length mirror, Ava stripped down to her underwear and looked at herself. The marks on her neck and shoulders had faded but the bruising on her hip and torso was a garish purple. She unwrapped the gauze on her arm and examined the cut. It had stopped bleeding, but she might need stitches. *God, what a mess I am*, she thought as she slipped a black Giordano T-shirt over her head.

Back in the lounge, she turned on her computer and connected to her email server. She sent brief messages to her mother, Marian, and Mimi, telling them she'd be back in Toronto the next day. As she scanned her other emails she saw one from Maria Gonzalez, inviting her out for dinner and dancing.

Dear Maria, she wrote, I'm looking forward to meeting you, but I think we should go for a coffee or something more casual. I'm flying back into Toronto tonight. We can discuss it in the next few days.

Ava had gone through the rest of her emails and was about to shut down the computer when one arrived from Mimi. Dim sum tomorrow?

Yes, Ava wrote back, just as a reply from Maria came through. What time does your flight arrive? she asked.

Ava hesitated, then wrote, 10:30, Air Canada from London.

Can I meet you at the airport? Maria wrote back a minute later.

I look like hell and I ache all over, Ava replied.

I'll bring a hug.

Am I ready for this? Ava wondered. Then she read over their correspondence again and smiled. I can use a hug, she wrote. See you there.

COMING SOON
from House of Anansi Press in February 2012

Read on for a preview of the next thrilling
Ava Lee novel, *The Wild Beasts of Wuhan*

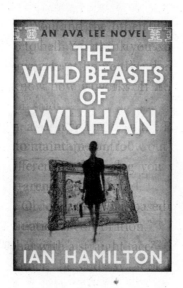

AVA LEE SAT ON A BENCH ON THE OTROBANDA SIDE of Willemstad, the capital city of Curaçao, watching ships from China, Indonesia, Panama, and the Netherlands come and go. The crews stood by the railings, waving down at the onlookers as their vessels moved almost rhythmically in and out of St. Anna Bay. Ava waved back.

It was mid-afternoon. She had arrived that morning on a cruise ship that was moored about a kilometre away, at a fort that had once guarded the entrance to the harbour. The fort had been converted into a tourist spot with restaurants, shops, a hotel, and a casino.

She was on vacation with her family: her father, her mother, and her older sister, Marian, who had also brought her husband, Bruce, and their two daughters. They were eight days into the trip, with six to go. Ava wondered if they would survive the long journey back to Miami.

The Lees were not a traditional family by Western standards. Ava's mother, Jennie, was the second wife of Marcus. Following tradition, he had married her without divorcing his first wife. They had lived in Hong Kong until Ava was two and Marian four, when Marcus had taken on a third wife. The new family dynamic had caused friction between Marcus and Jennie, so she and her daughters had been relocated to Canada. It was an arrangement that suited them both. He looked after all his families financially, spoke to Jennie every day by phone, and visited her for two weeks every year. Although Ava and Marian had grown up without the physical presence of their father, they knew that Marcus loved them. So, traditional or not, their time together was enjoyed, if only because everyone knew the rules and had the appropriate expectations.

This cruise, though, was a first. Marcus's visits usually consisted of a stay at Jennie's house north of Toronto, lunches and dinners with her and Ava, and a two-day trip to Ottawa to see Marian and the girls. The extended holiday had been Marcus's idea; the cruise, Marian's. In hindsight, Ava thought they should have known better. It hadn't taken long for discord to surface.

The main combatants were Jennie and Bruce. Bruce was a *gweilo*, a Westerner, and a senior civil servant with the Canadian government. But the fact that he wasn't Chinese wasn't the issue; it was the kind of *gweilo* he was — uptight and anal. The kind of person who got up early to secure deck chairs for the day. The kind who pre-organized a full day of activities at every port of call. The kind who made sure to use every facility and perk offered by the cruise. The kind who had to be in line at five forty-five for a six-o'clock dinner.

Marian and the girls were used to Bruce's ways and didn't think twice about it. Marcus and Ava had rolled with the punches for the first few days before politely begging off some of the group activities. But from the moment she stepped on the ship, Jennie Lee had refused to fall in line. She declined to go on any of Bruce's planned excursions, and she arrived later and later for every lunch and dinner. She never came to breakfast, being too tired from late nights at the gaming tables.

By day three, Bruce and Jennie had stopped talking. He had taken to glaring at her and she pretended he didn't exist. It was hard on Marian, and Ava felt sorry for her. Marian had always had a more difficult relationship with their mother than Ava did.

"Why did she come?" Marian demanded.

"What choice did she have? Daddy wanted to take us on a family holiday and you talked him into booking the cruise without discussing it with her first. Did you expect her to stay in Toronto for the two weeks of the year she has with her husband?"

"I thought it would be different."

"It's never different with her, or with Bruce," Ava said. "So don't make it one-sided. Neither of them is easy."

When they berthed at Willemstad, Bruce had organized a tour of Curaçao; a driver was waiting for them at the dock. Jennie didn't show. Marcus went on the tour, grudgingly. Ava had said she wanted to spend a quiet day in town.

She shifted on the bench and gazed at the Queen Emma Bridge, which connected the Otrabanda and Punda quarters of the city. Willemstad was a busy commercial port — Curaçao was a major oil refiner and exporter — and the bridge was in constant motion, opening and closing for vessels coming in and out of the harbour. She looked across the bay, admiring the rows of two- and three-storey stucco buildings painted in pastel blues, greens, and yellows, all of them topped with red slate roofs. The slate had originally served as ballast on the ships that had brought Dutch settlers to the Caribbean in the seventeenth century. Ava felt as if she were in Amsterdam, in one of the old neighbourhoods built on the canals.

The cruise had come after a two-month break from chasing bad debts halfway around the world. Chasing bad debts was what Ava, a forensic accountant, did for a living, and after back-to-back jobs that had taxed her both physically and emotionally, she had needed some time off. She had spent time with friends, danced at salsa clubs, eaten more than she should, burned off the extra calories by running, eaten some more, and gone to her regular bak mei workouts. She had also been exploring a growing relationship with a Colombian woman named Maria Gonzalez.

Maria was an assistant trade commissioner at the Colombian consulate in Toronto, a newcomer to the city. Ava's best friend, Mimi, had met her at a function and done some matchmaking via email. The two women had connected while Ava was travelling, and when she flew home, Maria was waiting for her at the airport. The physical attraction had been instantaneous. Emotionally, Ava was still feeling tentative. She and Maria had vacationed in Thailand for two glorious weeks, and they had managed to end every day wanting to see each other the next. When they got back to Toronto, Maria had begun to hint that they move in together. Ava was relieved that the cruise would give her some breathing space.

The sun was higher in the sky now and the pastel buildings glistened in its light. She got up and walked towards

Kura Hulanda, a hotel, conference centre, and museum complex that Dutch businessman and philanthropist Jacob Gelt Dekker had created out of what were originally the city's slums. The original street layout, including the cobblestones, had been kept intact. The old housing had been demolished, and colourful new stucco and wooden houses had been built that now functioned as stand-alone hotel units.

Ava headed for the Kura Hulanda Museum, which was famous for a collection that described the history of the slave trade. The museum was made up of several low-lying buildings linked in an L shape; its dark painted walls and small windows made the edifice look gloomy.

She walked through the galleries, admiring the sculptures, masks, weapons, and descriptions of the societies and cultures of West Africa. All the exhibits were drawn from Dekker's private collection. The final section of the museum presented the two-hundred-year history of the Dutch slave trade. Curaçao had been an auction centre for slaves sold into the Caribbean and all of South America. *Kura hulanda* was a Papiamentu term meaning "Dutch courtyard." As Ava walked out the front door of the museum, she found herself standing in just such a courtyard, on the very spot where hundreds of thousands of enslaved people had been bought and sold. She shuddered.

She walked back into the bright sunlight and crossed the Queen Emma Bridge over the harbour to Punda. There she found an outdoor Italian restaurant and ordered a glass of Pinot Grigio and a plate of spaghetti *aglio e olio*.

She recognized an elderly couple from the cruise sitting at the next table. The woman kept looking at her until Ava finally said hello. They introduced themselves as Henry and Bella from Singer Island, Florida, via New York. "I've seen you on the ship with your family. So attractive, all of you," Bella said.

Ava smiled. "Thank you."

"Your mother's name is Jennie, right?"

"It is."

"I thought so. Such a pistol! She and I close the casino most nights," Bella said. "What are you doing this afternoon?"

"I don't have any plans," Ava said, digging into her spaghetti, which had just arrived.

"Henry and I are going to the Snoga Synagogue. It's the oldest synagogue in the Western Hemisphere." She turned to her husband. "Henry, when was it built?"

"Sixteen something."

"In the sixteen hundreds. Crazy, huh?"

"Sephardic Jews from Amsterdam," Henry said. "They modelled it after the Esnoga Synagogue there."

"It's not far from here," Bella said. "Would you like to join us? It'll be interesting."

Ava was in theory a Roman Catholic. She had been raised in the Church and her mother and sister were still devout. But in her mind the Church had rejected her with its views on homosexuality. She now preferred to think of herself as a Buddhist — live and let live. But she couldn't explain why she still prayed to St. Jude in times of crisis and wore a gold crucifix around her neck.

"Sure, why not?" Ava said.

They paid their bills and left the restaurant. After walking past stores, cafés, and small office buildings, they stopped outside a bright gold stucco building. It was three storeys high, with a red slate roof; the windows and double doors were painted white. Henry and Bella led her into an inner courtyard, where they were greeted by a woman seated at a table.

"The synagogue is there to our right," the woman said. "It was built in 1692, and some additions were made in 1732."

Henry and Bella walked tentatively towards the entrance, Ava trailing behind them. As they stepped inside, she heard them gasp. Ava peered over Bella's shoulder and saw an almost perfect jewel box of a building. A straight line from the doorway led to a wooden pulpit at the opposite end; along either side of the aisle were rows of dark wooden benches. Just above, balconies ran down both sides, and four marble columns extended upwards to an arched ceiling from which hung three huge chandeliers.

They took several steps into the synagogue. As she entered, Ava noticed that Henry and Bella's eyes were transfixed by the floor. She looked down and saw that it was covered entirely in thick white sand.

She watched as Bella and Henry pressed their feet into the sand. Then Bella began to cry. Henry put his arm around her shoulders and started to sob as well. Ava didn't know why they were crying, but she felt their emotion all the same.

"The sand is the Sinai Desert," Henry said. "They brought it here to remind them of Sinai." He kneeled, picked up a handful, and pressed it to his lips.

"This isn't common?" Ava asked softly.

"There's maybe one other synagogue in the world with a floor like this," he said.

Ava was about to follow Henry and Bella farther into

the synagogue when her phone rang. She apologized and excused herself, stepping outside. "Ava Lee," she answered.

"Ava, it is Uncle."

Uncle was her partner and mentor; they had been in the debt collection business together for more than ten years. He was in his seventies, but he showed no signs of slowing down and still maintained a massive network of contacts that provided them with business and support. It was a common rumour that in his past life he had ties to the Triad. Ava didn't know for certain; she had only the deepest respect for the man she knew.

"Uncle," she said, glancing at her watch. It was 2 a.m. in Hong Kong, and he was usually asleep well before that. "You're up late."

"Am I disturbing you?"

"I'm in Curaçao. I'm sightseeing."

"Still on that cruise?"

"Yes."

"Can you talk?"

"Sure."

"Are you ready to come back to work?"

She took a deep breath. "That depends on what you have. I have no interest in chasing after some scumbag from General Santos City who cheated people with tuna sashimi that's been gas flushed twenty times."

"So you are ready."

"What do you have?"

"How soon can you get to Hong Kong?"

"Uncle, is it that important?" she asked, knowing already that it probably was.

"Wong Changxing."

"The Emperor of Hubei?"

"He hates being called that. Even if it is said respectfully, he worries that it is offensive to the government and military officials whose support he needs."

"I'm sorry. Do you know him from Wuhan?"

Uncle had been born in Wuhan, the capital of Hubei province. He had escaped the Communist regime and fled to Hong Kong when he was a young man, but he still maintained close ties there and had built a big enough reputation that his Wuhan roots were a source of pride to many people who lived there. "He knows me from Wuhan," Uncle said.

"Ah."

"He has a problem."

"What is it?"

"I am not sure, but he sounded distressed."

"Something personal?"

"Certainly pressing, if I read his manner correctly."

"So it's urgent?"

"He asked us to come to Wuhan to talk. He offered to pay our expenses and a fee of fifty thousand dollars for our time."

"I'm still on the cruise for another week."

"He said he needs to see us as soon as possible."

"You mean, Uncle, that he needs to see you."

"No, Ava. He was very specific that you come with me."

"How does he know —"

"That doesn't matter. He does."

"The cruise —"

"When he says as soon as possible, he does not mean a week from now."

Ava paused. The idea of working for Wong Changxing

intrigued her, and if her father hadn't been on the cruise she wouldn't have hesitated to leave for Hong Kong. But she couldn't abandon him so easily. "I'll have to talk to my father," she said.

"He is a man who has always understood the demands of business," Uncle said.

"Perhaps, but I still need to talk to him, and I can't assume he'll be that understanding. So let me call you back."

"I will wait up."

She called her father's cellphone, which he answered on the first ring. She could hear kids shouting and water splashing in the background.

"Can you talk?" she asked.

"I'm at a dolphin sanctuary, or show, or something. Bruce paid several hundred dollars so that he, Marian, and the girls could swim with the dolphins. They're in the water now. I'm supposed to be taking pictures."

"Something has come up," she said.

"Business?"

"Yes, I just got a call from Uncle. He wants me to go to Hong Kong right away."

Her father had heard the rumours about Uncle's past and was quietly disapproving about her association with him. "Is it that important?"

"Wong Changxing."

"The Emperor of Hubei."

"I'm told we shouldn't refer to him as that."

"It doesn't change the fact that he's the most powerful man in the province."

"No matter, he's asked us to go to Wuhan for a meeting. I asked if Uncle could go alone, and he said Wong had specifically requested that I accompany him."

"And you're calling me to ask for permission."

"Yes."

"You don't have to."

"Yes, I do. This is your holiday, and if you think that my absence will cause any disruption I won't go."

"This holiday was the worst idea —"

"I've spoken to Marian about Bruce."

"And I've spoken to your mother."

"Two immoveable forces."

"Bruce is a bureaucrat, professionally and personally. Your mother is every bureaucrat's nightmare. He wants a plan for everything and your mother can't think past her next meal."

"So do you need me? Do you want me to stay?"

"No, you go," he said quickly. "I'll try to spend as much time as I can with Marian and the girls and hope time flies."

"I love you."

"Me too. Be careful."

Ava went inside the synagogue to say goodbye to Henry and Bella. They were sitting on one of the benches, their eyes closed. She left as quietly as she could and made her way back to the ship to look for Jennie Lee.

She found her mother in the casino, sitting at the baccarat table with a stack of twenty-five-dollar chips in front of her.

"I have to leave," Ava said. "Uncle just called. We have a client in Wuhan who needs us."

"No."

"Yes."

"Your father won't be happy."

"I spoke to him first and asked his permission. He told me to go."

Her mother shook her head. "You can't leave me alone with them."

"Marian and the girls love you to death. And Daddy is still here."

"You are the only one who understands me."

You mean who tolerates you, Ava thought. "That's not true," she said.

"Stay until we get back to Miami."

"I can't. It's a crisis."

Her mother stared at her. When Ava didn't capitulate, she said, "I think Bruce may try to throw me into the sea somewhere between here and Miami."

"He probably thinks the same of you."

Her mother had kept on playing as she talked to Ava, her stack growing larger as she doubled her bet on the banker. When she won, she doubled her bet again, with success. "I suppose I can't stop you from leaving, can I."

"No."

"Well, have a safe trip and call me whenever you can."

"I need you to do something for me," Ava said.

"What?"

"My clothes — I brought this ridiculous suitcase with me and I have all these clothes that I can't wear anywhere else. Can you take them back to Toronto for me?"

"What will you wear?"

"I'll take my running gear, some T-shirts, my toiletries, and some jewellery. I'll throw everything in my carry-on. I can buy some business clothes when I get to Hong Kong. I need some new things anyway."

Her mother sighed and passed her room key to Ava. "Leave your case in my room."

Ava leaned over to kiss her mother on the forehead.

"Be careful," Jennie said.

Ava went to her room and turned on her laptop. She found a flight that landed at 8 a.m. in Hong Kong with a stop in Newark. She booked it and then called Uncle. He didn't react when she told him she was coming, and she knew he had probably expected nothing less.

"There's an early Dragonair flight from Hong Kong to Wuhan," he said.

"No, Uncle, I'm sorry. I have no business clothes with me and I need to shop. See if you can book something for later in the day."

"Where do you want to shop?"

"There's a Brooks Brothers store in Tsim Sha Tsui," she said, knowing that his Kowloon apartment was no more than ten minutes from the popular shopping district and tourist destination.

"I will send Sonny to meet you at the airport. He will take you wherever you need to go. Wong will have to wait." Uncle paused. "I hear that his wife is very attractive and a real power in their business. They should know that we have the whole package too."

IAN HAMILTON is the author of *The Water Rat of Wanchai*, the first Ava Lee novel. He has worked as a journalist, a senior executive with the federal government, a diplomat, and a businessman with international links.